TERMINAL LUCIDITY

A Chilling Medical Thriller With The Tug Of Romance

JO LOVEDAY

https://www.JoLoveday.com

Cover and Interior Design by: www. formatting4U.com

Published by Tall Leaf Press
Printed in the United States of America

ISBN, Digital: 979-8-9906431-09
ISBN, Print: 979-8-9906431-16

Praise for Terminal Lucidity

"A prescription for suspense: where medicine meets malevolence."

— Deborah Shlian, MD,
award-winning author
of medical thriller *Silent Survivor*,
and biographies in *Lessons Learned - Stories from women in STEM*

"Author Jo Loveday brings to life her real-world hospital experience in crafting this realistic medical thriller. Love, betrayal, and moral conflicts are woven into the plot and characters as nurse-turned-amateur-sleuth, Ariel Savin, is unwittingly framed for a recovery room accident. The deeper she digs into the privately funded neuro unit at her hospital, and the closer she gets to the truth, the more her own life is imperiled. Fans of Robin Cook's blockbuster, Coma, have a new heroine to route for."

— Victor Acquista, MD,
award-winning
Venom and Flame
thriller series author.

For Jeff,
my husband, friend, partner, and the love of my life.

Chapter 1

Another accident with the patient clinging to life—a usual shift in my day at Palm Beach's Becham Hospital. Except… my gut tells me this one is anything but normal. "My turn!" I yell, waving the gurney carrying the post-op FedEx delivery man over to my cubby of medical equipment.

"Ariel," the anesthesiologist hollers to me over the noise of the busy room. "This is Robert Young. He had a craniectomy for a bleed into his brain stem when his truck rolled. They don't want to keep him in an induced coma."

I place an oxygen mask on my patient, note his stable heart rhythm. Lifting the covers for a head-to-toe, I snort the metallic scent of dried blood out of my nose. Trauma victims carry a unique smell that's never good. His major systems seem functional, but in my years as a recovery room nurse, I've developed a sense of impending doom with some patients. There's something up with Robert.

Dr. Harold Goss, the lanky lead neurosurgeon strides in, and his sharp gray eyes land on me. "I explained what was done in surgery to Robert's family," he says, "and told them they can see him in an hour on his way to ICU. How's he doing?"

"He looks good, but his respirations are a little fast." I pop my stethoscope into my ears, then listen to clear breath sounds as his chest rises and falls.

"His injuries are minor, considering."

"Will you be in the hospital just in case?" I tuck away my stethoscope.

"I have a meeting at the lab," Harold says as he heads for the locker room. "Jake's here if you need something."

Jake Garcia, Harold's physician's assistant, steps over at the mention of his name. His curly brown hair and squat form are in obvious contrast to Harold's.

Jake surveys the heart monitor, does a pupil check. "I don't see a problem."

I look down at the sleeping face, barely scratched, his head wrapped with a turban of gauze. "Something's not right. I can't put my finger on it." I scan the heart monitor again.

"She has good intuition," Chelsea tells Jake while she hooks the intracranial pressure set to the monitor. Chelsea hasn't been here long, but she's earned my trust as a good nurse and has fast become my BFF.

Jake nods. "Is he waking up?"

"Anesthesia has worn off only enough to breathe," I say.

Chelsea's jet-black bob sways past her slender shoulders as she clicks a fresh cap on the digital thermometer. "His temp is ninety-six. I'll get a warm blanket."

"I'm going to change my scrubs. Back in a minute." Jake traipses along with Chelsea toward a blanket warmer near the exit.

I check Robert's pupils. They react as they should, but they look dead. The uneasiness in my gut ramps up a notch.

As Chelsea places the blanket on Robert, a blip appears over my shoulder, and the heart monitor screams. A saw-toothed, pulse-less line snarls at me from the screen above me.

"Chelsea, zap him." I check the patient's airway to make sure he's breathing as Chelsea runs for the red metal crash cart and defibrillator.

"Belinda, call the OR and get Dr. Johnson from anesthesia back here!" I holler to our nurse manager as my heart pounds.

The defibrillator shrieks—it's ready.

"CLEAR!" Chelsea yells from my right.

I step back from the patient's head. Chelsea hits the button—the sawtooth snarls across the screen.

"Anesthesia started his next case!" Belinda shouts.

"He stopped breathing." I pick up an Ambu bag, crank the oxygen wide open, pump in a couple of breaths, and watch the heart rhythm deteriorate. "Belinda put in an overhead call for Dr. Goss. He may not have left the building yet."

"*Doctor Harold Goss to PACU, stat,*" rings through the speakers.

"Ramping the juice up to three hundred and sixty joules." Chelsea holds the paddles in place.

The full-charge screech from the defibrillator triggers a hyperfocus in me that drowns out the chaos.

"CLEAR!" Chelsea pauses to make sure no one is touching the stretcher.

I jump back, bag in hand.

A bolt of energy surges. The monitor spikes from the jolt, goes flat in a heartbeat-less blur. Not good.

I resume bagging. A blip appears on the screen and another. The heart monitor continues to scream. His color is dusky. "He's got a rhythm, but it's erratic."

"I'll pump." Chelsea sprints to my right, climbs onto the stretcher, and starts chest compressions.

I squeeze a breath into Robert's lungs while the IV monitor chirps out its incessant beep.

Footsteps come running. "V-tach. We've zapped him twice," I blurt as Harold arrives on my left.

He eyes the heart monitor. "Give him a milligram of epinephrine."

"Yes, sir." Belinda appears at Harold's side, grabs the epi from the cart, pushes the drug through the IV.

Harold watches the screen. "Where's anesthesia?"

"In surgery!" I holler over Chelsea as she counts aloud during CPR.

"Give three hundred of amiodarone and get me an ET tube," he says.

"Amiodarone is in!" Belinda shouts.

I hand Harold the Ambu bag so he can breathe the patient. I step left to fetch him the laryngoscope as he slips into my place.

"Come on, Robert, rally," I whisper as I prep the ET tube.

Harold squats behind the head of the stretcher to get his sight line. "It's been a long time since I've done this. Chelsea, stop for a second." He guides the tube in.

I fill the balloon, hook tube to bag, and squeeze.

The patient's chest rises.

"You've still got it, Harold," I say.

"I need to prove that to my poor wife." Harold steps to the side, brushing his finger over the patient's wedding ring before tugging the blanket over his hand.

I resume my place at Robert's head while I push another breath into his lungs. I check the blaring EKG monitor. An erratic line continues. "Nothing yet."

"Go ahead, Chelsea, pump." Harold slides his sterile gloves into the trash and turns to Belinda. "Give another milli of epi and another three hundred of amiodarone. Get an EKG and cardiac enzymes."

I glance at the face of my thirty-something patient and picture a wife and kids in the waiting room outside. "Come on, buddy."

"How's it going?" Dr. Johnson calls as he rolls his patient out of the OR.

As the EKG tech arrives, Harold steps back from the crowded stretcher. "Not great."

Sam Johnson hurries over, tripping on the cord for the EKG machine. He puts his hand out to brace his fall and pulls the oxygen tubing out of the flow meter. He fumbles to reconnect it. "Why is the oxygen off?" Johnson's gaze lands on me.

My stomach tightens. I look at the oxygen meter on my right. "I had it wide open."

"The one on the other side of the stretcher is wide open, Ariel. The one that's hooked up to the patient is off."

All eyes fall on the flow meter. Everything goes dead quiet except for the soft *whoosh* of oxygen pumping into the room.

I grab the tubing, plug it into the running oxygen, squeeze the Ambu bag as fast as I can. "I turned this on when I got out the Ambu bag."

"Apparently not." Dr. Johnson looks at the pitiful lifeless line on the patient's monitor.

The air is thick with sweat and blame.

"Chelsea, hold compressions for a second," Harold tells her.

I shove another breath deep into the patient's lungs. A blip appears on the screen. "He's getting a rhythm back."

"Thank goodness for that," Jake blurts.

Harold fixes the comb-over that covers his bald spot, leans in to check my patient's pupils. "His heart may be working, but his cerebral function doesn't look great."

"No!" I drive in more oxygen, pushing it deep into the lungs.

Harold clears his throat. "Maybe he'll be all right. We

can slow down his brain activity and ventilate him for a couple of days, see how he does."

"It sucks to tell the family this." Jake's gaze feels like he's excising my innards with a scalpel.

The wrinkles around Belinda's lips tighten. "We'll have to report your patient's incident to the risk manager, Ariel."

"I know I turned on the correct one." The scene scrolls through my head. I watch myself crank the flow meter wide open and tighten the tubing for the Ambu. Chelsea was on the opposite side, Harold and Belinda near the one turned off. Harold was right next to it, but I have no proof. We need a camera in here—stupid HIPAA privacy laws.

Sam Johnson pats my back. "Not to worry. He'll be okay."

Don't worry. How can I not? I try to quell the uprising in my stomach.

"Give it time. Maybe it will all work out." Chelsea tacks on the smile she uses for encouragement.

"I knew his respirations weren't right," I mumble as I stare at the lifeless brainwave. "I didn't think it would lead to this."

"It's not you," Chelsea tells me. "You checked everything before he arrested. I was there in the beginning. I saw you turn the oxygen on."

"Why didn't you say something?"

Chelsea's eyes drop to the floor. "I… I don't like everyone's attention on me." A new patient is wheeled into recovery. She bolts to her assigned spot, waving the OR team over.

It's okay that the attention's on me?

*

Ben Guthrie, neurosurgeon and the love of my life, strides to my side. His thick, sable hair looks bothered, like his OR cap is on too tight. He puts his hand on my arm, soft as a caress, and I notice how slight he's become in the past few years. He was no stranger to the gym in college, but med school, residency, and his constant workload have taken a toll.

"I heard. I'm so sorry. How are you doing?"

"Terrible. I don't know how this happened. The oxygen was on."

Ben scans the monitor. "Maybe the damage is only short-term. After a couple of days in ICU, we'll know more." He offers a sympathetic look.

I smile in return, hoping he's right.

Harold glances our way. "Ben, have you got a minute?"

"I'll see you at home." Ben gives my arm a squeeze, goes to join Jake and Harold.

"He's dead. Effing dead." Jake's voice spills from the far side of the recovery room. Nurses glance at each other, start to busy themselves with their patients. "What am I going to tell his wife? 'Your husband survived horrendous trauma; the surgery went well, but some nurse killed him?'"

His words shake me to the core. I know I didn't do it, but the patient *is* brain dead. My temples throb as a headache starts.

Harold runs a palm through greasy hair. "You had a rough night on call, Jake. Take a breath. Ariel is one of the best nurses here. I'm sure she didn't mean to do it. Things happen."

Jake snorts. "That's what we can say, 'Sorry, shit happens. Have a nice day.'" He gestures so big that he bumps one of the rolling stools. Its chrome legs shudder and settle at a crooked angle.

I adjust the patient's curtains, so Chelsea and I can see

them from our side of the room. "Hospitals are supposed to be a place of healing. They're also worse than a high-school lunchroom for class warfare, jealousy, and petty grievances," I groan.

"Don't overlook gossip." Chelsa giggles. "It's ridiculous, yet we're all caught up in it. Here for either the power or a paycheck."

Ben takes off his OR cap, twists it in his hands. "Do you want me to tell the family?"

My heart goes out to Ben. He's still compensating for the fact that he got into med school when Jake didn't. And Jake's been cranky about Ben spending time with me and not doing guy things like they did in college.

Harold puts one hand on Jake's shoulder, the other on Ben's. His lab coat opens to show a pen with a heart-topped Caduceus tucked into the inner pocket. "I'll take care of it. You do rounds on the rest of the post-op patients we didn't check on when we dropped everything for this one."

"I'll stop by ICU to check on Mr. Young when I'm done." Ben ducks around the corner.

Jake turns his back to the rest of the room, big, wet half-moons showing under his arms. He clears his throat. "The Weebly family wants to discontinue the program and donate their daughter's organs."

Harold leans hard on the stool Ben got up from. "They can't quit," he blurts, his voice low. "I only have ten days before the deadline. We'll stall them. Do whatever it takes. Getting brain stem regeneration is so close. I've got to save those people, especially my wife."

Chapter 2

The headache that started an hour ago pounds. My eyes blur. My patient is dead. And, to make it worse, that death contributed to a program everyone knows I hate. As I slog down the long, beige hall back to the recovery room, I brace myself for a conversation with my patient's wife. Before taking Robert into the ICU, I let her look at him, telling her he'll be there for observation.

My headache ramps up another notch. Jake said they have two kids at home. How is she going to tell them their father is brain-dead? I *know* I didn't do it, but how do I live with the fact that I didn't prevent it?

I can only hope Robert's brain waves improve after a couple of days in ICU so that he doesn't end up in the neuro unit as one of Harold's experiments. I feel so sorry for those people, withering away on a respirator, tubes protruding from every orifice, pumped full of IV antibiotics that give them days of debilitating diarrhea as they fight off pneumonia and bladder infections. It's like they're trapped, unable to die with dignity because Harold convinced their families that he might be able to regrow their brains.

The smell of old coffee greets me from ten steps back. I pause outside the room, which is full of sagging blue-and-ecru plaid chairs covered in the coffee stains of anxious loved ones waiting for miracles. I don't want to go in, don't want to face her.

My mouth is a desert. I swirl my tongue around and swallow. "Mrs. Young, your husband's nurse is getting him settled in his room right now. She will come and get you in thirty minutes or so."

A woman next to her with salt-and-pepper hair and bright pink cropped pants nods. Mrs. Young doesn't look up. She looks fifty, not the mid-thirties I know she is. I'd look old in this situation, too. Her long, blonde hair is uncombed, and her olive skin is blanched. The worn blue T-shirt she's wearing is soaked with tears, while her hands are pressed together between her knees like she's praying.

I'm halfway down the hall when I hear, "Excuse me, nurse?"

The throbbing in my head bangs with each footstep as Mrs. Young walks toward me. Her plain face shows the strain of a hard life.

I want to turn and run but force myself to head in her direction. How can I possibly explain what happened? Did Harold say it was my fault or a complication of the accident? Does she understand her husband's brain has infarcted? That it's dead, and his heart is beating because it doesn't depend on the brain? Is she going to scream at me? Punch me in the face?

"Dr. Goss said that Robert needed some tests. What's he going to get?"

The breath I didn't realize I was holding seeps out. I gather myself. "They'll do an EEG. It's kind of like an EKG where they hook up leads and read a graph, but the leads are on the head, not the chest. They'll also do an MRI, probably tomorrow."

Her lower lip quivers. "Do either of them hurt?"

I can feel the weight of her aching heart and wish I could transfer all her pain to me. "No, ma'am. They don't hurt a bit." I want to say more, to explain myself, but I can't wait to get away.

"Thank you." Her swollen blue eyes fade to the floor, and she turns back to the waiting room.

I continue along the dreary hallway, wondering what will happen. Will my reputation of being top-notch with critical care be ruined? Could I lose my job?

When I arrive at the recovery room, Chelsea has already tidied my station. I spot her in the supply room. "Thanks for taking care of the clean-up for me."

"No problem. You'd do the same, Bes."

I smile at her Filipino *bestie* nickname for me as I pump a wad of soap onto my hands and scrub. "I'm freaking out about this whole thing."

"You didn't mess up. They'll find out the truth." She offers a quick smile.

"I replay the scene in my head: me at the patient's head, you on his right, Harold and Belinda on his left. Jake is at the foot. The EKG tech goes to the right side, and Dr. Johnson comes in from the right side."

She glances past me into the main recovery room. "Do you think Dr. Johnson did it?" Her voice is hushed.

I shake my head. "The patient's symptoms started before he tripped."

"A respiratory rate that's elevated doesn't mean someone is going to arrest." She unclips her name badge so she can clock out.

I sop up the water on the sink with a paper towel and follow suit. "His lungs were clear, so that wasn't the problem."

Belinda walks into the room. Her cropped chestnut hair is gelled straight out from her head. A wad of papers and a red incident folder are tucked under the arm of her starched white shirt. "Ariel, meet me in my office before you go home," she spouts.

Chelsea shoots me a glance and whispers, "Good luck."

"Thanks." Re-clipping my ID badge, I notice my hands are shaking. I shove them deep into my pockets and go to meet my boss.

Belinda's office is stark: a desk and khaki vinyl chair with box legs inside four beige walls, no photos of family, nothing sentimental.

There's a rap on the door, and the risk manager walks in. He's got mousy brown hair slicked back with gel and a blue, pinstriped suit. There is no other chair, but he looks like he's happy to stand because he's shorter than both Belinda and me.

"Hi, Ariel, I'm Mike." He sticks out his hand.

I give it a good shake. "Nice to meet you."

Belinda shuffles her papers. The wrinkle at the edge of her downturned mouth looks cracked and inflamed. "We need to talk about your patient, Ariel. This is not a small mistake."

"I didn't make a mistake."

Mike straightens. "We understand that things can happen. No one has come forward saying they found the oxygen tube on the floor during the code and reconnected it in the wrong place. Since you were the nurse in charge of Mr. Young at the time of the incident, your name must go on the report. We are very concerned about potential fallout from the family."

Thoughts of joblessness race through my head, and my legs fold to hit a hard seat. "I know I had the correct flow meter on. Chelsea saw me open it. Something happened."

"We don't have any proof of that, Ariel." Belinda examines my face like she's looking for evidence that I'm lying.

"I feel terrible for the family, but I know I didn't do it. I'm not sure how to demonstrate that fact. You were there, Belinda. What did you see?"

"I saw a code-blue situation where Dr. Goss saved the day by intubating the patient when the anesthesiologist was unavailable. He and I were on the left of the of the patient. Chelsea was the only one near the oxygen flow meter in question."

I glance at Belinda. "You were near the flow meter that was running wide open. You didn't hear it?"

Belinda clears her throat. "Let's not try to shift blame, Ariel. Things happen. Mistakes are made. The hospital has a risk manager to deal with the consequences of an event like this." She flips through the stack of papers, looking for something.

"I have a form you'll need to fill out." Mike hands me an incident report document.

I stare at the paper. It's what every nurse dreads. It's a huge smudge on your reputation. I've never had to fill one out before. "If the patient had no oxygen for a short time, it's usually not a problem. That means it had to have happened early on."

"Possibly," Belinda says. "The other nurses in the room said they saw nothing untoward. They mentioned Chelsea pumping, me doing IV drugs, Dr. Goss intubating, Jake at the foot of the bed with EKG, and Dr. Johnson coming afterward."

"You're missing the key detail." I start the form, feeling defeated.

"The event will have to be reported to the Risk Management Review Board," Mike tells me.

"You'll be watched for further episodes in the future." Belinda's voice is stern.

I feel myself shrinking under her glare. I hurry to finish and hand Mike the completed sheet.

"Okay," he says as he glances through it and tucks the paper into his folder.

"You can go." Belinda stands from behind her desk. "So, you know—ha, that rhymes." She laughs at her lame humor. "I'm keeping my eye on you."

I clock out, trudge down the hall. I can't get the lost look in Mrs. Young's eyes out of my head. The queasiness in my stomach ramps up. Could I possibly have made that mistake? No, I couldn't, and I didn't. I will my gut to calm.

The clunk of a heavy steel door brings me back as Harold dashes from the neuro unit and then down the stairs toward the doctor's parking lot.

When I reach the top of the stairs, I hear a male voice echoing up the stairwell in a whisper. "It's done. Nobody knew a thing."

The hair on my arms bristles. What's done? Could that be Harold? The whispering masks who it is. Doctors and the Neuro ICU staff are the ones who use this stairway the most.

I shove a pen in the door so it won't snap shut and creep down the stairs. A truck with a loud diesel engine pulls up outside, making me strain to hear the voice.

"The problem they should have taken care of with the driver is fixed. His squash is gone. We have what's necessary to compete."

Does *squash* mean brain? It's only one voice. It must be someone on a cell phone. Did he say *compete* or *complete*? I stretch my neck toward the sound.

"I'm working in the canis field tonight."

I wonder what a *canis field* is. Did I hear the right thing? Between the whispering and the truck, it's hard to tell. Could he be talking about Robert Young? Only a few people know about the patient's condition, or is he talking about the truck that's making all the noise?

"I tell you, I'm working on it," the voice hisses.

A door slams, followed by silence. I race down a flight-and-a-half of stairs to the ground floor. Bursting outside, I spot Harold, fifty feet away, hurrying to the doctor's lot, near a large cloud of smoke from a white semi-trailer delivering food supplies.

As I approach my car a minute later, I'm swarmed by flies that have inundated the east lot this past month. Scrambling to shut my Camry door, I swat frantically and notice Harold watching me from a window next to the stairs. My spine quivers. I thought he was outside. Did the smoke hide him while he turned around and went back to the hospital? And why is he watching me?

*

The front door of our one-bedroom apartment squeaks open, and I hear Ben flip on the lights and drop his keys on the kitchen counter. Climbing out of the bathtub, I wonder what's been said to him. I slip on my robe and pad to the living room. The fact that it's small afforded us the luxury of buying a good-quality, deep-pine-green, velvet sofa with a matching white-and-pine, tufted, cotton chair that we can later move to a house. A round dining table with teak trim and four white chairs was all we'd needed after that.

"Hey, there." Ben enfolds me in his arms.

I nuzzle his chest and feel my problems lessen. Out of habit, I cover the scars on his left hand with mine. The burns he got in our freshman year don't seem to bother him anymore.

This time, he takes my hand in his. "Tell me what happened."

I drop his hand, pace the living room. "The patient came out of the OR, and I knew something was wrong. The only thing off, and not by much, was his respiratory rate. Within a few minutes, he went into V-Tach. I turned on the oxygen to my right and bagged him. Chelsea shocked him. Harold intubated because Dr. Johnson had started his next case. The patient kept deteriorating. Dr. Johnson came back and noticed the oxygen plugged into the flow meter on my right was not turned on. The one on my left was."

"Did anyone vouch for you?" He plops onto the sofa, stretching his long legs out to the glass coffee table.

"Chelsea did."

"Thank goodness for that." Ben pats the seat beside him.

"I can't sit. Belinda and the risk manager don't believe me."

"You'll work it out. I have confidence in you."

"Glad *you* do." Should I mention what I heard in the stairwell? Could my imagination be working overtime? I take another lap around the room. "This may sound bizarre, but I'm wondering if it could've been Harold."

Ben pushes himself upright on the sofa. "Harold would never do that."

"Harold is the only one powerful enough to get away with it. He was at the head of the bed to intubate. The only others were Belinda, Jake, and Chelsea. Sam Johnson came after."

"Maybe it was Chelsea."

"She wasn't close to the head of the bed. She was running for meds and doing CPR."

"Maybe you were too busy with the patient to notice her."

I shake my head. "Jake came to mind because he's been so grumpy, but he was far away at the foot. Something else—I heard someone in the stairwell talking about a driver whose squash is gone and a canis field. Do you know what that's about?"

"Not a clue."

"The driver could be Robert, although the food delivery truck outside was loud," I say to myself more than to Ben. "When I got to the exit, I saw Harold on the phone, going to his car."

"Harold's always on the phone. Besides, you'd recognize his voice."

"It was a man, but he was whispering. Harold happened to be near the stairwell exit." I stop myself from saying that he'd magically reappeared in the window to stare at me.

"He juggles calls from the lab, nurses, and patients' families." Ben grabs some sparkling water from the fridge. "His reputation as a neurosurgeon is huge. Now that he's busy in the lab with his brain regeneration work, I'm getting all the surgery. My school friends are jealous that I've been able to advance my career so quickly."

"I get that you're happy. I'm just frustrated."

Ben leans in and kisses me on the head as I pace past. "I have good news for you. I called Jackson in Miami. My buddy is going to see if your dad can get into their program."

"That's wonderful. Thank you. I wish Dad would agree to come to our hospital for his ALS treatment."

"Maybe he prefers a big hospital with a big reputation over our small hospital."

"I get Dad's dilemma with stem cells since he's a former priest, but I could keep an eye on him and help Mom if they were here." I stop. A cloud in the red evening sky has morphed and mushroomed like a big bomb. The glitch in my stomach worsens.

Ben grabs my hand, tugs me beside him onto the couch. "You're far away."

"I can't stop thinking about the code and the whispers. Something shady is going on, and I've been blamed. You know Harold doesn't like the fact that I detest what he's doing to those poor brain-dead patients. They're living cadavers that he's experimenting on."

"How could you think it's Harold? He would never do anything to mar his surgical record. He's focused on restoring his wife's lucidity." Ben fidgets with the bottle in his hand. "Harold is the nicest guy around. He tells everyone you're so smart that you should have been a doctor."

"Very kind of him, but that reminds me, I *don't* screw up on something so major."

"Ariel, we all make mistakes."

"Sure, forget where you put your phone or maybe drop food on your shirt. Our Ambu bags are tucked behind the oxygen flow meters. I can't touch one without touching the other. Why would I turn on one that's three feet away?"

"I get your point. Maybe the oxygen got bumped, and someone reconnected it, not realizing that the flow meter was off."

"You'd think they would come forward."

"Maybe they forgot. You know how hectic a code blue can be."

"I have great focus in an emergency. The adrenaline rush amplifies all my senses. I would have noticed someone do that." I sigh and rest my head on his shoulder.

"That's true, I've seen you in action." Ben tickles the underside of my chin. "My vote is on Belinda. She feels threatened for some reason that you were friends with Jake and me in college. With Harold bringing me in as a surgical partner, she seems to think you have one up on her."

"I don't know why. It seems kind of juvenile, but she sure has been irritated as of late."

"Harold is at the pinnacle of his career. He's got too much to lose." Ben props his seltzer on the table and gives it a tap. "Someone will have seen what happened. Give it a few days. For now, put your feet up, relax, and forget about it. I'll order us some dinner."

My feet go up, but my mind is still reeling.

*

The pre-op area of our Becham Hospital is quieter than post-op but has the same beige windowless walls. The room is smaller since patients are usually here for a shorter time. I'm happy for the change of pace this morning.

I insert a syringe of morphine into the IV tubing in hand.

Pushing down on the plunger, I watch my elderly gentleman patient's eyes lose focus, and his lids slide closed. Kevin Quigly has been here so many times, we know each other's names. I pity the patients who come in here with peripheral vascular disease. They have a toe amputated, then another, and another. After that comes a below-the-knee amputation, followed by above-the-knee. It's not the first time I've wondered if what we do here is as humane as everyone insists.

"Good morning, Ariel. How are you doing?" Harold's voice is gentle like he's addressing a sister.

"I'm okay, thank you for asking." Not wanting to let him read my face, I finish placing the last piece of tape over Mr. Quigly's IV dressing without looking up.

"Dr. Goss." Belinda rushes to Harold's side. "The meeting about yesterday's incident is in a few minutes in the doctors' lounge."

"I'll be there. Ariel, would you mind getting Dr. Johnson from the OR?" Harold's eyes turn up with his smile, one of the characteristics that makes everyone like him.

I eyeball my patient, check his vital signs before clicking the stretcher's safety rail into place. "Sure."

Belinda glares at me. "You heard him, Ariel. Go find Dr. Johnson."

Picking up a dirty needle I'd dropped, I dispose of it in the appropriate box. "Can't leave anything sharp and contaminated around." I flash a grin as I tuck my ponytail under an OR cap.

I find Sam Johnson near suite ten, scrolling through his phone. "There's a meeting about the patient from yesterday starting in a few minutes," I tell him.

"Ugh, I hate those things," he moans.

"I guess we're all being summoned."

"I'll be right there."

When I return to Mr. Quigly, his eyes are shut, and his mouth is open in a snore. I hurry with his pre-op checklist so I can get to the meeting.

Ben appears at my side. "Whatever you're doing seems to be working."

"Morphine."

He places a soothing hand on my back. "Where is this meeting supposed to be?"

"It's over here." Belinda floats by with an extra big smile.

"Chelsea, will you keep an eye on Mr. Quigly until he goes to surgery? He can have two more milligrams of morphine if he needs it," I call.

Belinda stops. "This meeting doesn't include the nursing staff, Ariel."

My jaw tightens. "Wait a minute. You're the one who said I was responsible for the patient."

"It's set up with the physicians," Belinda retorts.

"*I'm* the one who got an incident report written up. I should at least be allowed to hear what's being said." I spot Jake walking into the doctor's lounge. "Jake's not a physician."

Harold pokes his head out. "Let's go, we need to get this started."

"Ariel, stay here and make sure your patient is ready for Dr. Johnson when we're done." Belinda rushes off.

"She is unbelievable," I grunt, piercing the bottom of an IV bag with tubing.

Ben shoots me an abbreviated smile. "I was only in on the surgery. You should be there, not me."

"Belinda's been a grouch in recent weeks. Maybe it's better I'm not going."

"I'll stick up for you," Ben pats my back and follows Belinda into the meeting.

Chelsea's round-cheeked smile sobers. "Whoa, Bes, she sure dissed you."

My cheeks heat. "That's so unreasonable. She doesn't like the connection between Jake, Ben, Harold, and me, but you know I'll be part of the conversation. It's annoying that she's trying to exercise her control by leaving me out." I busy myself reloading IV poles for the incoming patients.

"She has been riding you a lot since Ben started working with Dr. Goss."

IV fluid piddles onto my foot as the unwanted air is chased from the tubing. "Plus, she's so syrupy-sweet with Ben. It's nauseating." I halt the IV fluid, jam a sterile cap on the end of the tube.

"Oh, the complexities of dating a doctor," Chelsea teases. "All I wanted was to find some guy to go to Alaska with." Her cute pronunciation using *p* instead of *f* makes me smile. "After hearing about all those tourists who disappeared whale-watching in the Bering Sea, I've changed my mind. Now, I'd be happy with a decent date."

I laugh. "That was odd. What do you think happened?"

"In my opinion, an iceberg must have capsized the boat. Although, a lot of my buddies at home in the Philippines say the people were abducted."

My mind drifts to the possibilities while we keep restocking in silence. The time drags as I wonder what's going on in the meeting. I slide over to check my patient. "How are you doing, Mr. Quigly?"

He opens his eyes, brings me into focus. "The pain is back."

"I'm sorry," I say, injecting a little more morphine in his IV. You'll be going into the OR soon." By the time I toss out the syringe, Mr. Quigly's eyes are drifting shut.

"Wish I could have done that to the last guy I went out with," Chelsea mumbles.

I let out a hoot as Belinda enters with an orderly.

"I don't know what's so humorous around here." Fire shoots from her eyes.

Chelsea turns so Belinda can't see her face. *Spike's back*, she mouths.

I roll my lips under and hold them in place with my teeth so I don't laugh at our nickname for Belinda's short, spiky hair.

"We're done. Dr. Johnson is ready for the patient, Ariel." Each erect strand of her hair vibrates as she punctuates my name.

I hurry to hit ENTER on the morphine dosage.

"Wait, let me check my calendar." Mr. Quigley winks.

Chelsea's hand claps over her mouth. I can't help but laugh out loud.

Belinda's knuckles redden as her hands ball up. "We have a schedule to keep here, Ariel." Her arms rest on the spare adipose at her waistline. "This unit needs to run with efficiency. Patients must go to the OR on time."

I wonder what was said in the meeting that made her so cranky. I think about the reputation I've worked so hard to build. "You're right." I look away, quell my thoughts of unemployment.

"I feel much better now, Ariel. Thanks for the pain medicine. You're a great nurse." My patient offers a genuine smile as the stretcher brake clunks off.

"You're welcome, Mr. Quigly." I pat his arm as the elderly gentleman is rolling toward the operating room. "Good luck."

He grabs my hand and fixes his gaze on Belinda. "Same to you, dear."

Chapter 3

A techno beat thrums in the background as Ben and I approach The Painted Muroid. The restaurant's lobby is bathed in giant swirls of Florida azure blue and lemon. A registration table is in place of the hostess stand with brochures about the hospital and small framed quotes from big donors. "Ariel Savin and Ben Guthrie," Ben tells a blonde woman in a gold cocktail dress who has a list of paid patrons in front of her.

"Dr. Guthrie, so nice to meet you." The woman scrambles to her feet. "I'm Brie, with the hospital foundation. I'm so glad that you've become part of our hospital family."

I fix my eyes on Ben so they won't roll.

"The proceeds of tonight's grand opening are being donated to the hospital, thanks to Dr. Goss. They're serving bite-sized portions of the entrées for you to sample." She pivots to the next set of patrons.

Splashing water can be heard as we enter a room encased in a deeper shade of azure that, in the darkness, appears cobalt. The water is close. It makes me feel stifled like I'm drowning.

My eyes adjust to see a five-foot waterfall cascading behind glass shelves lined with high-end vodkas at the bar. It's beautiful but somehow unsettling. The tables and chairs that would normally fill the room have been removed. Brightly colored abstract art perches above white leather booths that encircle the perimeter.

Ben tugs down a sleeve of the navy blazer he's had since high school. His eyes roam from group to group, giving a smile or a nod to colleagues he recognizes.

I squirm under the stares of those who don't know we're a couple. "Can we go home now? I'd much rather be alone with you."

"I like being the guy with the smartest woman in the room, who also happens to be the best arm candy."

"Come on, Ben." I poke him in the ribs with my elbow.

"Since you were the one who got me the job with Harold, it's important to show face at these things so the movers and shakers in town know who we are." He waves over a waiter in a black bowtie toting a tray full of pre-poured glasses of white wine.

I snag one that's a little fuller than the rest. "Thank you."

"Sir?"

"No thanks." Ben flashes a charismatic smile.

"Harold must have a hidden charm school tucked away in that neuro unit."

Ben laughs. "Watch out, he may sprinkle some magic dust on you, and you'll have fun at this party."

I chuckle as I take another sip from my glass. "The wine's working. Don't you want one?"

Ben shakes his head. "Since you got me straightened out freshman year, I've only started having the occasional drink at home. Besides, I'm on call. Time to meet some bigwigs." He nabs a tenderloin slider from a tray going by, tugs me in a beeline to the bar. "Sparkling water with lime, please."

"I know some of the faces, but I'm not comfortable talking to a bunch of strangers."

He spots an arm-wave in the back. "There's Harold." Ben secures my hand and maneuvers his way through the crowd. "Please hold your opinion of the Unit."

"I'll try to, but you know I'm a protector of innocents."

Harold puts his arm around Ben's shoulder, pulls him close like they're best buds while a tiny woman in a black cocktail dress, dyed blonde hair coiffed to perfection, chats away. "This is a wonderful party, Harold. I hope it helps the hospital," she gushes. "It's so sad that Evelyn can't be here with us. She would be very proud of your new passion to enhance the lives of others."

Harold's smile sags. "I know Evie wants to be here with you and all of her friends. Thank you." He shakes her hand. "Ben, glad you could make it," Harold interjects as the woman slips away. "And you, Ariel." He dips his head in greeting.

I've never met him at a large social gathering before. I can call him by his first name, like we do in OR and recovery but would never out on the hospital floors. I don't want to hug him or look like the subordinate nurse, and he detests people shaking his surgeon's hands. "Nice to see you, Harold." I go for the classic air kiss.

He pulls away with a grin that appears pleased.

Ben fidgets with his shirt collar. "I'm on call. I may not be able to stay long."

"I wish I could use that excuse." Harold moans. "A lot of my surgical patients are here to give their support. Even though I'd rather be in the lab, I'm here to schmooze." Harold turns to his side. "Ben, this is Simon Worthington. He works for Regrow Corp., a group of investors very interested in our research."

Simon looks younger than Harold and a lot more tanned. The sun has reddened his dark brown hair. He's fit but not bulky, so his worsted wool suit falls perfectly like it's custom-made.

"I have a lot of admiration for what Harold is doing. He's mastering the illusion of life and death." Simon smiles.

I shoot Ben a look, wondering what the heck that's supposed to mean.

Ben ignores it, slides his arm around me, and brings me into the fold. "Simon, this is Ariel Savin."

"Ariel is a nurse in post-anesthesia," Harold tells him.

Simon's eyes trace every inch of me down to my heels. "Nice," he murmurs.

My face flushes. I look to Ben, whose grin shows he's enjoying the offhand compliment way more than me.

"The world needs people like you, Ariel," Simon finishes.

Is that like the world needs janitors?

While I try to figure out a reply, he tugs on a girl behind him. She's got waist-length, bleached-blonde hair and a tight red dress with a push-up bra displacing things so much it must be painful.

Ben has a joke about two cups of lies. He bumps my shoulder with his, our personal wink. I don't dare look at him.

"I want you to meet a friend of mine, Sparky Brooks. Sparky is an organizational genius. She's already helped me organize my closet and my pantry."

"Hi," Sparky giggles.

I apply my version of the charm-school smile as I wonder what else Sparky arranges.

Ben gives me a squeeze.

"This is Natasha." Simon scoots forward an ebony-haired woman sporting a neckline that terminates at her navel.

Natasha's over-siliconed lips border bleached teeth. She shrugs like she doesn't know a word of English.

I think about practicing my rudimentary Russian on her, but *why bother?* trundles into my brain. "Nice to meet all of you."

"Girls, there's a booth. Will you grab it for us?" Simon shushes them in the direction of the empty seats and table. "Ben, I believe Harold's research is going to wow the world."

A huge smile crosses Harold's face, his chest puffs.

"Details of his study are creating quite a stir at the hospital," Ben exclaims.

Harold nods. "The world can't wait to get their hooks into this information."

"That's a real hooker, all right," I say with a smirk.

Ben coughs. Simon laughs loud as Harold sucks in a breath and smooths the front of his shirt.

I tell myself I shouldn't have said it, but the opportunity was too good to pass up. I scramble for an idea to help Ben save face. "Simon, what do you feel is the most advantageous feature of Harold's research?"

A grin crosses Simon's face. "Definitely the brain stem work. To assist in restoring lucidity from a terminal brain state for the good of mankind is very humbling."

Ben tugs his phone from his pocket. "Head trauma in the ER, I need to go. It's been a pleasure to meet you, sir." Ben shakes Simon's hand.

I smile, extend my hand. "Nice to meet you, Simon. Have a lovely evening."

Simon clasps my hand with both of his like he appreciated the truth I spit out. "It's been a real pleasure, Ariel."

Harold drops back where Simon can't see him and gives me a scowl.

"You, too, Harold," I say with a grin.

"Come on." Ben cinches his arm in mine. "I'll drop you off on my way."

Ben leads me back through the crowd, nodding to colleagues and smiling big for the old ladies. "You've got your schmooze down. They're eating it up." I laugh.

In the car, Ben turns to me with a stern look. "I can't believe you said the guy had hookers right to his face. The hospital needs all the donating big shots it can get."

"What kind of tasteless troll brings not one but *two* hookers to a fundraiser? It was so ridiculous I couldn't resist. Simon seemed to think it was hilarious."

"He was being polite."

"He took my hand like he appreciated what I said."

"That he did, but Harold is my partner, and he needs Simon's connections. The money from a restaurant fundraiser is nowhere near enough to sustain the neuro program."

My arm bumps into the door as Ben cranks his Honda Civic into our parking spot. "Maybe he should look for associations elsewhere."

"You don't sabotage a deal because you think the guy is a low life with hookers."

"How would that ruin anything?" I climb out of the car.

Ben backs out and rolls down his window. "I've got to work with Harold every day. I don't want to make my life more difficult than it already is. Please hold the comedic quips."

*

I shed the high heels and stiff taffeta dress, climb into my pajamas. My unfinished drawing of sunflowers sits beside our little teak desk crammed in the corner of the bedroom. Working on it would be soothing, but slimy Simon is fixed in my mind. Why would a guy like that be interested in patient welfare?

Flipping open my laptop, I plug in his name. He lives in a fancy neighborhood in north Miami Beach and is divorced. Not surprising. It looks like Regrow Corp. is out of Delaware.

I go to Delaware businesses. Companies registered in that state don't need US bank accounts or documentation of who owns them. "That's not surprising," I tell Victor, our hairless cat, who's perched on the windowsill.

"Enough of Simon's antics. It's time to check on Mom and Dad." I follow Victor's sightline. He's watching cumulus clouds clash in the distance as I hit speed dial. "Dad, how are you doing?"

"Let me put the speaker on so your mother can hear," he tells me. "Ben's friend called from Miami. They'll have a spot for me in a month."

Crosswinds are starting riots in the sky overhead. "A month is a long time."

"I agree," Mom says from a distance. "We got a walker for your dad yesterday."

My stomach drops. The thought of Dad's muscles deteriorating 'til he's hunched in a wheelchair and can't feed himself is unbearable. "What if you come to our hospital? The neurology program is getting good results with their stem cell treatment for ALS."

"I'm not doing that. I'd rather die than put the cells of a dead baby from an abortion clinic in me. Just because I left the priesthood years ago doesn't mean I'll go against my beliefs."

"Dad, they don't do that here. Stem cells can come from plenty of other places, even you."

Mom shuffles in the background. "This is your life we're talking about, Paul."

"I don't want to have any part of it," he snaps.

A lump, thick like a rain cloud, sticks in the back of my throat as I think about the slow, painful demise of his disease. "Dad, with ALS, the sooner you get treatment, the better."

"What I want is in Miami."

"That's sixty miles away. If you were here, I'd be closer to help both you and Mom."

"Don't worry about me, I'm fine," she blurts.

"I thought you were on my side, Mom."

"Whatever he decides, I'm going to support your father."

I wish she wouldn't go along with everything he wants. If she brought him here, it would fix everything—I hope.

*

Chelsea meets me in the parking lot of the community center for our Saturday morning tennis. She's got her hair pulled back in a ponytail with a visor tucked in at her hairline. Her Golden Retriever, Cecil, has his tail going so fast, his whole body is wiggling. I kneel beside him, and he covers me in slobbery kisses.

"Cecil is a sweet dog. Petting him is so comforting."

"I can have them watch for a cute pup for you at the Humane Society."

"I'd love to, but Ben's allergic to fur."

"I forgot that's why you have a purless cat.

I smile at her *p* instead of *f.* She's relatively new to the recovery room, but we've become friends fast. "Ben and I have talked about finding a bigger place where I could have a garden. Maybe if we had a yard, Ben would be okay with a hypoallergenic dog."

"Sounds like you have the ring and the house already planned. I'll have to let him know," Chelsea teases.

"Haha. Don't do that." The gate of the eight-foot chain-link fence squeaks open. "I do love him, though."

Chelsea makes her way onto the tennis court, shoes swishing in the newly brushed clay. She leans on the taut net as she pops open a can of fuzzy yellow balls. "Aside from Ben, how are you doing today?"

"Freaked out about Robert Young. He was my patient and I'm the one who wonders if those brain-dead patients are in misery or are conscious on some other level. I didn't do it, but I feel like such a failure. I wonder if I should find another career."

Chelsea sets up to serve. "You're good at what you do, Bes."

"Yesterday makes me wonder if a job selling shoes wouldn't be better." I return the volley. She sends it back to me and I slam it into her court.

"Ben does like having you in the hospital. He won't care if you get another job, but maybe not in shoes, though." She grins about my exaggerated point.

"I don't know. I've spent all these years developing my career. Hospital nursing is a stable field. Even in a recession, I'll never have to worry about being homeless." My mind goes to the brief stint our family spent living in the car when Dad lost his job.

"That's one way to think about it." Chelsea lobs it to my backhand.

"What I really want is to focus on Ben. He's my top priority."

*

Tip-toeing into our tiny, white kitchen so I don't wake up Ben, I slice fruit for breakfast on the extra-thick cutting board my parents gave us as a housewarming gift. I know how hard working all night can be. I hear Ben stirring in the bedroom and poke my head in.

"Hey, babe." He stretches, pulls the pillow down under his head.

"I wasn't sure if you'd be up yet."

"What time is it?"

"Around eleven." I climb across the green-and-white duvet cover, prop my head in my hand. "How did your case go last night?"

"Gang shooting. The guy got a bullet lodged in his spine. He's going to be a paraplegic."

"That's awful."

"No kidding. Jake came in to help me finish the case. I guess Harold and Simon had a meeting after they left the restaurant last night. Harold took Simon to his lab and explained his research in depth. Simon asked a bunch of questions and whether Harold can have the cells of the brain stem erase memory and start over again."

"Can they do that?"

"Jake said Harold stayed up all night working on it. He called Jake as we finished up in the OR because he was excited. He'd figured it out."

"Harold is going to wipe the memories of all the patients like a frontal lobotomy?"

Ben shrugs. "Simon said his investors think it would be advantageous for new cell growth."

"What about Harold's wife?"

"He refused to wipe her memory."

"I would hope so. Still, it seems like a creepy request."

"I agree. It bothered Jake, too. He said he wouldn't be able to sleep. He decided to stay at the hospital and do rounds."

"Wouldn't the hospital board have something to say about that?"

"The ethical board members all quit. The ones left seem to be more interested in how much money Harold is bringing in."

Or they're paid off. I keep it to myself because if I say it, he'll get defensive. "The patients have been lying there for months, even years. They have no muscle tone or motor function. How does wiping their memory help?"

Ben props himself on his elbow. "With rehab, they could rebuild muscle tone."

"And to what end?" I interject. "How much cognitive function would return? It's so cruel, forcing those innocent people to lie there day in and day out. Harold is starting to get on my nerves."

"You can't let this stuff get to you, Ariel. If he's able to bring those people back to a normal resemblance of life, it would be a miracle. Who are we to judge whether it's right or wrong?"

"Who are we *not* to judge?" A long sigh seeps out, and I lay my head on his chest.

Ben's fingers rub my back. "Don't you remember the fights Harold had before the unit was built and all the board members who resigned? What it comes down to is that the hospital needs the money. Harold's fundraiser last night made five hundred and twenty thousand dollars for the hospital."

My eyes fall on Ben's red scuba diving flag. "I could see twenty thousand from people in the community. Five hundred is a lot of money for a function like that. The balance must have come from Simon's people."

"If Harold's program can flourish, it will help the hospital a lot."

"It bugs me that Harold is working you non-stop. He's turfing extra call to you all the time. You're up all kinds of hours and you're exhausted."

"Everyone needs to pay their dues in the beginning. If Harold succeeds, he says he'll quit doing surgery, and I can take over the practice."

I trace the lines of the new wrinkles on his forehead. "Your residency is over. Harold wants you to do everything so he can play with his research."

"He's advancing my career, Ariel. I'm building my reputation, getting credit for the success I'm having with my surgery."

"I worry about you."

"I don't love being up all night so often, but I don't want to be groveling for another position somewhere, with Harold smearing my name because you disagree with him. Besides, maybe the research will be able to help people who get Transverse myelitis like my mom."

"Your mother has done so well. Recurrence is rare; she seems to be in the clear."

"True, but if it weren't for that, I might not be a doctor."

"What would you be?" I roll up close, rest my chin on his chest.

Ben strokes my hair as he thinks about it. "Maybe I'd be a scuba guide."

"Really? I know you like diving, but I didn't think you liked it *that* much."

A lopsided grin crosses his face. "I could study the habits of the North Atlantic Slippery Dick."

I burst out laughing.

"There *is* such a fish you know," he deadpans as he pulls me on top of him.

"And my swimming ability won't affect my learning about it?" I run my fingers along the side of his face.

"It lives around coral reefs." He circles my breast with his tongue.

I feel my heart pound against his chest as my nipples tighten.

"It's an aggressive, carnivorous fish." He nips at the skin of my shoulder.

I slide my hand down his chest, across his belly, to the fullness of him. "Hmm… let me guess. It gets its name from being so slippery?"

"How did you know?" He slides inside, and I forget my retort.

Chapter 4

A yawn escapes as I sink into a chair at the long, wooden conference table. This room is technically a doctors' lounge, but it's shared with the recovery room staff in case a bunch of patients finish surgery at the same time during lunch. It's not very loungey, but the upholstered teal chairs are cushier than they would be in a regular lunchroom, and the TV is a nice bonus.

My feet ache from being here for seventeen hours and back at work by six. Being on call sure messed with yesterday's plan of a relaxing day with Ben. I pull another chair close to rest my feet on.

"Hi, Ariel. How's everything?" Jake pours himself a cup of coffee.

I'm still peeved about his rant that the incident with Robert Young was my fault. "Tired feet." I glance at the TV to avoid him.

He plops down into the chair beside me. "I got kind of carried away the other day, sorry. I was tired from being up all night with a patient. I hate giving families that news, and I thought Harold was going to turf it to me."

"Seriously, Jake?"

"Okay, okay. I owe you and Ben a dinner out."

"And…"

"And I know you didn't kill the patient. For as much as

I hate to admit it, you're smarter than that." He laughs. "Someone must have knocked the oxygen off during the code and reconnected it on the wrong side. It wasn't me. I was at the foot of the bed the whole time."

"If I hadn't known you for so long, I'd think you're a real jerk."

"Well, since you know I am, are we good?"

I think about how he used to flirt in college. I'd almost dated him before Ben had shown up. He kept on flirting for a while after Ben and I were dating making me wonder about his morals. "I guess." My mind goes to the meeting. "What happened at Belinda's meeting the other day?"

Jake's shoulders relax. "Not much. She asked who was where during the code and if we saw anything strange."

"Anything about me?"

"Only that an incident report had been filed under your name since you were the nurse responsible for the patient while he was in the recovery room."

Jake takes a sip of coffee. "I spent all day with Harold and Mrs. Young yesterday. She signed Robert over to the program."

My stomach tightens as the guilt returns. I picture the petite woman in the hall, her shock, her disbelief. "Poor thing, she's still thinking of Robert as he was. I feel so sorry for her."

"She wants the best for him."

"Harold has you buffaloed, too. She doesn't realize what she's in for."

"Come on, Ariel. Harold will be able to reinstate brain function like a salamander re-grows its tail. His idea of an implanted neurotransmitter in sync with stem cell regrowth is brilliant."

I roll my chair over to the fridge to grab my lunch. "You still don't know what the patient's personalities will be like even if you can get them up and walking again."

"We have to get to the walking part first."

"That's my point. It's cruel to keep those people alive on respirators."

"They're brain-dead. They've met the nationally set legal criteria. Those people don't respond to stimuli, they can't breathe on their own, and their reflexes are shot. They feel nothing."

"Those patients meet the criteria of fixed and dilated pupils and no reaction to pain, but how do you know if they don't have another level of consciousness and are trapped in their bodies?"

"They don't have Locked-In Syndrome, where their brains, and for some reason, their eyes, work, but they're otherwise paralyzed. That happens in stroke patients, not brain-dead ones." He eyes the strawberries as I pop the lid off them. "Wow, those look good."

"Have some." I slide the bowl over, knowing he has no retort. "I read an article on alternative treatments a while ago. It got me wondering if patients shouldn't get a more natural approach sometimes. Treat the whole person, not just the organ systems."

He plucks one from the top. "This kind of thing comes up all the time with Harold's patients."

"Light therapy, along with turmeric or green tea in tube-feeding, can decrease brain swelling."

"That stuff's a bunch of voodoo," a voice roars from the coffee bar.

I whip around to see Belinda filling her mug.

"You believe that?" she levels at me.

"What?" Harold grabs a throw-away cup, and Belinda pours for him.

She dumps a hefty dose of sugar into her coffee. "Sounds like Ariel thinks witch doctors know more than real doctors."

My jaw tightens as I fight my burning tongue.

"Hmm." Harold snags a donut from a pile he brings for the staff every day. Red jelly oozes onto his lip as he bites down.

"You're a surgical nurse, Ariel. Don't go telling our patients any of your cockamamie ideas, or you'll have families sneaking in kitchen spices, thinking they're pharmacists." Belinda takes a sip—Grumpy from The Seven Dwarfs sneers from her cup.

Harold wipes the jelly from his face. "Everyone has a right to their opinion, Belinda."

Is he sticking up for me? It must be to keep his nice guy image going. He knows I disagree with his ideological fanaticism.

"Ariel needs to keep her opinions to herself, not broadcast them to the rest of us."

Harold downs his coffee and doesn't respond. "Let's go, Jake. Anesthesia is ready to start." He disappears into the OR.

I'm left sitting with Belinda. I think about the trouble I'm in, the way she snubbed me the other day. Now, she's riding me again for no apparent reason. I need to speak up, or she'll never stop.

I take a deep breath and blot my palms on the legs of my scrubs. "Belinda, we're all supposed to work as a team. I should have been in that meeting about Robert Young."

"Your presence in that meeting wasn't necessary. The destiny of the patient was obvious at that point."

"You're calling me responsible, even though I didn't do it."

"Ariel, I'm proud of what we do in this hospital. Dr. Goss's program to save neurological patients is genius. He's such a nice man, yet you've berated his endeavor since day one."

What you really mean is if Harold fails and the money flow stops, your position will be combined with another manager's, putting you out of a job. I open my mouth to protest.

She does a STOP with her open hand, plunks down in front of me with what looks like an out-of-character genuine smile. "Maybe if you worked with the patients in the neuro unit, you'll discover the huge obligation Dr. Goss has undertaken."

"What?"

"I got a call from the nursing supervisor. They need help over there today. You can see for yourself the kind of care the patients get."

"Since when do we have to float to areas that don't belong to the OR and recovery?"

"The hospital administration wants all nurses to be available for other areas."

"Other nurses don't know how to recover patients. When we need someone here, we have to cover ourselves. It's not fair."

"Is it fair for the patients to not be able to get the care they need when somebody calls in sick? You're a good nurse, Ariel."

"I happen to be the first one available, right?"

"You know how to handle patients on respirators. I think you'll come back as delighted as me to be contributing."

I dig my fingers into my kneecaps and don't answer. My eyes fix on the abstract print I've made on my scrub pants. It looks like someone screaming.

*

Walking into the neuro unit feels like going into a funeral parlor, with a fake lemon smell masking the odor of diarrhea instead of formaldehyde. There's a heaviness to the too-cheery-yellow walls while the only sound is of respirators clicking on and off in stereo. A chill envelops me as I read inspirational posters hung on the walls.

I tell myself it's only one day. I'll take care of these people the best I can and hope the nurses are friendly enough to give me a hand moving and turning them. But the underlying stillness is unsettling. It's like a scene in a movie when a cat is about to jump out of a closet.

I head for the central nurses' station. Three of the twelve rooms are empty, and there's not one gray head in the place. Odd for anywhere in a hospital other than obstetrics and pediatrics.

Passing a converted closet set up as an office, I figure it must be Harold's. I wonder how much he uses it since he's in the lab more these days.

"I'm Ariel Savin from PACU. Heard you need help today," I say to a nurse with thin brown hair slicked back in a ponytail.

Her eyes are sunken and shifty, and her scrubs are light pink, a color usually worn in the nursery. A baby toe is about to tear its way through the fabric of her sneakers.

"I'm Rebecca," she says in a low voice.

They even talk like it's a funeral home here.

"Thanks for coming over." Rebecca lowers her head and all but whispers, "Ashley and Jessica quit yesterday. We're strapped for help."

"I didn't know that. Did something happen?" I say in a soft voice, thinking of how fast I would quit a job in this horrible place.

The chair she's in swings side-to-side without pause. "You know the argument around our brain stem subjects. The situation is too much for some people to handle."

Subjects? They don't even consider them people. "Why are you whispering?"

Her eyes shoot to room number one. “Dr. Goss doesn’t want his wife disturbed.”

“Is that Evie over there? I heard she had a complication after her brain aneurysm that caused brain death.”

“Shh! And we call her Mrs. Goss.” Rebecca gives me a look to make sure I get the point. “Dr. Goss sits at her bedside, holding her hand, telling her how she’s going to be well soon. It’s sad.”

“It’s got to be hard on all the families.”

“A lot of the subjects are indigents from the streets. Families of the others come a lot in the beginning, but the visits become less and less, until it’s only holidays and birthdays except for Dr. Goss. He’s in Evie’s room twice a day, stroking her cheek or reading to her. He’s dedicated.”

“I’ve never seen that side of him.”

“He hides it.” Rebecca turns back to me. “The care here is pretty straightforward. Because of the ventilators and IV meds, we have no aides or LPNs. It’s just the two of us. Are you familiar with vents?”

I nod, thinking how painful it must be for the families to see their loved ones artificially breathed and fed, to watch their muscles deteriorate to living skeletons.

“Good. You have rooms six through nine. The night nurse is finishing up. She’ll give you report.”

I scan the area, listening to respirators clicking on—whooshing air into patients’ lungs. The sound bounces off the windowless walls.

The night nurse, sporting the same pale pink, flops into a chair. Her eyes hold the heaviness of being forced to stay open against the body’s normal diurnal rhythm. “Thanks for coming to relieve me. Doing another shift after night shift is torture.”

Tortured staff and patients… that’s novel. “This isn’t an easy place to work. How do you do it?”

"I decided a long time ago that it's not my place to judge. I do my work and go home, happy that my patients never complain." She clicks open a computer screen to give me report on my new charges.

I feel for her as she trudges her way past each patient on the way out, but all those young patients are the ones I pity.

Heading to room six, I notice the rooms have a similar setup to the regular ICU. A monitor, oxygen, and suction are on the back wall to the right of the headboard. A respirator is parked next to the oxygen. To the left of the bed is another suction and oxygen flow meter with an Ambu bag.

The respirator sighs out a greeting as I examine my first patient, a female named Tina. Her hair, once bleached blonde, has grown out with two inches of brown and is secured in a pigtail on top of her head. It's freaky that brain-dead patients can't think or breathe on their own, but their hearts beat, their hair grows, and they digest food. They can even carry and deliver a baby. The thought makes me shudder.

I do my usual head-to-toe, checking each system to see if it's functioning properly. I suction out her lungs, turn her, and check for bed sores. I figure I'll go back to bathe her, change dressings, tubing, and sheets on the second round.

My second patient, Mary, has scars over large dents in her scalp where pieces of skull were bashed in. The tip of her nose points to the right from a break, and her left cheek has a jagged four-inch scar.

"I'm sorry this happened to you," I say.

Checking her eyes, I notice pupillary movement. The hair on my arms bristles. None of these patients should have reactive pupils. Did I make a mistake? I check again.

The left pupil responds with a slight constriction when I shine a light in it. My stomach flips. I rush to the door. *Hey, Rebecca* is on my lips, and I hesitate. Sinking into a chair at the bedside, I stare at the woman.

Has Harold been able to restore brain function? You'd think I would have heard about that. If these patients are waking up, they're comatose, not brain-dead, which means they have brain activity of some sort. I check the chart. The woman has been here four months. Pupil checks were discontinued after the first month. Could it be that nurses aren't checking pupils, assuming that the diagnosis is complete? Was this overlooked from the beginning?

I bathe Mary while I think about it. Should I ask Harold or Jake what's going on when they finish in the OR today? I don't know if I can trust either one of them.

I recheck the pupils, the left one has a one-millimeter reaction again. The knot in my gut tightens. I zip back to Tina, recheck her pupils, and find she has an almost imperceptible reaction in her left eye. It's so slight I wonder if it's my imagination. I wish there was a pupillometer in the unit because it's so much more accurate. That's not going to happen with the budget crunch around here. I check again. It's there.

Moving on, I assess Zora, a gunshot victim from Jackson. Both pupils constrict even though they're sluggish. Her brain is starting to work. She doesn't respond to pain, so her motor responses aren't present yet.

Weebly is next. No pupil movement. No apparent brain activity in this girl. Do her parents know the plan and that's why they want her out of here?

Three out of four patients have one or both pupils reacting to light. Dang. Harold is waking these patients up. I need to find out more.

"Hey, Rebecca, will you hold Zora over while I change the sheets?" I call out to the desk, making sure to keep my voice down.

"No problem," she whispers.

I close the sliding glass door, pull the curtain behind her, then roll Zora's stiff body toward me. "The people I'm taking care of aren't on any medications. Is that true of everybody in the unit?" I cradle my patient, trying to sense any seizure activity as Rebecca tucks the old sheets along the patient's back and prepares the new linens.

"Pretty much, unless they get an infection and need antibiotics or something for an acute situation. We don't give them any long-term sustaining medications." Rebecca finishes the sheets on her side of the bed.

"Do any of them get any type of sedation?" I ask as I roll the patient toward her, pulling out the old linens and tossing them into the laundry.

Her face puckers. "They're brain-dead. They don't need any sedation."

I fish crumpled sheets from under the patient's back. "Do you do pupil checks or anything to reevaluate their brain function?"

"We do palliative care here. They've had a final diagnosis by the doctors after a ton of tests. We keep them from deteriorating."

"What if something changes?"

Her lips tighten. I watch her jaw set. "We would notice." Her voice goes a tone deeper. Rebecca rolls Zora toward her. The tube on her tracheostomy pulls, stimulating her cough reflex.

I roll the respirator closer to relieve the tension on the tube, and the patient's coughing stops. "Has Dr. Goss completed his research to start helping these people?"

Color flares in Rebecca's jowl. "Dr. Goss only discusses his progress with the administration and the families when necessary."

"So, he's not yet working on reversing the brain stem damage that's keeping patients here?"

"Not that I know of."

I wonder if Harold is lying to them or telling them to lie.

I tug the wrinkles out of the sheet, secure it well under the mattress. "Thanks for your help, Rebecca."

"Not a problem." She steps back, and something in her jacket catches on the railing.

It's a penlight for doing pupil checks.

Chapter 5

"Ariel, what are you doing here?" Jake speeds toward me, the onyx curls on his head bouncing with each step.

I slip out of Zora's room and close the sliding glass door behind me. If she has anything left in her brain, Zora doesn't need to hear our conversation. "The nursing supervisor sent me to help since the unit is down on staff."

"Are you here for the whole day?" His tone has a touch of worry.

"I guess so," I sputter, wondering why this feels so awkward.

"Which patients are you assigned?"

Rebecca jumps into the conversation. "I gave her rooms six to nine."

Harold walks into the unit, and Jake's shoulders relax.

"Have you found your way around, Ariel?" Harold asks with an extra-wide smile. "Did Rebecca give you a tour?"

Rebecca's brow shoots up.

"This layout is very similar to the ICU, so I am familiar with it." I study his face, trying to figure out the dynamic here.

The wrinkle in Harold's brow unfurls. "Perfect. It's delightful to see you again, my dear."

My dear? That's never crossed his lips before. Something's up.

"What do you think of my neurological intensive care unit?"

I roll over in my mind whether to be honest. I know he wants to hear me say he's amazing for being at the forefront of saving lives, but I'm not going there. "It's absolutely fabulous." I offer my own exaggerated smile.

Harold rubs the back of his neck. "It took a lot of work to put this together."

The truth smolders in my throat. I want to say what he's doing is *so* wrong, but I think about Ben and remind my tongue to stay in check.

Harold studies my face. His hands fist up. "You do know about my wife?"

"It was tragic. I'm sorry."

Harold smiles, shakes his hands loose. "The families here thank me all the time. They understand we're on a path that can twist the very fabric of humanity to restore their loved ones."

I cough at his absurdity and hold back my thoughts that he's forcing physical existence on these poor people, keeping them in a perpetual hell.

Patches of red bloom on his cheeks. "Do you know how hard it is to lose your wife to a freak incident like post-op brain sag when you're the expert who should have recognized it? Every day, I come here and see my Evie lying in a critical care unit instead of in my bed."

"I'm sorry for your loss, Harold. I truly am."

He turns to Rebecca. "Will you make sure that Ariel has everything she needs today?"

Rebecca tucks her hands in her pockets. "I'd be happy to."

"Good, I'll be in my office." Harold pivots toward his cubby, and Jake follows.

A pang of guilt digs at my insides. It must be tough for him.

*

As I fill a basin to bathe my next patient, I think about Mrs. Young, wondering if she'll be in later. This place is so creepy it would make me want to stay away.

My phone beeps with a text from Chelsea:

How are you doing over there?

Harold and Jake came by. We discussed our feelings regarding this place.

Oh boy. I wish you would keep your opinions to yourself.

I did. It was hard. They could read me, though. Should I tell her about the pupils? Maybe I'd better keep it to myself.

How many patients do you have?

They gave me four. I'm on the second one. I've glanced in on the others and got a set of vital signs.

Hang in there, Bes. I'll see you when you get back.

Harold motions to Rebecca as he leaves the office. She checks to see where I am and meets him in the supply room.

I tiptoe over to the linen closet next to it. I can use the excuse of getting sheets and towels if they see me. Propping the door open with my foot, I leave the light off to avoid drawing attention.

"This is outrageous." Harold hisses. "I'm going to have words with that nursing supervisor."

"Dr. Goss, we need nursing staff."

"Rebecca, you know…"

Harold's voice gets muffled like he turned the other way. I wonder if he saw me come in here. I pile sheets from a rolling cart onto my arm.

"I can't… sir." Rebecca's voice is softer, too.

I strain to hear as I stretch for the towels.

"This is very tender cargo we're carrying. I don't want that nurse anywhere near…"

Harold knows I disagree with his experiment. Is that why he is making a fuss, or is there something else?

My foot slips. The room goes as black as the inside of a trunk. My throat tightens. I scramble for the knob. Wondering if they heard me, I ease it open.

"Yes, sir," she answers in a low voice.

"They're ready for me in the OR. Remember, keep her away."

Keep me away from what?

Harold heads toward the double doors. While I wait to hear where Rebecca will go, I consider what he meant by "tender cargo." I wish I could have seen Rebecca's reaction when he said it. I check to make sure they're both gone and head back to my patient's room with an armful of linens.

Out of sight behind the white curtain, the withered form of my patient greets me. Eyes taped shut so they won't ulcerate, spittle running down her cheek. I can't imagine how difficult it would be to see this if this were someone in my family.

Rebecca pokes her head past the privacy curtain.

I gasp and drop the linens.

"Are you all right?"

"I wasn't expecting you."

"Could you help me with turning?" She eyeballs me as I scoop the linen off the floor.

I wonder if she saw me or if she truly needs a hand. "Sure." I dump the clean linen in with the dirty laundry.

Rebecca eyes the bin. "We don't like to be wasteful with supplies."

"It hit the floor. I'm not compromising for my patients."

"Figures," Rebecca grunts.

Her patient has a mangled leg that has since healed. Should I ask what the circumstances were or leave it alone? I spot a picture of a soldier on a nightstand and figure asking about a photo wouldn't pose a threat. "He's a veteran?"

"Yes. Did a tour in Iraq, was a prisoner of war, and ended up homeless after he came back."

There's a twinge in my chest. The picture of us living in the family car flashes by. "I understand the pain of homelessness, but I don't know how prisoners of war survive. The confinement… Being at the mercy of your enemy… Having no control whatsoever…"

I roll the patient to me, hold him balanced on his shoulder and hip while I check out the leg. "Those were some nasty wounds. They look pretty recent."

"We're not to discuss things."

"Why?"

Rebecca avoids my gaze. "You know, the HIPAA privacy laws."

"Patient history is necessary for proper care."

Rebecca rolls the man toward her, cradling him. "That changes when they arrive here."

I duck behind the patient to hide my surprise while tugging the balled-up sheets from under him. Do they not talk about histories or erase them?

Harold parts the curtains and steps in with a smile. "Aren't you curious?"

I mirror his grin. "Being observant regarding the people we care for goes with the job."

"That's what makes you such a good nurse. I admire watchful people. It's something I do myself."

Is that a compliment or a threat?

*

Back with my patient, Mary, I think about Harold's words. Is he watching me? Did he know I was in the linen room? How about on the stairs?

As I organize my supplies, I wonder if the patients have more going on mentally than we recognize. Could there be a level of consciousness that we're not aware of? Patients talk about out-of-body experiences after being resuscitated. Is that type of experience prolonged because they're being kept alive?

The idea sends a shiver up my spine. I need to find out more about the people in this unit. Maybe I can figure out if there is an underlying state of awareness. I hurry to finish re-taping the tubes that protrude from Mary's body.

Examining her chart, I find nothing unusual. The standard course of testing has been documented, and consents were signed by a sister in California. The only change is the level of assessment by the nurses has gone to that of palliative care. I stare at the living skeleton stretched out on the hospital bed before me. If she has some kind of brain activity, is it enough to know she's stuck here, dependent on us for everything, but unable to communicate?

I need to read all the charts in this unit and look for anything other than a vegetative state.

I peek out at the desk. Rebecca's at the computer.

I can't get her patient info with my password. How do I chase her away? Can I get an alarm in one of her rooms to go off without her seeing me? If she reports me to Harold or the administration, I could lose my job.

What if I'm mistaken? Maybe it was a trick of the light in the room, a reflection off the sliding glass door that made me think her pupils reacted?

I check with my light again. Her large pupils contract with the slightest movement. Not just the left, indicating damage to only one side of the brain, but both equally.

No mistake.

I head for the supply room, grab a new urinary catheter and bag since Zora's is due for changing. Gathering my courage, I slip into one of Rebecca's assigned rooms and shake the foot of the bed.

The heart monitor goes off, showing static. Rebecca looks up.

"Do you want me to check?" I ask from the hallway.

"No, I'll take care of it."

I tiptoe to the nurse's station and watch for Rebecca's feet showing under the curtain. Slouching below the central computer, I check the screen. She left the chart open under her ID. I'm in.

Her patient in room two, Lydia, is from Jackson in Miami. A twenty-two-year-old in a car wreck. She was sent here after a month. She'd lost fifty pounds before she arrived, up four since she got here. I wonder if it's fluid related or if Harold feeds them better.

There's an italicized *P* in "*P*atient" in the nurse's comments. I sit up. Zora has the same thing. It must stand for pupil reaction. Interesting that in the chart, these people are not called subjects.

I hear movement, so I check on Rebecca. She's still behind the curtain.

Scrolling back in the chart, I look for when the *P* started.

My breath catches. It was today.

I punch in Evie, wondering if she has a *P*. She's password-protected. Shit.

Popping my head up, all is clear. I scan fast through Robert Young. He has a urinary tract infection with a high fever. Geez, she said he was all right.

There's a thud from Rebecca's direction. It's the lid from the dirty linen bin. She must be done. I close the chart and head back to Zora's room.

As I change out her catheter, I think about common threads. Two patients with *P*, one from Tampa, one from Jackson. We have another patient from Jackson with no *P*. All patients who were in-house were pronounced dead by Harold. Not surprising because they were surgical patients… or is it?

Chapter 6

My mind is spinning with recent events as I hit the button for the double doors to the recovery room. A couple of patients are keeping the other nurses occupied. Chelsea and Jake are in a corner, whispering.

When Jake spots me, his cheeks flush, and he zips through the back door into the operating room.

That was odd. “What are you doing, Chelsea?”

“Looking for jobs in case you need one.” She leans over an open *Journal of Peri-Anesthesia Nursing*.

Didn’t look like it runs through my head. “Seriously?” My eyes follow Jake’s trail. He’s such a cheerleader for Harold. Could he be trying to get me to quit? We have our differences, but I’ve always felt he was more aligned with my side than Harold’s. Maybe that’s changed.

She crosses her arms and tilts her head toward me. “Even though you’re one of the best nurses here, Belinda has decided to put you on her shit list.”

“I may be a bit unconventional sometimes, but I stay within the rules. She’s never fired anyone for that.”

“Ariel, I overheard her this morning. You shouldn’t be talking about natural, alternative treatments they don’t do here in the hospital. You’ll lose your job.”

I feel my shoulders tighten. “She can’t fire me over an opinion that doesn’t affect the care I give to my patients.”

"You'd better watch out. She's been on a rampage against you."

I know I shouldn't mention their huddle, but something about it is annoying. "Does Jake have inside information on that, or is he trying to get rid of me?"

Chelsea's nose wrinkles. "No on both counts."

My rational self reminds me that she's my friend, that she wouldn't betray me. I direct my attention to the MH cart, and do the daily check of all of our malignant hyperthermia equipment. "We haven't had anyone in an MH crisis for a long time."

"Thank goodness for that. It's so scary."

"Some of these drugs expire tomorrow. I'm changing them out now." I get new ones and pull over a cart with IVs, gloves, and electrodes to start restocking the drawers beside each stretcher.

"Stop it. It's past your time to leave. Go home. You got sent to that awful unit today. Go have a nice bath and relax."

I want to say that I can't stop. I need to do something rote and familiar while I absorb all the things that are going on in this hospital. "Ben's second case today got delayed because of blood work," I tell her while I tow the supply cart to the next stretcher. "He's cramming in three cases tomorrow. He'll be all charged up in the morning, and I want to make sure I have everything I need to start."

"I'll do that. Get out of here." Chelsea nudges me away from the cart.

I grab an IV bag, pierce it, and chase the fluid through the tubing. It's moving slowly, like it will never get to the end. I feel the same.

Chelsea puts a hand on a hip. "Are you trying to tell me what I said about your job has sunk in, and now you're worried?"

"I'm not worried."

"Ariel, when you get the sense something's up with your patients, you're always right. I know you want to pursue that, but you need to be careful about your job." Chelsea nods like she's agreeing with herself.

"Maybe you're right," I say to placate her.

"You know I am, but it's time for you to go home." She tugs my ID badge from my shirt and slides it through the computer to clock me out. "Get out of here."

"All right." I snatch my badge back. "I'll see you tomorrow."

A light breeze swirls around me as I step into the sunshine. I spot my car in the first space, remembering how happy I'd been this morning to find such a good parking spot.

The flies find me and follow me to the car. One gets in and divebombs straight into my ear.

"Get out! Get out!" I claw at the live buzz saw trying to bore into my head. I yank the fly out. It lands on the windshield, and I flatten it with my hand. I peel the thing away with a tissue as the sun glints off a window in the neuro unit, flashing at me like a beacon.

*

"You're home early." I put my bag down next to Ben's laptop and a pile of papers he has splayed across the dining table. "I can't remember the last time I saw you before dark on a weekday." I run my fingers through his hair, kiss him full on the mouth.

He pulls away. "For as much as I'd like to dump this project, I can't now."

"Does Harold have you doing research for his brain regeneration program?" I stay close.

"He wants me to start doing lectures to bring in more surgical patients. I thought I'd get a jump on it while I have some time today."

"Seems to me that you guys are pretty busy already."

"I know. His plan is to keep the hospital administration happy with revenue."

So they don't snoop into what he's doing. I grab a LaCroix from the fridge. "Want something to drink?"

"No thanks." A long sigh seeps from Ben as he shuffles through his papers. "How was your day?"

"Belinda sent me to the neuro unit. Two nurses quit yesterday."

"I heard about the nurses."

My thoughts turn to the neuro unit: the creepy feeling, the reactive pupils, my questions about patient awareness. "It seems like there's more going on in that unit than the staff talks about. What's Harold up to?"

"Same as usual."

"Did you know they call their patients subjects?"

Ben groans. "It's a new term Simon started."

Simon has a bigger role in this experiment than I'd expected. "Two nurses quitting at once seems odd, don't you think?"

"Nurses quit all the time, especially when other hospitals offer big sign-on bonuses." Ben picks up an issue of the *New England Journal of Medicine*. "All I know is this periodical holds Harold's dream. He talks about his work being published in it all the time, how he'll silence the naysayers, make himself noteworthy and rich."

"And you're okay with being recruited into his pursuit of flashy glory?"

"I've agreed to the lectures to increase my reputation as a professional in the community. I'm talking about common neurological problems and fixes, not reanimating living cadavers."

I want to ask about the reactive pupils, but I don't want to piss him off and start an argument. "Do you know if he started any of his regenerative work yet?"

"He said he found more research that'll help him, but he needs some sort of product not available in this country to make it work."

I tug the silver tab on the can as I think about the secrecy between Harold and Rebecca. The tab is stuck, doesn't want to open. "You have any idea what that might be?"

"He said it's supposed to help regenerate protein chains."

The can opens with a pop. "Is he doing some sort of spinal cord work in the lab?"

"I don't know." His eyes drop back to the journal in his hand.

I crank the tab back and forth, wondering if that's true or if he doesn't want to talk about it. "Where is the lab?"

He drops the magazine on the table. "Ariel, I've got to get this presentation written. I don't want to know where the lab is. Why don't you draw? Getting absorbed in your art might take your mind off all of this."

The tab snaps off, piercing my finger with its sharp edge. "I'm afraid it will turn dark."

*

"Looks like we're going to finish early again," I say to Chelsea as I check the operating room schedule.

"I hope Belinda doesn't send us home. My paycheck's been dwindling." She checks her watch.

The OR janitor whizzes past our door. His cap is askew,

and his scrub shirt is damp with sweat. "George, you're mopping double-time. Have you got a hot date you want to get to?"

"I wish." He pauses to refresh his mop. "I gotta clean the neuro unit 'cause they fired the guy who use to."

"What happened?"

"That guy don't know how to keep his mouth shut. His mouth's what got him in trouble."

"That's too bad. What was his name again?"

"Bill. Bill Weston. I feel sorry for him. He got a bunch a young kids."

"He's a nice guy. I hope he finds something soon."

"Me, too," he calls from down the hall, his mop swishing away.

Jake strides into the recovery room ahead of Harold's next patient coming from the OR.

"Jake, what happened with Ashley and Jessica, the nurses who quit the neuro unit?"

"They had a disagreement with Harold and left. They were traveling nurses. He didn't like that they would be short-term to start, but the director of nursing pushed him to try them out."

The patient's stretcher clunks across the OR threshold. I focus on the sleeping body gliding toward me. Something's not right. "Anything special I need to know about your patient?"

Jake shakes his head. "No. Healthy guy, injured in a car wreck a few months ago. I'm going to tell his family about the surgery."

Dr. Johnson swings the gurney over to me. "Anterior cervical fusion of C 6-7. Nothing unusual. He can have fentanyl if he needs it."

A cloud of humidified oxygen swirls around me.

Moving my arms through the haze, I apply the oxygen while Chelsea hooks up the monitor and BP cuff. My eyes are fixed on the patient's chest.

"Something's up." I lift the covers and do a head-to-toe. His breath is shallow, not uncommon in recovery. There's a weird wrinkle on his lip. It looks caved in, like he has no lower teeth. I readjust the oxygen mask, inspect his mouth. All his teeth are there, no cuts or bleeding.

Dr. Johnson checks the monitor above my head. "His vital signs look good. No medical history. No problems in surgery. He'll be fine, Ariel."

I nod, but don't look up.

Chelsea hits the button for another blood pressure reading.

Sam Johnson eyes the vital signs one more time. "This was my last case. I'm going to change. I'll stop back before I leave for home."

I stay focused on the patient, re-check the monitor. "Everything looks good except this strange wrinkle on his mouth."

Chelsea leans over. "I wouldn't have even noticed that."

I lift the covers to scan my patient again.

A tiny squeak escapes his throat.

I reach behind the neck brace then thrust his jaw forward to keep his airway open.

A screech like a clogged vacuum cleaner bounces off the walls, vibrating terror.

Laryngospasm.

I grab an Ambu bag, crank its oxygen on all the way. "Get Dr. Johnson from the locker room!" I holler. The monitor above me screams as the patient's heart rate accelerates.

I peel the face mask off to place the Ambu's soft edge over his nose and mouth. Spreading my hand across it, I hook my fingers under his jawbone. With my other hand, I squeeze the bag hard.

Air escapes out the side of the mask.

A high-pitched shriek fills the room.

My patient's throat pulsates with desperate attempts to suck in air.

Another screech.

I stretch my fingers wide, clamp down on the mask like a vice. Squeezing the bag as hard as I can, I shove fresh oxygen past the restriction.

The patient's chest rises.

Chelsea arrives at my side and draws the curtain behind her.

I push another lungful of oxygen in. And another.

The stridor subsides.

I hear running.

Dr. Johnson appears with stethoscope in hand. He listens to the patient's lungs. "Looks like you've got it under control, Ariel. Good work."

I hesitate, with the Ambu bag still over my patient's nose and mouth. I know the incident is over, that the patient can go back to the oxygen mask, but I can't get the picture of Robert Young out of my head. I recheck the oxygen tubing and the flow meter. Everything is in place and working. I scan the monitor, watch all the numbers as they return to normal.

"You fixed it, Ariel." The elderly anesthesiologist puts a reassuring hand on my shoulder. "He'll be fine."

Chelsea nods. "Yup, you caught it, Bes."

I reapply the humidified oxygen mask and stare at the patient's chest, listening to his even breaths. I hope Dr. Johnson doesn't see how much my hands are shaking as I place my stethoscope in my ears to hear the patient's wheezy, even breaths for myself.

Taking a peek at his eyes, I note the only problem is they're still glassy from anesthesia. All is good.

"Start an aminophylline drip. That should clear up the bit of wheeze that's left."

"I'll get it." Chelsea hurries off to the medication room.

Harold glides into recovery. "You don't usually sprint around here, Sam. What's up?"

Johnson tucks the stethoscope back into his pocket. "A little laryngospasm, that's all."

Harold scans the monitor. "He's all right now?"

Dr. Johnson shakes his head. "Ariel cleared it up before I got here."

Harold touches my hand, pulls back before I can shake it away. "Thank you, Ariel."

Fire etches its way into my face. Is he being nice or proving he knows I'm rattled? "Just doing my job."

*

"You're sweating." Chelsea hangs the IV with aminophylline, setting the drip rate on the machine. "Laryngospasm might make other people sweat, but not you. What's up?"

"Harold makes me nervous." I wipe the tiny beads from the sides of my nose. Doesn't she think it's weird that, every time something happens to a patient, he's here?

"Ariel, you're being paranoid. He's showing his appreciation because you did the right thing." The IV machine starts to beep.

"It's odd."

"You're angry with him, that's all."

"You would be, too." I flick a bubble out of the IV tubing and the beeping stops.

Chelsea pulls up a stool to sit beside the stretcher. "Why would he do something to harm his own patients?"

"I'm not sure. I need to poke around and find out."

"I'll buy you a magnifying glass. You can tail him." Chelsea laughs.

"Very funny." I grab my stethoscope to listen to my patient's chest again.

"You could use that to eavesdrop through doors." Her chortle grows louder.

I can't help but grin as I write down a fresh set of vital signs. "Cut it out. Here he comes."

"How's my patient?" Harold's voice rumbles from the doorway, a cup of coffee steaming in his hand.

I straighten. "Lungs are clearing up."

As he gapes at the monitor, I figure now is my chance. "Is laryngospasm common with anterior cervical fusion?"

Harold checks his phone. "The larynx is manipulated more with this surgery."

"I don't recall that happening with any of the others."

He keeps his attention on the phone. "You'll have to catch up on your reading."

"It seems kind of unusual," I press.

"Can I see the chart for this guy?" Harold turns the monitor to an angle I can't see and starts scrolling through the pages. He sighs and closes the chart. Leaning over the patient, he takes a long look at the dressing that is obviously free of blood. "Thank you for taking care of the problem, Ariel."

Harold's smile is saccharine-sweet. It makes me want to barf.

"Isn't that patient due to go to his room now?" Belinda glares from the entryway.

Harold ducks into the OR. Chelsea winks and slips into the medication room.

"I want to keep my eye on him for a few more minutes," I answer.

Belinda groans. "You and Chelsea need to finish up and go home. The OR schedule is done."

I hurry to pack up my patient, so I don't get in any more trouble.

As the orderly helps me whisk the stretcher out the door, Chelsea whispers, "I saw Harold change something in the chart."

Chapter 7

Back in the recovery room, I'm helping Chelsea finish up with her patient so he can be transferred. I can't stop thinking about what she said regarding Harold. "What did you see Harold change in the chart?"

"I don't know what it was. I thought I saw him hit delete and then type something in."

"Was it on the recovery room sheet?"

"I couldn't tell, the screen was at a strange angle."

"Was he typing numbers or letters?"

"I don't know. It's not like I was looking over his shoulder."

"That's not very helpful, Chelsea. You tell me something, get me all worried about it, and then say, 'I can't help you.'"

"Sorry. I thought you'd want to know. Would you call some muscle so I can get this guy out of here?"

"Sure." I find the orderly.

As he and Chelsea roll the patient away, I'm left wondering whether medical records have the original transcript. I'm pretty sure I logged out, but I don't trust Harold. I can check while I pick up my lunch.

On my way to the cafeteria, I hear Harold's voice in a one-way conversation by the elevator. I slow down. He must be on the phone. He's around the corner, so he can't see me.

"I'm anxious to get this going, too, Simon. You need to understand that dozens of trials are done on animals before humans," Harold says as the elevator *dings* its arrival.

"I've given you a lot of money." Simon's voice is loud through the phone, and it sounds like he's angry.

"I get it, but I'm pushing the limits already," Harold says.

"Push harder."

I walk past to see Harold looking at his phone. Simon must have hung up on him. The elevator door shuts. Harold was making excuses. Why is he unwilling to cross Simon? I know the money is important, but it's Harold's program. My stomach rumbles, and I head for the cafeteria to get my lunch.

The door to medical records is locked when I arrive. I spot an intercom on the wall and hold down the button. "Hi, I'm Ariel Savin from PACU. I need to look at the surgical dictation for a patient I had today."

A buzzer sounds, and I let myself in. The door locks behind me with a loud *click*. I shudder because the room is as dark as a basement lair. "They give you mood lighting down here," I joke, noting the burnt-out bulbs above my head.

A snowy-haired woman in a worn purple sweater and bright red lipstick spread way past her lip line grunts. "And not a window in sight. I'm ready to bring some light bulbs from home so I can see."

"I hear ya," I laugh, checking the space for spider webs.

"At least it's quiet. No patients hollering. No hissing and farting of machines. Who's your patient?"

"Mel Hasner."

She reads her computer screen through wire-rimmed glasses. "The transcription is finished. You can check it out on the monitor over there."

"Thanks." I don't know if she can see the first computer

in the row of cubbies from her desk, but I don't want her to watch what I read. I settle in at a screen halfway down as her cell phone rings. She leaves the room to take the call.

Since she's not here, I decide to check my recovery room record first. Nothing has been changed. Thank goodness for that.

As I pull up the surgical record, I hear the door to the outside hallway *clunk*. I pop my head up from behind the cubby and see that it's Harold. He's looking at the desk and doesn't see me. I duck back down, scan the document.

His footsteps come my way. They're heavy, purposeful.

I read faster, trying to examine every word, looking for things that are out of sorts.

The footfalls are closer. Did he follow me? My skin prickles.

I speed up, skipping words. A shadow falls across my computer, and I click out of the chart.

"Hey, Ariel." Harold leans over the partition, sporting a huge grin. "I didn't expect to find you here."

My cheeks burn as I build a lie. "A friend asked me to check her brother's ER record from the weekend. I know we're not supposed to do that because of privacy laws and all, but you know…"

"I guess we all cheat a little, don't we?" He laughs and takes a seat.

What does he mean by that? I stand to check what he's doing. "What brings you here?"

"I forgot to sign the surgical dictation on my last patient. I put in an addendum and wanted to make sure it showed up."

I pick up my lunch, showing I plan to leave, and watch while he pulls up the original dictation. Sure enough, no signature.

"There it is," he says as a red blip of signature comes on

the screen, showing the chart has been changed. "Okay, done." Harold stands up beside me.

I do a nervous two-step. I'm not sure what to say. How lame it is that I'm down in the bowels of the hospital, checking his work? I fumble with the Styrofoam container in my hands.

"After you." Harold smiles and holds an open hand toward the exit. "This hospital needs to start making some money. It looks like a dungeon down here."

*

Chelsea's halfway through her food by the time I arrive in the lunchroom. There's no one else here, which gives us a chance to talk. I settle in at the big table.

Chelsea picks up her sandwich. "What did you discover?"

"Wild goose chase. He only forgot to sign his dictation."

"Ugh!" she grunts between chews.

"At least I got to see the medical records department. I've never been down there. It's pretty creepy."

"That and the morgue. They make a perfect pair."

My arms chill.

"Geez, Bes. You look like you've seen a ghost. What's that about?"

I drop my gaze and push around the lettuce in front of me. Shoving a forkful of salad in my mouth, I gnaw on a memory.

Chelsea leans in closer. "Well?"

"Every time I walk past the morgue, it reminds me of when my parents had to go ID my brother."

"I'm sorry, Ariel. What happened?"

"He OD'd at nineteen." A long sigh seeps out. "I could have prevented it if I'd told my parents about the people he was hanging out with. I kind of got into the partying with him. I pulled back when my grades dropped. He kept going."

"How old were you?"

"I was sixteen."

"You were only a kid. You can't blame yourself."

My mind goes to when Ben had started partying too much in college and ended up in a bad spot. Jake had been a big help then. He believes he's still helping me somehow. "After all we went through in college, it feels like Jake's flipped against me."

"Where did that come from?"

"Harold is getting creepier all the time. Jake knows it, yet he's not saying anything to help me out."

"That's his boss. He doesn't want to lose his job."

I stare at the wall, knowing that she's right, but I can't lose the spook I got in medical records. "Harold is way too powerful. He's put me under surveillance from all the big shots, and I can't do a thing about it." *And he has the ability to kill off a patient and get me blamed for it.*

"You're getting ahead of yourself, Ariel."

Taking a long sip of cool water, I let her thoughts dissipate. "He even managed to know I was in medical records and showed up at the same time." I don't tell her how he had seemed to be going to his car yesterday and yet had appeared in a hospital window, watching me.

Chelsea straightens. "You never said he was down there."

"He came in right after me. The timing was uncanny. Couldn't he call them to check or look at the chart tomorrow when he goes to see the patient?"

"You need a vacation, girl. Get out of town and put all this behind you."

"My dad's too sick for me to take a vacation."

"Maybe go up to see your parents and enjoy the Carolina mountains' fall colors."

"What Dad needs is to get out of North Carolina for some treatment." I shove my chair back, and it bangs the wall as I trash my empty lunch container. "I can take the heat, in here and outside."

"I ate too fast. I need some air," I tell Chelsea and head for the hospital's duck pond out front. It has a soothing fountain people sit by to reflect. The air is heavy with humidity, the sun blocked by gathering clouds. I can't get my mind off my dad's ALS. I hit the speed dial for Mom.

"It's surprising to hear from you this time of day. Is everything all right?"

"I'm fine, Mom, just thinking of you. How are you?"

"We got back from the doctor's office." There's a wrinkle in her voice. "Your dad's getting worse."

My stomach knots, and the food I ate threatens to come back. "Oh, Mom." Images of Dad and withering patients flash through my head. "What happened?"

"He fell again. He didn't break anything, but it scared him because he smacked his head."

I stare at the pond, water from the fountain crashing down like giant tears. "Mom, I'm so sorry. How are you doing?"

She clears her throat. I hear her swallow. "I'm okay."

"Did they offer anything that will help him?"

"A wheelchair and rest."

My heart crumples, and I suck in a breath. "His pride must have been crushed." I picture her phone gripped in one hand, a tissue in the other, blotting the tears streaming down her face. "If I can get a bed for him here, would he come?"

"I don't think so. He's set on the ALS program in Miami." She sounds exhausted.

I feel so bad. "Mom, see what you can do. I'll call you later."

"Okay, honey." A muffled sniff comes through the speaker as she clicks off.

I check the time. Almost two o'clock, one more patient.

Dad can't wait a month for Miami. I need to get him in here, even though he hates the idea of stem cell treatment.

I trudge up the stairs. The neurologic program is a far cry from Harold's neuro unit and has a completely different staff. It could work out well for him.

As I enter the recovery room, Belinda eyes me. I wonder what she's up to.

"The nursing supervisor wanted me to let you know you did a great job in the neuro unit the other day. She's thankful for your willingness to float."

My dad's dying, and she wants to lay on the bullshit? I remind myself to hold my tongue. "You can tell her she's welcome." I smile.

"Not all nurses have the wherewithal to take care of that kind of patient. That's why I chose you. You are a good nurse, Ariel."

She'd better not be sending me back right now. "Thank you. I'm glad you feel that way."

"A friend of mine is about to come out of surgery. She has her PhD in Nursing and is quite well-known in the academic world for her theories. Everyone else has a patient now. You'll have to take care of her."

She says it like I'm the last resort. "No problem," I say as a tiny woman with flaming red hair is rolled in front of me by the OR team.

"Ariel, this is Sandra Garner," the anesthesiologist informs me. "She's had a total hysterectomy under spinal with sedation. No significant medical history. She can go to her room once she has movement in her legs and feet."

"Thanks, Dr. Johnson." I hook up the patient to our machines.

"How are you feeling, Sandra?" Belinda asks as she applies a blood pressure cuff.

I've never seen her do that before. She's putting on a show.

"Grrreat!"

"I have a meeting that started a few minutes ago, but I wanted to make sure you were settled."

Sandra's lids start to fade over her green eyes. "I'll nap." A light snore filters from her throat.

"Text me when you transfer her." Belinda cranes to see if the flow meter is on as I apply oxygen.

My jaw tightens. Damn that Harold.

I wake Sandra up every half hour to see if she has movement in her feet. After a couple of hours, there's still nothing.

"I'm leaving, Ariel," Dr. Johnson tells me as he stops to check in on Sandra. "Why don't you take Belinda's friend around the corner into the pre-op area so she doesn't have to listen to all the commotion in recovery?"

Sandra's eyes flutter open while I slog the gurney she's on into the next room. "What got you into nursing?" she asks me.

The sedation is wearing off, thankfully. I place her stretcher in the quietest part of the room. "I wanted to be able to help people get better."

She rolls her head to read my face. "Is that working for you?"

I jolt back. "I beg your pardon?"

"How do you feel about working in a hospital after having done it for a while?" Sandra asks, trying to focus on my face.

Dad comes to mind. I certainly want everything known

to medicine to be performed to make him better, but there's this niggling.

Sandra's eyes are blurry. She won't remember this conversation with the amnesic Versed in her system. I decide to be honest. "I wonder if what we do is more detrimental than beneficial to patients sometimes."

Sandra blinks to focus. "That's the reason I got a PhD in nursing. I got burned out on the everyday and felt that I could touch more people in the teaching world."

How refreshing. I decide to proceed with caution. "There's a lot to medicine and patient care that can be done on the preventative side."

"That's what I teach in my nursing theory classes."

I examine her eyes to see if she's stringing me along. They're shades of green and brown that complement her brick-red hair… and they're truthful. "I didn't even know that existed."

"Nursing theorists strive to open people's thinking to new concepts," Sandra blurts with such force her toes wiggle.

"I like that. Perfect timing," I say as Belinda walks through the door. "Sandra's feet are moving, and so is she."

"Ariel, I know it's your time to leave, but will you stay with Sandra and take her up to her room?"

Is she joking? "You don't mind the overtime?"

Belinda grabs the other end of the stretcher. "We want her to have consistency of care. I'll help you."

"Sure." I smile as Belinda steers a wobbly course down the hall to a private room at the end of the surgical floor. The western sun streams through the window, making the room feel too warm. Faded beige-and-green vinyl wallpaper peels from the corners where the sun hits. A worn sand-colored vinyl recliner sits next to the window. We roll the stretcher in place to slide Sandra over.

"I'll raise the bed," Belinda says, pushing the control.

"Wait, there's an overlap," I call.

The bed lifts the edge of the gurney. The stretcher tilts, IV pole catching on the over-bed light. The bag rips, and Sandra screams as she's saturated in IV fluid.

"I can't believe you did that!" Belinda barks and grabs a towel.

I open my mouth to retort and wonder if it's better to take the hit. Getting wet won't kill Sandra. If I take the blame, maybe it will improve my standing with Belinda. I hurry to lower the bed, align it with the gurney and hear, "I'm so sorry, Sandra," come out of my mouth.

Belinda blots the face of the woman. "She's soaked, Ariel."

How can I allow Belinda to do this to me? Because I want her off my back, and I don't want to have to look for another job. I tell myself to take a deep breath, clean the mess up, and I'll be out of here in ten minutes. "Sandra, I'm going to slide you toward me, and I'll get you cleaned up." I grab the sheet and pull her into the dry bed without waiting for Belinda's assistance. Blood backs up into the IV tubing.

"Hold this." I hand Belinda what's left of the IV bag and race down the hall to the nurse's station. "I need a liter of D5LR," I say to the nurse who will be taking care of Sandra. "The other one ripped on transfer."

"You don't need to be so panicked, honey. It's not the first time that's ever happened to anybody."

"Except this patient has her PhD in nursing and is my nurse-manager's friend."

"Yikes." She hands me a new bag.

I hurry back to the bedside, thinking it's unfortunate that patients who are connected get an extra level of care.

"Sandra, I feel terrible. I'll get you cleaned up right

away." I plug in the new IV. As I hang it on the pole, a large air bubble traps in the tubing. I pinch the tubing and flick the bubble with my finger, trying to get it out. The bubble won't rise up like it's supposed to. The IV doesn't stop.

"Get that out of there!" Belinda yells as a two-inch space of air inches toward Sandra's arm.

I dig my fingernail into the tubing and grab a sterile needle from my pocket, shoving it into a port to vent the air. The bubble rolls right past the needle.

"Get rid of the air." Sandra's face is panicked. Her hands fist the sheets.

"It's supposed to go out the needle. I don't know why it didn't work." I move my fingers lower and pinch the tubing next to her skin. The flow of fluid doesn't stop and pushes the bubble into Sandra's arm.

Belinda glares at me. "Do you know what can happen from an air embolus?"

My stomach churns. "I'm sorry. It was an accident. You saw me. I did everything possible to get that air out."

Sandra closes her eyes and, with a move that looks like some kind of Zen meditation, she breathes in through her nose and out through her mouth. Her eyes flutter open, and she offers me a genuine smile. "It'll be fine. We all know that happens sometimes. It wasn't a whole tubing full; it was only a small amount."

Belinda touches Sandra's arm where the bubble went in as if to make it go away. "How could you do that to her?"

"Ariel didn't mean to," Sandra intervenes.

I want to crawl away and hide. I know it happens, but this was really bad timing. "I'm so sorry, Sandra. So sorry. Using the needle always worked before."

"It's not a big deal." Sandra smiles.

Belinda's jaw pulsates as she loosens the brake of the

stretcher and shoves it out of the way. "I'd better put the side rail up myself before you do something to make her fall out of bed." She slams the railing into position.

With shaky hands, I hurry to snap a fresh hospital gown onto Sandra and cover her with a dry blanket, making sure the IV is running properly. "I need to give report. I'm sure you'll be happy to have a new nurse."

Belinda leans toward me, her face twisted in a snarl. "I won't forget this."

I wonder what I'll have to do to pay for this mess.

Chapter 8

At home, I climb into a pair of soft blue jersey shorts and a shirt, Dad on my mind. I need to do more research on ALS treatment before my tennis game with Chelsea. I would love to disappear into my artwork, but don't have the time.

As I settle in at the computer, Victor hops onto my lap and begins to purr. I feel my blood pressure going down as I run my fingers over his head.

"It's hard to believe that Dad is sick, Victor. He's always been so energetic. Why couldn't he get something that could be cut out? I know all the best surgeons."

Victor lays his head down and continues to purr.

Opening my laptop, I find it's still on Simon in Delaware. A headline at the bottom jumps out: *The Russian oocyte program for irreversible brain damage terminates when patients develop aggressive personality changes.*

Oocytes must have something to do with ovarian cells. I skim through the article. *After two years of physical therapy, Vladamir Planov's family was shocked when he started disappearing for hours and returning home blood-stained. "The first time he said he fell, then it was because a dog bit him," Planov's mother stated. She contacted a woman she knew from the hospital brain regeneration program and discovered similar things happening with her son. The women reported it to the Russian Medical Society, and the program was shut down.*

"It doesn't mention Simon, but it's strange that this is on the same page. The woman with Simon at the restaurant was Russian. That can't be a coincidence, Victor. Are Simon's investors Russians trying to recreate that same program here? I know a lot of Russians live in north Miami Beach."

The cat starts to knead my legs with his paws like he's trying to massage the idea. "I'll have to think about this later." Plugging in info about the ALS program in Miami, I find they're using a protein garnered from stem cells exposed to ultraviolet light and a protein chain. They've partnered with a hospital in Massachusetts to get the product. "Huh."

Half an hour later, on my way to tennis, I swing by the apartment complex on the back side of the hospital where they house the traveling nurses. I asked around in the hospital to see if the two girls who'd quit had taken an assignment on a different floor, but they hadn't. A twenty-something woman with wavy, long, blonde hair wearing green scrubs and white runners comes out of one of the apartments.

"Hi," I say. "I work in PACU. I'm looking for Ashley and Jessica. Do you know which apartment is theirs?"

"That one was." She points.

"What do you mean, *was*?"

"It's like they left in the middle of the night. No one saw them load up, but their cars are gone. It's surprising because we have to prepay our rent for three months. It's super-cheap rent, but the hospital wants to make sure we stick around for the length of our contract."

"That does sound odd. Does anyone have a phone number for either of them?"

"No. They worked the same shift. They'd go to the beach or clubbing together."

I knock on the door. It goes unanswered. "Were they close to anyone else in the building?"

"Not that I know of. Why are you asking?"

"I got floated to the area they worked in after they quit. I wanted to ask their opinions on some things. Do you think I could look in the window?"

"Don't see why not. They're gone."

I cup my hands and peer in. The cabinet doors are open and empty. There's not a personal item in sight, only the basic furnishing provided. "It does look like they're gone. If they happen to show up, here's my phone number." I pull out a scrap of paper and scribble it down.

"Okay, I'll let them know."

Getting back into my car, I wonder why they left. What about losing the rent money? Most nurses can't afford to do that. Could they have been threatened?

*

I hammer my tennis ball against the painted practice wall at the Community Center. Heat radiates in waves from the asphalt surface as it bounces back to me. I swing harder. How many slams against the concrete will I need until I feel better?

My eyes burn. I wonder if it's from worrying about my dad, anger over Belinda's friend and Robert, or plain old sweat. I set up a serve, smack the ball so hard it breaks open.

"You destroyed that ball, Bes," Chelsea calls. "I'm not sure I want to play against you today because you look like you're ready to beat the crap out of anyone who comes in range." She leans against the wall, racquet resting in the crook of her arm. She looks effing perfect in a new navy tennis skirt with white-lined pleats. I look like a drowned rat with my hair soaked in sweat and a shirt with a hole in it.

"I have to get all of this out of me somehow." I wipe the sweat from my eyes.

"I heard about your incident with Sandra."

"Which one? The ripped IV bag Belinda blamed on me or the air bubble that wouldn't get out of the tubing even though I used every trick that exists?" I grab a new can of balls. "I sure know how to make a good impression with the bosses."

"Don't worry about it, Ariel. She's a nurse. I'm sure she's had an air bubble in a patient IV at some point," Chelsea soothes as we make our way to the court. "Did you get a chance to talk to your dad?"

"I'm afraid if I talk about it, I'll burst out crying."

"I hear ya. Tell you what, I'll give you first serve and choice of side."

First comes out *pirst,* which makes me smile inside. "I feel better already." I flash her a wide grin. "Between Belinda's gaslighting, my dad's illness, my patient dying, and the problems with the neuro unit, it's like my head is going to burst." I hit the serve. It whizzes by Chelsea.

"Geez, Bes, I didn't even see that ball. I'm not letting you get to me this time."

We go at it for a while, and the score stays close. I hit one deep to her backhand and she misses.

"I need to get that stroke in shape." Chelsea lifts her sunglasses, dries her face with her towel. "Good match."

"Thanks. I feel better with something positive in my day." I slide my racquet into its sleeve and plop myself in the shade.

"Loser buys." Chelsea laughs as she tugs two bottles of water from her bag, hands me one. "I ran into a guy I know who's with the police department. He was at the scene after the hit-and-run on your patient, Robert. He said a huge mess was created by packages spilled all across the ditch in the rain."

I think about Robert, the strange circumstance of me

being blamed, the whispers in the hall. I take a long drink of water and wonder if Robert's truck could have been hit on purpose. "Was anything missing?"

Chelsea looks down. "He said the boxes and labels got wet and were falling apart. It was hard for them to track the packages."

I lean closer. "So, something was missing?"

"He's not allowed to talk about an open case outside of the office." Chelsea's lips twitch as she looks over her shoulder. "I'm not supposed to say anything, but…" She fans herself for a second. "It turns out a biomedical box that was unaccounted for."

My heart, which had been slowing, begins to pound again.

"A camera at a nearby business showed a black pickup sideswiping the truck. Another guy was waiting behind the building and took a box from the scene."

"Have they ID'd the guys?"

"They both had black hoods and sunglasses on. Covered the license plate, too."

My mind goes to Harold and Rebecca whispering in the unit. When he'd said *tender cargo*, I thought he'd meant patients, but maybe it was the box. My arms chill. "Could Harold have something to do with it?"

"There you go again, back to Harold. Do you know how unlikely that is?"

"With Harold, anything could happen."

"You should go buy a lottery ticket. You might get a hit there, too."

"Why do you keep sticking up for him?"

"Why would you jeopardize your job?"

"My reputation is on the line, and I can't live with this guilt."

"You need to let that go. It's all you talk about."

"That's not true." I take another swig of water.

"You're consumed by it like it's more important than your dad or Ben."

Heat pulses its way into my neck, across my cheeks. "How would you know?" I glare at her.

"Because that's all you talk about."

"You're the one who brought up the cop. If I force myself to focus on the box, maybe the nightmares of Dad and my patient dying won't be in my face all the time."

"You're going to get in more trouble at work to take your mind off your dad?"

I jump off the bench, jam my water bottle in the trash. "If that's what it takes because I *will* find out about that box."

*

A wailing valve in our showerhead greets me when I walk into the apartment. I know I should do something about it, but it'll have to wait. Dropping my bag on the countertop, I stash my racquet in the closet. The door bangs closed.

"Is that you, Ariel?"

"Should I call out, 'Honey, I'm home' when I get here?" I laugh.

"That would be great. I'd know you're not a disgruntled patient with a machete."

A wave of steam hits me when I poke my head in the bathroom. "Are you kidding? Your patients love you. I'm ready for a glass of wine. You want one?"

"Sure. I'll be out in a minute."

On the counter are a couple of bottles of our usual Two Buck Chuck. I know I should open one. Ben is being frugal because he wants to pay off our student loans before we buy a house or new cars. I reach past them for the bottle of Seven Deadly Zins we've been saving for an occasion. Ten dollars isn't going to make a difference in my life right now.

I plop on the couch and take a sip of wine, feeling the muscles in my neck start to relax.

Ben arrives in a towel, skin glistening, smelling of his favorite bay rum soap.

"That's nice to come home to."

He grins, grabs his wine, and settles beside me. "I heard about your dad."

I straighten. I'd waited to tell him, figuring he was busy. I hate when the hospital gossipmongers talk behind my back. "From whom?"

He takes a gulp of wine, realizing his mistake. "I saw Chelsea in the OR right before my last case. She thought you'd told me."

She didn't admit it when we played tennis. My mind goes back to my dad. "It's hard to believe this is happening."

"The Miami team had a big setback when a new synthetic peptide they were using got lost in transport."

The stolen box. I can't ask because he'll think I'm crazy. "Do the neurologists in the decent half of the neuro building have anything new for ALS?"

Ben slides closer. "I talked to the head guy today. They have a new drug they're trying along with stem cell work."

I drop my head on his shoulder and stare at the wall. "I bet none of that is covered by Medicare."

He cradles my chin. "They're doing clinical trials. We can get your dad in for free."

"If he'll go." I swirl the red wine in my glass and mumble, "The metaphor for blood."

Ben picks up my phone, hands it to me. "Let's talk to your dad."

There's a bump, a grating noise on the line before Mom's, "Hello."

"Hi, Mom. I have you on speaker with Ben. You sound frazzled."

"Your dad fell again a few minutes ago. I got him into bed."

"Dad, are you okay?" I ask, knowing Mom always puts her speaker on at home.

"Bruised my ego, that's all." His voice sounds weak.

"What about the wheelchair?"

"If you think I'm going to use that thing like some old man, you're wrong."

Ben inches the phone closer. "I'm sorry for what you're going through, Paul. My friend, Dave Martinez, is doing work on ALS. They have new medications they are using, as well as other treatments that he says work well for people like you."

"That would cost a fortune."

"It's a clinical trial, so you won't have to pay for it, and you can do only the meds if that's what you choose."

Dad sniffs. "The program in Miami has a better reputation."

"This new drug has the potential to surpass the Miami treatment," Ben says with conviction.

I cross my fingers. "I could keep Mom company."

Ben nods at me with a wink. "We would both feel better if you were here, Paul."

"I can't keep falling all over the place. If it's only drugs, no stem cells, I'll give it a try."

My breath lets loose. "Thank you, Dad."

"That's great, Paul. Dave said the sooner you get here, the better."

"We can pack up tonight and leave in the morning." Mom's moving around like she's already started.

"It will all be arranged when you arrive." Ben gives me a nod.

"I can't wait to see you both." I hang up and hug Ben. "You certainly have a way with him."

Ben kisses me on the forehead. "This has got to be hard for you."

"I wish he would accept the fact that stem cells do three-quarters of the work, and the drug does only one." I let my head flop back onto the cushion.

"A lot is going on with nerve regeneration these days. That can help a lot, too. You need to do what makes you happy and forget about the rest."

"I like that idea." I stare at the ceiling, glad the issue of bringing Dad here is resolved. The rest of my problems come flooding into my mind. "Chelsea shared with me that a box went missing when Robert was run off the road. Do you think Harold could have anything to do with it?"

"Will you stop? Harold is at the forefront of helping a lot of people, while you're creating this whole conspiracy in your head. How can you think a random missing box and Harold could be related?"

I prop up on one elbow. "Chelsea said medical supplies were in the box."

"So, some homeless dude who's sleeping in the bushes sees a box of syringes roll up beside him. He figures it's a gift from heaven and stashes it."

I push myself upright. "That's not what happened. Why do you always defend Harold?"

"Because I want to succeed as a neurosurgeon."

"Anything could be in that box."

"Drop the subject, Ariel." His look is stern. "Besides," he says, and runs his fingers along my thigh, "you shouldn't be messing around with Harold and his neuro unit. You should be messing around with me."

I want to talk about ALS treatment and tell him about the patient's eye movements. "Ben, it..." I touch his wrist. His skin is soft. Warmth radiates through me, melting my thoughts, my focus.

With a swift move, his arms engulf me. "You need to let go of all of that," he whispers, breath hot in my ear.

My mind goes back to flipping between Dad and the neuro unit. "You're right, I do."

"I can help you." He takes my hand, plants kisses up my arm as he leans into the curve of my neck.

The smell of bay rum and excitement fills my lungs. I squeeze my eyes shut and fling away all thoughts.

He trails his tongue along my jaw and parts my lips. His body presses inward. I feel my breasts yield against his firm pecs, his heart pounding against mine.

I run my fingers through his curls and fuse my lips to his, telling myself to put it all aside.

Ben peels away my clothes. He lays me down on pine velvet.

Chapter 9

I'm in a tunnel. It's dark. Someone's chasing me. Running, running. A phone is ringing. I can't find it.

"Ariel, your phone." Ben elbows me awake.

I grab the phone and notice it's Mom. "Mom, are you okay? It's five thirty in the morning."

"We're an hour away, and we're fine."

"What? You drove all night?" I climb out of bed and switch the phone to speaker.

"I figured your father couldn't change his mind if he was sleeping, so I made a thermos of coffee and got to driving. Where should I take him?"

Ben sits up. "We'll meet you at the hospital. The main entrance."

"Sounds good. Looking forward to seeing you." She clicks off.

Ben rubs his hands across his face. "I hope I can get him in. When I said it, I'd presumed."

My eyes wander past the blinds to the still black sky. "Mom must be desperate."

"Let me make some phone calls." He bolts to the kitchen.

Hurrying to shower, I think about Mom and Dad in their younger years. They were so active, so vibrant. It's sad they have to endure this illness when they're enjoying retirement so much.

"There's nothing available," Ben tells me as I climb out of the shower. "Word got out about a free clinical trial, and it filled up yesterday."

"Shit."

"I checked with Miami, too. No room there."

"This is terrible. I can't leave Dad hanging." A horrible feeling overtakes me. I know what I need to do, but the thought nauseates me. It would be creating a lie and cheating someone else out of their chance to live. It would be everything my dad spent his life teaching me not to do. It would make Ben and I indebted and vulnerable to the person who is already trying to ruin me.

With my stomach in knots, I inhale deep. "Could you ask Harold to pull some strings?"

Ben's phone alarm discharges, splitting the air. He rushes to turn off the wake-up call. "I hate to do it, but it looks like that's our best option."

*

The sun is rising as Mom parks their silver Honda Pilot under the hospital portico. Harold managed to get Dad a bed. I wonder if we'll both pay for that favor. I rush out with a wheelchair to greet them.

Opening the door, Dad pivots and plunks his feet on the pavement one at a time. He's pale and gaunt, with two quarter-sized bruises on his left cheek. The bald spot in his ash-brown hair had been silver-dollar-sized a few months ago, and now it's the size of an orange.

I drop to my knees and throw my arms around him. His shoulders are bony. His clavicle feels like the end of a boomerang. He must have lost thirty pounds. "Daddy, I'm so glad you're here. We're going to get you all healed up and home in no time."

"It's good to see you, Ariel." He pats my back. "I sure hope so." He scoots to the edge.

I bring the wheelchair closer. "Let me help you."

"No, I've got it." He pushes himself upright and teeters.

I move closer just as his legs buckle. I grab him by the waist and haul him into the wheelchair.

"Paul, you have to wait for help." Mom runs from the other side.

"Who says you need to go to Disney for a great ride?" He adjusts himself in the chair.

"Looks like some things don't change, Mom." I laugh and give her a hug.

Her shoulders sag like she's been holding them upright well beyond tonight's thermos of coffee.

"I booked a room for you at the Residence Inn down the street with my hospital discount."

As she pulls back, I notice the weight of her lids, the drooping below her eyes. Her salt-and-pepper hair looks shapeless and tired. Her sturdy frame is clothed in sweats and a T-shirt, not her usual snappy dress.

"Thank you," she says in a weak voice.

"I can check Dad in if you want to go and sleep."

Mom opens the trunk, tugs out Dad's suitcase. "I'll wait until he's settled."

The automatic doors jam on our way through. I retry the button, nudge the door open. It tries to close again. Holding it with my elbow, I glide the wheelchair in.

"Gee, it's like they don't want me in here," Dad jokes.

I laugh, thinking how close to the truth he is. What if he finds out? Would he ever forgive me?

I remind myself of all the reasons my choice was necessary. "Dad, I got the paperwork done ahead of time. All you need to do is sign."

"Give me my glasses, Katie. I never sign anything without reading it." Dad scrolls through the pages. "I'm not getting stem cell treatment. I told you that."

"You don't have to. Ben talked to the head of the program, who said you can take the new drug only."

"I don't see an option with no stem cells. I'd be agreeing to whatever they want to do to me."

"They have parameters laid out that they're required to stick to. The description is on page ten."

Dad continues reading. "I'm not doing this. The side effects can include heart attack, stroke, blindness, and dementia. Why don't I eat all the junk food you've taken away and drink myself blind? That seems like a better idea. I'm going home to wait for the Miami program."

"Dad, it doesn't mean that's going to happen."

He starts pushing the wheelchair toward the car. "You know how much I love reading. I'm not going to go blind."

Mom grabs a handle of the wheelchair and whips it around. "Paul, I know it's hard being sick, but you have to trust Ariel."

His face blanches, terror in his eyes.

I drop to my knees and take his hand. "Dad, they're required to tell you those things, like on a drug commercial when you're watching the news. It doesn't mean that's going to happen to you." I know potential side effects are rare. I pray none of them happen to him.

Mom clears her throat. "We've come a long way, Paul. We're not going back."

When he looks at her, his face softens. "You're right, Katie." He grips my hand tighter. "You've got to take care of me, Ariel."

He looks so scared. What if he *does* get a bad side effect or the drug does nothing? It'll be all my fault.

I can't think about it now. I squeeze back. "I'll do my best, Dad. Let me cross out the part about stem cells." Maybe in a couple of days, he'll consider the use of some of his own stem cells.

One step at a time.

Dad reaches for the pen. "Good. I'll sign now."

Chapter 10

Belinda's on the in-house phone at the desk when I clock into the recovery room. I check to see which slots I'm assigned and make sure I know the oxygen is attached, the flow meters work and all the supplies I need have been restocked. Chelsea has a post-op patient already. I plop down in a seat nearby to wait for a patient of my own.

"Ben got my dad into the clinical trial for the new ALS drug. He's on his way up to his room now."

"Yesterday, it wasn't even a possibility. How'd you manage that?"

My chest tightens as I think about being indebted to Harold. "With compromise, but I'm glad he's here."

"It's got to be a relief that he can start treatment right away."

Belinda pokes her head up from behind the desk. A wave of guilt runs through me for not checking on Sandra as I'd planned to. "How's Sandra doing this morning, Belinda?"

"She's having some pain. She's all but forgotten about the IV incident last night." She strolls toward us. It's a slow amble like she's thinking about what she's going to say. Is she going to put me on some kind of probation for two incidents in a row?

Belinda parks her shoe on the footrest of my stool, towering over me. "The neuro unit called for help again.

Everyone here has a patient, and the rest don't come in for an hour. Harold won't be happy, but you'll have to go. You know ventilators the best anyway."

Seems her job is more important than Harold. If I play it like I don't want to go, maybe she'll send me more often so I can find out what's happening. "Doesn't anybody else have to take a turn around here?"

Belinda clears her throat. "I planned to send Allie, but she changed shifts with one of the other girls."

My mind goes to the box. If it's there, I can find out why it was so important that Robert's truck got rolled.

I stow my coffee cup in the cupboard and keep my eyes on the floor like I'm upset. "I'd be happy to go."

The neuro unit smells different, less antiseptic, more like rotting clay pots. I wonder why. Looking around for a plant that's been overwatered, I find none. It might be the smell of deteriorating flesh. I shiver.

"Thanks for coming to help us, Ariel," Rebecca says. "You can have the patients in rooms six to nine again."

Is she being nice, or does she not want me snooping around in any of the other charts? "That does make it easier. Thanks, Rebecca."

Walking past each of my patient rooms, I make sure nothing is out of order before I start. It's so quiet in here. If not for the ebb and flow of the respirators, there would be no sound at all. After a quick head-to-toe on Tina in room six, I record a set of vital signs and reach for my penlight.

"What are you doing here, Ariel?" Harold's voice is crisp. He looks different. Darker. "Belinda told me she rotates the nurses that are floated from the recovery room."

"Belinda seems to have her own agenda." I smile.

In an instant, Harold's at my side, eyes locked on my hand. "What are you doing with that penlight?"

Why is he so defensive if he's trying to wake these people up?

I lift my chin and make a point to speak clearly. "I'm checking the level of consciousness."

The hotness of his anger radiates toward me. "Consciousness is what goes away when they undergo anesthesia. It comes back when they wake up. Your job here is to bathe the patients and change the sheets."

"A nurse assistant can do that. Your patients are on ventilators and need complete nursing care. That's why no aides work in critical care areas. Part of that care includes evaluating levels of consciousness."

"You leave that to me." Harold's jaw sets.

I can almost hear his teeth grinding against each other.

"Some thanks." He pivots. "I'll be in the OR if you need me, Rebecca."

He means thanks about my dad. *Great.* Should I go after him? It's not a good time now. Shit, I messed up again.

I slide the penlight back into my pocket, plug my stethoscope into my ears. Placing the end over the patient's lungs, I try to focus on giving good care.

Harold was more riled than I've ever seen him. It wasn't about my dad; it was the light. Why would he be so upset about a penlight? I thought he wanted these patients to wake up. Unless he's trying to hide something.

I move to my next patient and check the chart for her history. Twenty-six-year-old Mary, car accident in Tampa. Other than Robert, who is thirty, and Evie, who I've heard is in her fifties, Mary is the oldest of the group. The rest are all in their early twenties. Is that intentional, or because young people do careless things that cause head trauma?

I write down a set of vital signs and finish my assessment. Both pupils are reacting. Last time it'd been only the left one. "Huh." Drawing up a syringe of ice water, I squirt it into her left ear. Her eyes look left. Another sign that she's not brain-dead. "Hang in there, Mary. I'm trying to find out what's going on so I can help." I whisper.

Gloving up, I plunge a catheter into her lungs to suck out the sputum she can't clear on her own. Her cough reflex kicks in. I hate this part. It would be so horrible to have a fit of coughing every two hours while all the air is sucked out of your lungs.

I consider my findings while I get Mary bathed. Is anything happening in this unit ethical? I can't report pupil reactions to an ethics board when treatment has already been approved. But I didn't think Harold would get this far so fast. The only thing I can do is watch and see if I can stop Harold somehow. But how?

As I finish Mary's dressing changes, Rebecca pops her head out from behind the curtain. "I didn't want you to be having all the fun over here by yourself." She chuckles.

"This place is a barrel of laughs."

"I can help you change the bed. Do you mind if I leave this open so I can see what's going on in the unit?"

Does she want to be helpful or to keep an eye on me? "Sure, thanks."

"Got your linens?"

"Ready to go," I answer, unfolding the bottom sheet.

Rebecca grips the patient by the shoulder and hip, rolling Mary toward her.

As I bunch the old bedsheet behind Mary's back, I spot a scar that looks like a boot print over her kidney. "She's been pretty bashed up."

"Of all the subjects here, she's my favorite. She's so mellow." Rebecca tosses the old sheet in a bin.

Subjects again. Other than Evie, Mary is older than the rest. Does that matter? "Do you refer to Evie as a subject?"

Rebecca winces. “Of course not. We call her Mrs. Goss.”

“Well, then, why the others?”

“It’s a new term that makes us more objective about their care.”

“Do you need to be that way because, aside from Mrs. Goss, all the others are young?”

Rebecca draws back and her eyes narrow. “How would I know?”

“I’m sure you don’t, but it seems like such a coincidence.” My mind hops to the fact that young adults have a strong chance of recovery after head injuries compared to only ten percent of seniors. “How’s Robert doing?” I toss out, hoping for a tidbit of information since I’m not supposed to know about his UTI.

“He’s fine. His wife and kids are still struggling. It’s sad to hear them crying.”

“It must be horrible for all of the families.”

“Yet they still maintain hope.” Rebecca digs out the other half of the fresh sheet and tucks it in on her side.

“What about Harold?”

“He’s the most hopeful of them all. He has a goal to have his wife up and functioning for their twenty-fifth wedding anniversary nine months from now.”

“Wow! I hope that works for him. Thanks for your help, Rebecca,” I say, wondering if Evie is ahead of the pack or behind with her level of consciousness.

“No problem. Would you mind helping me with room two?”

“I’ll be right there.”

As she walks away, my mind churns. Do I have time to check out Evie in the room next door while she goes for linens? I’ll only have twenty seconds, and Harold is already mad at me.

I'm in a heap of trouble. I really should do my work and go home. But this is so unfair to the patients I can't stand it. To stop Harold, I need to know everything that's going on in this unit.

I inch my way to the sliding glass door, peek outside. Rebecca steps into the linen closet, and I dash to Evie's room.

Counting backward, I cross the threshold. Eighteen. I dig out my light and pull her right lid back. Fourteen. The pupil is large, but my pen light gets no reaction. Twelve. I try the other one. Nothing.

Eight. I need to know for sure. I glance up, looking for Rebecca. Six. I recheck the right, no reaction. Four. I do the left eye, nothing. Evie's the only patient in the unit with fixed pupils. I've got to get out of here.

As I hurry from the room, Rebecca emerges with an armful of linens. I duck down with the nursing station between us, hoping that she didn't see me.

"Are you all right?" Rebecca materializes beside me.

"My shoe's untied." I blurt, fumbling with my laces.

A deep frown stamps onto Rebecca's forehead. "Your shoe looks fine to me." Her index finger points at my face. "You may not know this, Ariel, but you don't want to mess with Harold Goss."

*

The silence is awkward as we change the sheets on Lydia's bed. I can't think of a legitimate excuse for being in Evie's room. My head is so full of the alterations in consciousness I've seen that small talk won't come to mind. I hustle to get the sheets done noting Lydia has huge scars from road rash like she was in a motorcycle accident or in a car with no seat belt. I rush back to my patient's room the second that we finish.

Rebecca's words about Harold swirl around me like a tornado. He is powerful, but how do I live with myself if I don't do something to help these people?

Mary's ventilator responds with a sigh as if it knows.

Was Robert's truck rolled to get a box? If so, what was in it? Harold's goal is to have Evie up and functioning in nine months for their twenty-fifth wedding anniversary. It seems like an impossible task. Could Harold be getting so desperate that he would have someone killed?

Having a team of thugs is not Harold. He wouldn't know where to find people like that. I wonder if Simon had something to do with the truck accident. If I knew what was in the box, it might give me an idea of how to stop them. I need to look in Harold's office.

What if I get caught? Harold would have me fired for sure. There would be complications for Ben, too.

Should I recruit someone to help me? Ben won't get involved, neither will Chelsea, and I don't trust where Jake's allegiance lies these days. What if Belinda never sends me to the unit again, and I lose my chance?

I peek at Harold's office from behind the curtain and mull it over. Well, like Simon implied, the world needs janitors. I inhale deep and plunge from the room.

Making my way to the far side of the nursing station desk, I plant a bag of tube feeding on the medication cart. I can say I got it out of the fridge to warm up and forgot it there. I position the dirty linen cart at the end of the desk as a blocker and sit down at the central computer to make it look like I'm charting.

Rebecca glances up when she sees the movement but doesn't acknowledge me.

Bowing my head, I watch until her back is to me and duck behind the desk. Shimmying along, my legs burn as I near the end of the long desk. I dip to one knee behind the linen cart, listen for Rebecca, and dash into Harold's office.

Scanning the room, I don't see the box. There's got to be something here. I slide his chair back and see some paper in the trash bin. It's wrinkled and frayed like it was wet at some time. My heart hammers against my chest. Hitting the button on my penlight, I notice it's an invoice. *MRNA peptides* catches my eye. Excitement and disdain course through my veins.

The pneumatic doors to the unit fling open with a hiss.

I freeze. So few people come in here; it can only be Harold. I dive from his office to scramble behind the laundry cart. Sliding the cart back to its original position with all the nonchalance I can muster, I blurt, "How did your surgery go, Harold?"

He glances up from his phone and walks right past me. "Is my door open?"

Glancing back at his office, I notice the door has not latched. My throat tightens. I snag the tube feeding and hurry to my patient's room.

Harold beelines to his office. He opens the door an inch, then closes it, giving it a rattle. He pivots to stare at me. Daggers shoot from him, boring into me, willing me to confess.

I focus on hanging the bag and checking the tubing.

The office door swings shut.

Is he going to come after me? I'm okay. I didn't touch the invoice. My fingerprints aren't on it.

I wish I'd grabbed it.

I sink against my patient's bed, mind racing to figure out a plan. I'll say I was looking for a lift to get the patient up in a chair.

A moment later, Harold is out of the office, talking to Rebecca. "Come here, Ariel." His tone is dark.

My hands leave sweat marks as I put up the patient's safety rail.

"What did you think you were doing in my office?"

"I thought it was a closet. I was looking for a Hoyer lift."

"It's in the empty patient room. You have no right to be in my office."

"I'm sorry; it was a mistake."

Harold slams his fist on the counter. "Cut the crap. Rebecca saw you in Evie's room. You know that's off-limits. I want you out of here right now. Never come back to this unit. Ever."

The fluorescent lights glare at me as I all but run down the hall back to recovery. What will Harold do now? What kind of trouble will I be in with Belinda? I don't know, but the box not being there tells me it must be in his lab.

Chapter 11

"Everybody's sleeping in the neuro unit, so they let you out early?" Chelsea jokes as I walk into the recovery room.

"Harold kicked me out."

Chelsea glances at the other nurses nearby. She grabs my elbow and steers me into the empty lounge. "They need staff over there. What did you do?" she whispers.

"He found out I was poking around his office and banned me from the unit."

"Why would you ever go in his office?"

"I wanted to find out more."

"Ariel, everyone knows we're friends. You need to stop nosing around before you get me in trouble, too."

"Are you kidding? Belinda loves you."

Chelsea frowns. "Belinda loves calm efficiency, not rebel nurses."

I grab the strands of hair that fell forward when she steered me in here and flip them behind me. "I'm not the only person in this hospital who thinks erasing memories and regenerating brains is not right." I step closer to the door. "I need to talk to the director of nursing before Harold does."

Chelsea leans against the oversized table. "Are you trying to commit professional suicide? You're already on Belinda's list, as well as Harold's. You'd better back it down before you get canned."

"The administration needs to know the truth. People are suffering in that unit. I don't care if Harold says they're brain-dead. It's wrong."

Chelsea rubs the back of her neck. "What if Belinda comes looking for you?"

"Make something up to cover for me."

She throws her hands in the air. "I am *not* losing this job over your craziness. It's like I'm stretching Belinda's patience by hanging around with you. If you're going to lie, you're on your own."

"Chelsea, I have to say something." I dip my head so I don't have to look at her and hike it down the hall toward the director of nursing's office.

The director's assistant sits in a sand-colored anteroom. The middle-aged woman, with deep wrinkles creasing her brow, is on the phone. She pivots her chair to fetch some papers, and I notice that the back of her blouse is damp with sweat. Beside her, a light blinks from someone on hold while a third caller rings. "She's on another line, sir. Yes, I will relay the message."

Could that "sir" be Harold? I lock my fingers together behind me and offer a polite smile while I wait.

"Can I help you?" the assistant asks me.

"I'm Ariel Savin from PACU. I'd like to see Janet Turner, please."

She glances at the blinking phone lines. "It's a busy time right now."

I don't know if this office is busy all the time or if this woman's job is to chase off nurses who come to complain. I wonder if I should make an appointment. "No problem. I can wait until things calm down."

"Ms. Turner's office. Can you hold?" She studies my face for a second, gets up, and goes into the attached office.

I'm surprised she didn't ask me what it's about. Maybe

the man on the phone was Harold, or maybe I look pissed off enough that she doesn't want to hear a rant. Either way, I'm glad I'm here. I need to get this off my chest.

"Go ahead," the assistant says, closing the door behind me.

Ms. Turner is on her office telephone, her face taut. Her suit jacket is thrown over the back of her chair. Her blonde bangs are askew. "It's five days away?" She holds an open hand to one of two gray wing chairs with white piping on the other side of her desk while she listens to the response. "What do they expect it to strengthen to?" She rolls her chair over to a bookshelf that matches the cherry-wood desk and pulls out a binder that reads *Hurricane Protocol.*

My stomach flutters. *That's* why she's so busy. Talk about bad timing. I don't have a good explanation for why I'm here. I don't have a recordable dispute against a staff member or Harold. No violations of standard practice have occurred, no laws broken.

My mind goes to hurricanes. I hate when our daylight gets blacked out by shutters, the stifling heat when the power goes out. I need to figure out a place for my car since the apartment doesn't have covered parking.

"We're on the outside edge of the cone. I'll be in touch." She cradles the telephone. "Hello, Ariel, what can I do for you?"

She knows my name. I know she doesn't know the name of every nurse in this hospital. Is it because Harold called?

I grip the edge of my seat and lean in. "I wanted to talk to you about the neuro unit." My voice is weaker than I'd like.

She flips open the *Hurricane Protocol* binder on the side of her desk, glances at the table of contents. "I know staffing problems have occurred. You're unhappy floating out of your area, aren't you?"

This is my chance to bail. I should walk out that door so

she can prep for the storm. "It's more about the patients themselves," I hear myself say.

She looks up, keeping a finger under the heading *Power*. "Oh?"

I hold the edge tighter. "When I was sent to the neuro unit last week, one of my patients had pupil reactions. If all those patients are brain-dead, that's not supposed to occur. I was floated there again today. It seems that a lot of the patients have reactions to light in their pupils. That would mean they're comatose in some form. It opens the hospital to even more ethical and, possibly, legal issues."

Ms. Turner sweeps her paperwork aside, places the binder in front of her. "It's hard to be out of your element. Sometimes, our minds play tricks on us when we're upset. I'll make sure that you are not required to float to an area you're unfamiliar with anymore."

"I am familiar with the patient care. I was an ICU nurse before I went to the recovery room."

Janet Turner leans back, crossing her arms. "I recall. And now that your boyfriend is a new partner, you and Dr. Goss have been butting heads."

I think about how I hate the hospital gossip chain and hold my head high. "Ben has nothing to do with this. The criteria for actual brain death are being violated here." My voice is too loud. I need to stay calm.

Ms. Turner taps her pen on the desk. "Dr. Goss is a renowned neurosurgeon. His notoriety brings a lot of recognition, as well as revenue, to this hospital. He's secured the funds to open the neuro unit completely on his own and deserves the right to direct the patient care as he sees fit."

I clear my throat and sit tall. "If patients have brain activity, how do you know what level of consciousness they're at? If they're having pain?"

"I know for a fact that Dr. Goss is keeping close tabs on his research and has plans for the enhancement of the human species." Her tone is stern.

"But I'm not the only person in this hospital who thinks keeping those people alive is unethical."

"Miss Savin, controversy always exists when new concepts are brought forth. I appreciate you expressing your concern. Since you are uncomfortable with the neuro unit, I will make sure that you're not required to work there." She leaves her desk, opens her office door. "You are signed up for hurricane call, aren't you?"

*

My mind races as I try to sort out all the events of the last week: my dad's illness, Harold trying to hide reactive pupils, dismissive administrators, switched oxygen tubing. It's so confusing. I don't know what to do next. I slump down on a stool beside Chelsea and her half-asleep patient.

"Did you get your exit interview done while you were there?" Chelsea deadpans.

"They didn't fire me."

"What did they do?" She eyeballs her patient, records a set of vital signs.

I force a cough. "Janet Turner pretty much told me Harold can do whatever he wants."

"That man has got some clout."

"Yeah. Now she's pissed off at me, too."

"You're starting to get good at that. You need to go home, relax, and chase all of this from your mind. I know it's tough, but you need to let it go."

I check my watch. "Shoot, it's past my time to go."

I clock out as Belinda flies in, waving the hurricane

manual in hand. "Attention, everyone!" she calls out to the entire room. "There's a hurricane out there, and we're in the cone. We're at stage one prep. It's about five days out, but you know they can speed up or turn. I want to remind you of your hurricane-call duties. Tell your families the hospital will be under lockdown."

Murmuring starts between the nurses.

"Ariel, I need to have a word with you before you go." Belinda takes a seat behind the nursing station.

Chelsea busies herself with her patient as I make my way over to Belinda.

"An angry voice message from Harold appeared on my phone half an hour ago, and a call from the director of nursing. You're making me look bad, Ariel, and I don't like it."

My eyes trace scuff marks on the toes of my shoes. *Maybe they'll fire you instead of me* runs through my head.

"You should go up and check on Sandra," Belinda directs.

"I clocked out already. My parents are here from out of town."

"Need I remind you of what you did to her yesterday?"

A flash of heat drills into my face. "I did every trick known to medicine to stop that bubble. The IV ripping and soaking her is on you. I said nothing at the time so you could save face."

Belinda snorts. "I recommend that you go upstairs and check on her." She waves the hurricane binder past my face. "As you can see, I don't have time for things like that right now."

Chelsea rolls her eyes, pulls the privacy curtain around her patient so she can hide.

"I'll say hello for you." I fake a smile, grab my bag, and head out.

"Good." Belinda flips the manual open. "You are signed up for hurricane call, aren't you?"

I hit the button for the automatic doors heading into the hall and don't answer.

I can't stand that she's making me do this. I know I messed up yesterday with the IV, but why can't she leave me alone? The problem is, I know that Chelsea's right. I have to suck up because I don't want to get Ben in trouble, and I need a job to pay my bills.

"Hi, Ariel." Sandra grins as I walk in. "It's so great to see you." Her smile is bright as the light streaming through the window.

"How are you feeling?" I plunk down into the recliner next to her.

"Terrific. I'm hoping they'll give me a late discharge."

An old man pushing an IV pole shuffles into the room, sporting hospital-issued socks. A loud fart pierces the silence. "Oops, wrong room." He scurries out the door, the back of his open gown flapping.

Sandra bursts out laughing and shakes her head. "I hate hospitals."

I try to hold back, but a wayward giggle sneaks out, and another, until my frustration is uncorked and spills like bubbles from champagne.

Sandra grabs a pillow, clutches it tight to her belly.

I leap from the chair. "Are you all right?"

She lets out a hardy horselaugh. "I often find that flipping a situation on its ear gives you a grand solution."

"I'll have to remember that." I chuckle.

"You never know when it will come in handy." She grabs a tissue, wipes her eyes. "Laughing at that man shows me the absurdity of hospitals, the opposite of my need to be here. Any time you are up against a challenge, think about how you can reverse the situation."

"Great advice, thanks. I'm glad you're feeling better. Can I get anything for you?"

"A ticket out of here."

I laugh. "Around here, my free passes have expired."

*

I walk into Dad's room in the Neuro building. It's painted a calming sage green. A shabby beige recliner sits next to the window and spa music rolls in from the hall. The room is higher than Harold's unit giving Dad a decent view. The wall clock tells me it's five-thirty. I'm glad I had time to get hurricane supplies, cash, and dinner for them.

Mom greets me at the door with big bags under her eyes. Her chin-length hair is washed and showing a lot more gray. I wrap my arms around her drink in the smell of her favorite Chanel Number Five. "How's he doing?"

She motions to the door.

I see my dad coming out of the bathroom in a wheelchair with an aide, his bare arms and legs withered. My heart sinks. He's such a proud man. It's got to be so hard for him. Without layers of clothing, he looks so skinny. Even his cheeks are sunken. "Let me help," I say to the aide.

She hands over the wheelchair and preps the bed for him while I shimmy the chair in place. Kneeling beside him, I fold him into a long embrace. His Old Spice aftershave lingers on my cheek. I wonder how many more hugs I may get. "The team here will have you running marathons in no time," I tease.

"Pretty good since I've never run one before."

I chuckle. He's using humor to hide his feelings. The aide and I each grab an arm, stand him up, and pivot him to the bed.

"You'd think I was a drunken sailor."

Laughing, I lock the safety rail in place.

His brow knits. "The weather was on a few minutes ago. Can they still do the treatment if there's a hurricane coming?"

I rock onto my heels. "Are you backing out on me?"

His lips flatten.

"Are you upset that you came here?"

"No, no. Half the time, the hurricanes stall or go into the gulf. Your mother has flashlights, a cooler, and extra cash. She even refilled the car."

"Wow, Mom, did you get any sleep? How are you holding up?" I ask while my back is to Dad.

"Hoping this works," she whispers.

I swallow hard. I was trying to help, but now they're mad at me.

I hold up the large bag I'd set on the side table. "I brought dinner."

"My favorite barbecue joint. Now, there's something good." Dad pulls his tray table over.

"You're in for some fine dining." I pass out paper plates and cutlery I brought from home. "If, for some strange reason, they don't let you stay here, you can stay at my place. Ben and I will be at the hospital."

"Oh." Mom glances at Dad. "You won't be with us?"

"If the storm comes, there's no way my boss will let me out of hurricane call."

My mother stares, unmoving.

"Are you okay, Mom?"

"It was a long drive. I'm tired. I'm going to go back to the hotel for a good night's sleep."

I stop serving. "You don't want to eat?"

"No, dear. It's fine. Good night, Paul." She kisses Dad on the head then disappears.

"Sleep well, Katie." Dad's lips smack as he licks the barbecue sauce off them.

I managed to get too much sauce on my plate. I try to balance it on my lap, so it won't spill. My fingers slip and the plate crashes on the floor. Sauce covers the bed, the wall, and his suitcase.

"I'm so sorry." I dive for a towel in the bathroom, start wiping it up.

Dad clears his throat. "Don't worry about the mess, Ariel. The room will be cleaned tomorrow. I'm ready to turn in. Thanks for bringing the barbecue."

I stop scrubbing. "Are you angry with me?"

"It's been a long day."

"Okay, sleep well." I shut the drapes, give him a hug, and shoot out the door after my mother.

Racing down the hall, I watch the elevator close as it sweeps Mom away. Is their reaction because the past few weeks have been exhausting, or are they sorry they came here?

*

Back home, I change into my running clothes. There's been so much going on I need a good run to clear my head. *Should* I have told them about my hurricane call? I've mentioned it every hurricane season since I've been here. I start down a trail along the canal next to our apartment and stop.

I forgot my phone. I look at the wildflower-strewn path that winds behind our apartment building, past the hospital and adjacent medical offices. All of them have cameras. The hospital has so many people going in and out; no one's ever alone. The scent of the wildflowers is intoxicating. It draws me in, soothes my mind.

This is a well-populated area. I'll be fine without the phone.

I get into a rhythm, lengthening my stride and letting go of my tension. It feels good to stretch my legs, let go of everything, and focus on each step. The light on the trail wanes, casting long shadows.

As I plod, a snake crosses my path. I jump to the side before I realize it's a wet reed. Further along, I spot a gator lurking in the weeds. I halt before discovering it's a pile of rocks. I hadn't counted on the light disappearing so fast. I wish I had my phone.

The flies are worse than ever. As I swat them, I weigh my routine of running back on a barely visible trail against heading out to the well-lit street for the run home. Prudence wins over, and I turn away from the quiet path.

Jogging into the bright light of the parking lot, I hear a whimper.

I stop, then hear it again.

To my side is a large blue dumpster with flip-up lids. Visions of stories about abandoned newborns flash through my mind.

Stomach churning, I hold my breath and flip up the lid.

A fresh swarm of flies escapes. The smell of rotting food and soggy newsprint engulfs me.

Peering over the edge, I spot clear plastic bags full of papers and magazines, to-go containers, and drink bottles.

Something moves under a bag on the other side.

I stifle a scream. Gathering my courage, I make my way to the other side of the dumpster.

The smell is awful, like being around a dead bowel in the operating room. Breathing through my mouth, I grip the other lid with both hands, fling it back, and gape.

Chapter 12

My stomach convulses. I take deep breaths, trying not to gag. Three dogs lay piled on top of each other, ET tubes sticking out of their mouths. Fur is shaved from a front leg on each where an IV is taped. The IV tubing has been cut and dried blood clumps on their fur.

"Who would do this?"

I reach for my phone and realize it's at home. How could I forget my phone with Dad in the hospital? I must be losing it. I case the parking lot, but see no one I can call for help.

Another whimper yanks me back. A brown-and-white spaniel is trying to lift its head. I notice the stretch gauze around its muzzle has loosened and its ET tube is almost out. "Take it easy, buddy. I'll help you."

The small spaniel is pinned under a boxer and a pit bull. I watch the chest of the pit bull and see it's not moving. Neither is the chest of the boxer.

I wish I had gloves. I don't know what killed these dogs. What if it's contagious? Another cry grabs my attention. Poor thing could be dead by the time I get help. "Hang in there."

I tell myself I've handled plenty of dead bodies, and I've been exposed to millions of germs in the hospital. This is no different.

I secure my foot on the side bracket and reach way in but get nothing. If someone dumped dogs, did they dump contaminated needles, too? I shiver.

I need a stick. If I tug the dog closer, I might be able to reach him.

Searching the parking lot, I spot a wooden pallet but can't get a board loose.

The dog whimpers again.

I drag the pallet alongside the dumpster. Climbing the boards, I balance on the edge. My fingers touch the pup, and its crying slows. "It's all right, buddy. I'm going to get you out. I need a couple more inches."

Raising my leg for leverage, I lean in, grasp the dog's thigh and tug. I lose my balance, start to slide in. I dig my fingers into the edge. My grip's not holding, so I land face-first in the dumpster.

"No, NO!" I clamber upright, feet sinking into a wet, squishy bottom. The stench is overwhelming.

I check my hands, my arms, my legs. "No cuts."

The dog whimpers.

"Here I come, buddy." I tug the boxer aside. Checking the pit bull for breathing again, I roll him away. The spaniel's eyes seem less panicked. The ET tube's balloon is down. It's half out but jammed against his cheek.

"With that tube in your mouth, it will be hard for you to bite. If I pull it out, will you?" I stroke the spaniel's head and gently peel off the Coban holding the IV in place.

He doesn't move or growl, so I peel back the stretch gauze from his face, grab his upper muzzle, and slide the tube out.

He pulls his dry tongue into his mouth and closes it. His eyes follow me, but he still doesn't move. Or he can't.

"Okay, here goes." I grab his front legs and tug him toward me.

The dog pees himself.

"Don't be scared." I stroke his back before sliding my arm under him.

His breathing is shallow. He doesn't make a sound.

I wonder if I should bind his mouth with the gauze remnants so he can't bite, decide he doesn't have it in him.

I kick a large bag of garbage to the edge. "Ready, pup? Here we go."

The trash bag collapses, and I lose my balance. Grabbing for the side of the dumpster with one hand, I almost drop the poor thing as the dog slips and dangles from my other arm.

He yelps but doesn't move.

"It's okay, I've got you." I slip my arm under his butt, slide him up on my shoulder, tug over two more bags of garbage, and stomp them down until they're compressed. "Get ready to try again," I tell the dog. I kick over another bag, test my weight. They seem to be holding.

Gripping the top of the dumpster, I spring.

The stack waivers and collapses. The dog and I fall into the mound of trash. He squeals in pain as something below me squishes and wet oozes its way up my back.

"Ugh." I leap to my feet. "This is *so* disgusting."

I want to throw up and claw my way out of here and into a shower.

I toss five bags against the side. My hand hits something hard. "An office chair," I call to the dog as I drag it up and position it against the side. "Okay, buddy, we're out of here," I tell him as I lift him to my shoulder.

Stepping onto the seat, I grab the edge of the dumpster. The chair teeters. I swing my legs over the edge and ease down off the dumpster, cradling the pup.

*

In the parking lot at my apartment complex, I lay the dog across my lap, turn on the hose, and hold scooped hands of water under his snout.

The dog drinks, and drinks, and drinks.

"That's enough for now, buddy. We need to get this garbage off us."

I peel off my socks and Asics, hose down my arms, legs, and back. Streaks of orange and brown flow in a putrid stream toward the storm drain. It's all I can do to not bolt for the shower. Thunder booms. A soaking rain would do us both good.

"All right, now it's your turn." I pat the dog's head as I run the water over his back to gently rinse out the grime. Holding him under his chest, I stand him up and find out he is a she. "Looks like us girls got into some deep shit." I laugh.

Her legs bend and flop, unable to hold her weight. "You are a mess, aren't you?" I say as I hose down her other side.

The dog rests her head on my arm and licks my hand.

My heart melts. "You're a little sweety, aren't you? Come on, a good shampoo always makes a girl feel better."

Victor leaps to his feet, back arched and hissing as I fumble with the door. "We stink, I know," I say as I hurry past him.

He bolts behind the couch.

We're almost done in the shower when I hear the front door close. "Hey, don't shut off the water, I'm coming in to warm up. It poured as I was getting out of the car. Talk about rain." Ben sneezes. "Jake got soaked this afternoon in a cloud-burst, too. I'll be happy when the dry season starts next month."

Ben sneezes again as he peels his clothes off on the other side of the smoked shower door. I rack my brain for a plausible explanation but find none. Time to punt. "I have a furry surprise for you in here."

"I like the sound of that." Ben laughs, slides the door open, and gapes. "What the heck are you doing with that dog?"

"She'd been tossed into a dumpster by the hospital with two other dogs. The other ones are dead."

Ben's face scrunches up as he gawks at me. "Say what?"

"All three of them had ET tubes and IVs sticking out of them."

"Did you call hospital security?"

"All I've done was come in here after hosing off outside. I didn't want to touch anything."

"What if she has something we can catch?"

"She kept crying. I couldn't leave her there."

Ben sneezes inches behind the shower door. "You should've called 911. They have hazmat suits."

"I was jogging and didn't have my phone." I set the dog on a towel. Her head sags in my hand as I dry her off. "The poor thing is shaking. Maybe that's a good thing because she didn't have the energy to do that before."

Ben scans her body and stops near her right front paw. "Is that where the IV was?"

"Yeah. Maybe I should have left it there. It was cut and coagulated. I didn't want anything else to get into her."

He hands me a pair of jeans and a long-sleeved shirt. "Put these on. They'll offer a layer of protection."

Donning my clothes, I wrap the dog in the towel and carry her to the kitchen, easing her to the floor. "You sure smell a whole lot better now, my friend."

"I can imagine," Ben calls as he gets dressed.

"I'm going to give her some milk and see if she holds it down."

"She does look pitiful. I'm calling the emergency vet."

I slide the dog's front legs over mine to get her head by the bowl.

Her nose slumps into the bowl as she laps up the milk.

Victor pokes his head out from behind the sofa to check her out.

"What about your dad? You can't be with him and a sick dog at the same time," Ben says as his phone rings.

My chest tightens. "I never thought of that."

"All Night Veterinary Clinic. How can I help you?"

Ben hands the phone to me. I explain what I saw and that I have one of the dogs with me.

The voice on the other end tells me, "Come in right now."

*

"Who would do something like this?" I ask Ben as we drive to the vet.

"Maybe some shady vet who doesn't want to pay for proper disposal. Dumping them at the hospital could make it look like it's a medical experiment."

"It feels like it's related to the hospital somehow."

"The hospital doesn't have any experimental labs." Ben rubs his eye with the back of his hand.

"Ben, I think we need to call the police. This is too bizarre."

"Ariel, the hospital doesn't need its reputation smeared by hypotheticals."

"You said five minutes ago I should have called 911."

"It was a gut reaction. Now, I've had time to think about it."

"Dead dogs with medical equipment sticking out of them are in the hospital parking lot."

Ben scratches his eye. "It'll be a media circus if you call the police."

"The police don't call their favorite newscaster on the way to a crime scene."

"Ariel, the news stations monitor police radios. We should be there with the appropriate people from the hospital when the police are called. We can call as soon as we're done here." Ben nods at me and turns into the parking lot.

"Okay." I hop out and gather my pup from the back.

"Dogs can bite when they're scared. Hold her head away from you."

"I think she's too weak for that."

"The smell of the clinic might trigger her." Ben hurries ahead to open the clinic door.

The emergency vet's office doesn't have the sterile feel of a hospital or the scent of rubbing alcohol. It smells like dog.

Ben sneezes even though the wood-look vinyl floors are spotless, and the wooden chairs are clean.

"I'm Ariel Savin. I found this dog in a dumpster by the hospital about an hour ago."

We're shuffled into an exam room with a stainless-steel exam table, a small desk, and two more wood chairs. The vet listens, wide-eyed, while I tell him the details about the dogs.

"Did you report it to the police?"

Ben clears his throat as he rubs his eyes. "We wanted to get the dog here right away. We figured we'd report it on our way back."

The vet offers his hand for a sniff, then dons a pair of latex gloves. "She's thin, but not totally emaciated."

I point to the dog's snout. "You can see some of her fur came off where I pulled the stretch gauze to get the ET tube out. She doesn't seem to have a fever, and she's drinking."

He draws a vial of blood, puts a drop in a monitor. "Blood sugar is normal." He sets aside the vial. "Will you hold her head?"

The vet strokes her with care as he feels the vertebrae of her spine. His hand rubs along her legs, stopping to examine the shaved area.

"That's where the IV was," I interject.

He nods, checks out the tape marks and lifts her lip. "You're being a very good girl," he murmurs to the dog, opening her mouth and peering in it with a light. "She's got a tooth broken here. There's redness on her tongue and inside her throat that's consistent with an ET tube."

Ben peers down her throat, too. He turns away to sneeze. "Who would do that? A shady vet?"

"Someone without a conscience, that's for sure." The vet closes the dog's mouth, slides his hands along her shoulder to her belly. "There's an incision like she's been spayed. It's newer, even though she's about two. Most dogs are spayed at four to six months. Keep hold of her noggin, Ariel, while I palpate her abdomen."

I hold the dog's head. She keeps her eyes locked on me.

"Her liver feels a bit enlarged, but she's not jumping at anything I'm doing here."

"Do you have someone in your clinic who will watch her overnight? I'm really allergic." Ben rubs his eyes again.

I pat the mop of fur puddled before me. "She's had enough trauma, Ben. Can't we take her home?"

"No." Ben shoots me a look.

"Other than rabies and kennel cough, dogs don't have infectious diseases, do they?" I ask.

"They carry MRSA," Ben protests.

"We're both exposed to MRSA every day at the hospital. I don't have any cuts on my hands, do you?"

"There's a scrape on your leg." Ben points behind my knee. "We need to get you a tetanus booster."

I wrench around and spot a three-inch-wide line of scratches on my thigh. "It's nothing." I say to reassure myself as much as him.

"Her lymph nodes aren't swollen. She has no fleas or mange," the vet tells us.

"Dogs can spread campylobacter and salmonella," Ben laments.

"She would have a fever and diarrhea," I counter.

"I'm checking her for worms and parasites," the vet interrupts, his voice louder as if to drown Ben and me out.

The dog flinches as he takes a stool sample, but she doesn't jump up or growl.

A smile crosses the vet's face as he tugs his gloves off. "I think this dog may be all right. I don't understand what the ET tube and IV were all about, though."

I flash him a grin and scratch behind her ears. "I need to come up with a name for you, doggie."

"She has a name and a family that's missing her." Ben's voice pitches up.

The vet nods. "That could be true, but I didn't find a chip in the back of her neck to look for them."

"I feel so sorry for her. After all she's been through, I hate to see her have to spend the night in a place that, to her, might seem like where she was tortured."

Ben slides his arm around my back. "It would be best for her to stay at a clinic, Ariel. That way, if something happens, they have the equipment to help her."

"That's true." The vet packs his samples into bags marked for the lab.

Three pairs of eyes fall on me. I keep picturing the dumpster with dogs piled in the rotten stench. "What has happened to her is so awful. I hate to leave her."

"When we go back home, she'll have to be alone. Your parents are here. I can't stay with the dog while you're with them."

As I stare at the dog, her eyes drift shut.

"She's exhausted, Ariel. She'll end up sleeping all night," Ben reminds me.

I sigh and give in. "You're right. It would be best."

As the vet scoops her up, I give the dog one last pat. "I know what I'll call you: Grace."

*

Walking out of the clinic, Ben trails behind, scrolling through his telephone. "This is Dr. Ben Guthrie. There's been an incident in the parking lot by the medical offices. Have security meet us in the southwest corner of the hospital in ten minutes."

I wonder what they'll say. I need an armband for my phone, but if I'd had it, would I have called the police? All I could think of was getting that awful slime off both of us.

Ben starts the car, reaches over, and takes my hand. "How are your mom and dad?"

I breathe deeply. "Dad is worse than I thought, and Mom is exhausted. Dad is on the verge of needing a wheelchair all the time. I hope your buddy Dave's clinical trial helps."

"This hurricane needs to turn. It could throw a wrench in the availability of staff and materials for the treatments."

"I've been avoiding thinking about that. Let's cross our fingers. The dumpster is on this side of the parking lot." I point as we get closer. "Park here and leave your lights on so we can see."

I scramble from the car. "Oh, no, the lid's on! Someone's been here. I left both sides of the lid flipped open." I call out to a security guard arriving on foot.

"Why does that matter?" he asks.

"I was jogging down the path a couple of hours ago. I ran past this dumpster and heard crying. When I looked inside, I found three dogs, all intubated with IVs in them. The boxer and the pit bull were dead, but the little spaniel was alive. I pulled her out and took her to the emergency vet."

The guard pulls a pair of latex gloves from his pocket and slides them on as we hurry to the dumpster. He flips the lid back, directing his flashlight inside.

"Oh my gosh. It's been picked up." I flip up the other side of the pair, scour the interior using the light from my phone. "It was full of garbage. The dogs were piled right here." I point. "I had to move the boxer to this corner, and the pit bull was there."

The guard follows my gestures with his light. All we see is flies picking at the orangey-brown wet in the bottom of a rusted dumpster.

My jaw aches for the words to say to prove I'm not lying. "I piled bags of garbage on this side and tried to climb out, but they kept smashing down. I finally found a broken office chair and climbed out this way, using that bracket to get down."

The guard shines his light on the concrete in front of the dumpster. "Looks like truck tires."

Ben scans the empty dumpster.

"I swear, Ben. They were right here." Something must be left. I squat, shining the light from my phone on the ground as I search for scraps of evidence. "The boxer and the pit bull were right here."

The guard shines his light back on the dumpster then on me. "Why didn't you call the hospital immediately?"

"I didn't have my phone with me."

"Women should always carry a phone when jogging alone, ma'am."

Ma'am. Geez, that's worse than the scolding.

I look to Ben for support. His eyes are in the direction of the hospital, following the nursing supervisor he'd summoned, who is striding toward us.

"Dr. Guthrie, you called?"

"It, um, seems to be a false alarm," Ben sputters.

The security guard comes forward. “This young lady found a dog abandoned in the dumpster. Anything unusual happen around the hospital tonight?”

The night shift nursing supervisor frowns. “I’m inside all night long. The only time I’m in the parking lot is to come and go from work unless the press is at the hospital for some reason. We don’t allow them inside.”

There’s got to be something. Doesn’t the hospital have cameras? Can you check the footage?”

“We have one on the south side that should cover this area.” The security guard points to it. “I’ll take a look.”

“I’d appreciate that,” I tell him. “I can’t believe they’re gone.” I go back to the dumpster and shine my light in for another look.

“What are you looking for?” the guard asks.

“For whoever came and emptied this out within the last couple of hours.”

“The vet did note what looked like an IV site on the dog’s leg and redness in her throat consistent with ET tube placement,” Ben says to the supervisor.

“Are any veterinary clinics nearby? Do you think one of them might have dumped them here, thinking the dumpsters handle medical waste?”

“I don’t know,” Ben answers. “We wanted to let the hospital know rather than call the police and have a huge media circus.”

“Where do we go from here?” I ask.

“I can file a report,” the guard says as his light shines in the vacant dumpster.

“Where does the report go? I don’t want it to disappear into the abyss,” I protest.

“It can be retrieved and investigated, if necessary,” the guard retorts.

"Can I come by the security office tomorrow to see what you found?"

"Sure," the guard tells me.

"Next time, call us immediately." The supervisor eyes me, heads back indoors.

"Yeah, *next* time." I climb into Ben's car. As I'm closing the door, I spot a little heart on the ground and scoop it up. The heart is red ceramic on the front and flat gold on the back. I know I've seen it before.

Chapter 13

Back at the apartment, I take the disgusting running clothes I'd bagged up after my shower and drop them down the garbage chute. The timing of that dumpster being emptied is too much of a coincidence.

I reach for the metal heart, roll it in my fingers. It's a quarter-inch wide and equally as long. The gold back has a pucker, where it must have been attached to something else. It makes me think of Grace, which brings a smile. I tuck it back into my pocket and head inside.

Ben pulls a beer from the refrigerator and pours me a glass of wine. "Here you go." He settles in on the couch.

"You do believe me about the other dogs, don't you?" I kick my shoes off, put my feet on the coffee table.

"Yes, but it's hard to prove when the dumpster you're talking about is empty."

"No kidding." I take a sip of my chardonnay, letting it roll across my tongue and warm the cold spot in my belly. "It'll be interesting to see what the security guard finds on the tapes."

"I see you went hurricane shopping. There's a ton of food here."

"I got gas and a wad of cash, too. You should fill up your car tomorrow morning before they run out. I sure hope the storm doesn't affect Dad's treatment."

Ben sips his beer. "It's a good thing you didn't keep the dog. You won't be able to get supplies for her before a hurricane."

"She's so sweet, I feel bad for her. Maybe I want something soft to cuddle with."

"I'm not good enough for you?" Ben slides his arm around my waist, pulls me closer.

"You can't curl up in my lap."

"I can get pretty close." Ben laughs, picks up a lock of my hair, and twirls it around his finger. "I heard you worked in the neuro unit today."

"Belinda sent me there again with the excuse that, even though it was someone else's turn, she thought I should go. Halloween is coming. I think I'll buy her a broom." I reach for a swallow of my wine. "There's something fishy going on with that neuro unit, Ben, whether you want to admit it or not."

"I know you feel that way, but it's bugging Harold. He's putting a lot of pressure on me."

"Ignore him." I shift in my seat to get a read of his face.

"He's threatening my job. If he finds you snooping around again, he said I'll pay for it."

"That's ridiculous. Your surgical skills have nothing to do with me."

"He doesn't care. He knows that he can get to you through me. You undermined him by going to the director of nursing. That pissed him off."

I pull back. "You know about that?"

His lips flatten. "I got reamed out for all of it. Can't you do your job and stay out of his business?"

"I'm sorry, Ben, but when I find something that's wrong, I want to correct it."

"It's your opinion that something is wrong. Not everyone shares your view, Ariel."

"Plenty of people do. Staff, patients, people outside the hospital."

"You're imagining all kinds of problems that don't exist."

"I didn't fabricate my patient's cardiac arrest. I didn't manufacture the story that a box went missing from Robert's truck and he mysteriously wound up as one of Harold's patients. Don't you think dead dogs are hardcore truth that something is wrong around here?"

"The problem is we didn't find the dogs. You're putting a negative spin on all of those things and blowing them out of proportion. I wish you'd look for the good in things."

"I wish you'd be more supportive. I'm swimming in the shit and dead bodies Harold's leaving around, and you don't believe there's a problem."

"Honey, you have no proof for any of it. People are beginning to wonder about your theories."

"What people?"

"The hospital is a big place. Gossip runs rampant."

"Somehow, our hospital has fallen into a *Lord of the Flies* society, with Harold at the top of the pyramid. Anyone who questions or threatens his standing is ostracized. It's such a high school mentality. I can't believe it."

Ben puts his beer down with a thud. "Stop, please."

"You want me to ignore the truth?"

He gets up from the couch, glaring at me. "I've worked hard to get to this place in life. I do not want to lose my job, Ariel."

"I can't disregard reality."

"After all we've been through, I guess your theory is more important to you than my ass is." Ben grabs his car keys.

The front door slams.

*

I sink into the sofa with a huge lump in my throat and the echo of the door slam ringing in my ears. The cat climbs on my lap. "Victor, why don't I keep my opinions to myself? They always seem to get me in trouble. Ben's a great surgeon. The patients and staff love him. Harold would never get rid of him. Still, I wish I had more proof." I watch his car as it leaves the parking lot. "I know he'll be back. This is his way of letting the air cool. I need to pick up a pencil and start drawing before I pick on Ben."

The cat purrs in agreement.

"I'll never get to sleep now. Maybe I'll go check on Dad." Leaving Ben a note to say I'm sorry and tell him where I am, I zip down to the car. The parking lot is still after the rain. It's quiet, almost too quiet.

Pulling up to the hospital, I don't see Ben's Honda Civic. Did he go to Jake's? Is he getting gas? I hope he's home in a couple of hours.

The hospital is still as I trek through the halls. I used to like this time when I worked the night shift. The visitors are all gone, the patients are settling in, and you're not yet to the point of the middle-of-the-night wrench in your stomach that comes with fighting to stay awake.

Dad is fast asleep, so I check the assignment board and track down his nurse at the main desk. The salt-and-pepper-haired woman in a pair of sky-blue scrubs and a daisy-covered jacket is doing her charting. "Hi, I'm Ariel, Paul Savin's daughter."

She eyes the ID hanging around my neck.

"I work in the recovery room. I came back to see my dad. He was supposed to have an MRI this afternoon. Are the results back yet?"

"The machine broke down again."

"Great. Dad gets cold easily these days. He's got the blanket tugged right up to his chin. Do you have another one?"

"We can only give someone a new blanket if theirs is soiled."

"We haven't had that problem in OR and recovery."

She places her mug of coffee on the mottled mica desktop. "You must be generating income. The entire neuro building has been affected. Dr. Goss needs more patients, too, or the board will terminate the program he set up to help his wife."

Harold needs patients splatters in my brain like grease in a hot pan. Does that mean Robert's accident was intentional? That smells of Simon. Harold wouldn't know how to hire thugs.

A patient down the hall hits the call button. The nurse stands.

"Thanks for the heads-up. What nights are you on this week?"

"This is my last." She adjusts her stethoscope. She looks older, more tired up on her feet.

"Are you retiring?"

She shakes her head, follows the call light. "My husband is an accountant. He says this hospital is in bad shape."

"How would he know?"

"He used to be in the firm that manages the hospital's books. He recently went out on his own."

"Tell me more."

"I've said enough. I don't want to compromise my husband's practice."

"Thanks for letting me know." I make my way to the recovery room. No wonder Harold is putting so much pressure on Ben.

Grabbing two blankets from the warmer, I hurry to Dad's room.

"That feels nice." Dad snuggles in, opens his eyes. "Ariel, what are you doing here?"

I tuck in the blankets and kiss him on the cheek. "I felt like I should check on you."

*

The sound of a dog barking wakes me. I bolt upright in bed. It's not Grace. She's at the vet.

Ben rolls over.

He didn't wake me up. I wonder if that means he's still mad or if he's over it. I don't want to wake him to ask. He needs all the sleep he can get.

I inch behind him, kiss his shoulder, and mold my frame to his, but sleep won't return. My mind keeps toggling between my dad, the dog, and Ben walking out.

At five a.m., I override the timer on the coffee pot, make my way to the shower.

Water trickles over my closed eyes. The picture of Grace lying under dead dogs, whimpering, keeps flashing through my mind, and guilt sets in. I should be thinking about Dad and Ben, not the dog.

I stick my face closer to the stream to wash the picture away. I'll call them both in a couple of hours.

At the animal clinic, I stand where the camera at the front door can see me. A buzzer sounds, and I walk into the lobby. It smells less like dog with none in here.

"I see we wear the same designer," a round woman in purple scrubs and a ponytail laughs.

"Except you're sporting the season's latest color, and I'm in plain old green," I chuckle.

"Your little dumpster girl slept all night. I can't imagine what she's been through. I woke her up once to make her drink water because the vet said she's dehydrated." She ushers me to a room with large metal dog crates.

Half a dozen dogs are in here. The scent of dog fur and Lysol is strong.

She takes me to my sleeping pup and unlocks the black mesh door.

"Hello there."

Grace opens her eyes and lifts her head.

I stroke the fur on her back. "You look like you're doing better today."

"I think she perked up because she saw you. She was terrified last night. She cried for an hour before she fell asleep."

"I was worried about that. Poor thing."

"She'll have to stay here at least until we get her lab work back. She's had a lot of muscle wasting like dogs we get that are trapped for a long time. There's something weird with her eyes that the vet can't figure out."

"Can she see all right?"

"Seems to, but what's strange is the way she shows emotion."

"What do you mean?"

"We don't know if it's from medication or something else, but her reactions are off."

Grace closes her eyes as I run my hand along her muzzle. "It's something neurological?"

"Maybe, or an issue with the eye muscles. I'm glad you came by. It's good for her to feel loved." The woman shuts Grace's crate.

The dog's eyes plead with me not to leave.

"I've got to go to work, girl," I tell her, turning away in a hurry so I can't see her pitiful look.

As I start my car, the clock says six forty-five, still too early to call Mom or Dad.

I hit the button to call Ben.

His phone clicks on, and I can hear him bumping around in the bathroom.

"Is everything all right?" he asks. "Where are you?"

"I came to see the dog before work."

"I was afraid you'd say that."

"I'm sorry about last night."

"That's okay. You're entitled to your opinion. I hope you're not planning to bring the dog home."

I wish I could hear some support in his voice. "She has to get checked out more before she goes anywhere. She's a little perkier this morning, but they said her affect is weird."

"Doesn't surprise me. You have enough on your plate right now. You don't need a dog that might be sick to worry about."

The sound of the shower door opening makes me wish I'd checked all the fur was rinsed away. "What's on your agenda today?"

"I'm in the office this morning and have surgery in the afternoon. Promise me you'll avoid Harold."

The car in front of me screeches to a halt. I brake hard. "Oh, shit!"

"Are you okay?"

"Some idiot in a red Porsche tried to get around a line-up for gasoline. He smacked into an SUV, and the road is blocked."

"That's what's nice about living next to the hospital." Ben sneezes.

"Bless you," I say, crossing my fingers. "I noticed yesterday that the dog was skinny, but I'd assumed it was from lack of food. The vet tech mentioned muscle wasting from inactivity. Now that I think about it, the pit bull's muscles were not prominent and the boxer was thin, too."

Ben sneezes again and again. "Stupid dog must have left dander on the bathmat." The shower door chugs open. "Ariel, there's a wad of dog fur stuck in the drain." He sneezes again.

Shoot. "I have a plastic bag under the sink. If you scoop the fur in and seal it, maybe it won't bother you."

The shower door bangs shut. "Forget it. I'll shower at the hospital. I hope this clears up before I have to start surgery."

*

I arrive at the hospital ten minutes late. Staff parking is full, and I have to go to the far side of the lot. As I run to clock in, Belinda spots me. "You've been racking up the tardies recently, haven't you?"

"I have a couple." The number four pops into my head.

"When you get five of them, HR puts it in your employment record, Ariel."

"Thanks for the reminder." I force a smile and head for the cupboard where we put our purses.

Chelsea appears as I check the equipment in my assigned slots for the day. "Heard Belinda putting the screws to you."

I glance toward the desk to see if she's there before I answer. "She is consistent."

"You're always on time. Everything all right with your dad?"

My conversation with the night nurse comes to mind, but I decide to keep it to myself. "You, Miss Dog Lover, will be happy to know that I went to see a dog."

"You're dog-sitting?"

"You won't believe this." I watch Chelsea's skin grow pale as I tell her about the dogs in the dumpster.

"Are you going to keep her?"

"Ben doesn't want me to."

"It's your apartment. If you want to have a dog, you should be able to."

"It doesn't quite work that way," I sigh. "I've never had a dog. I know nothing about them." I plop down onto the stool next to her. "You're good with dogs—would you take her?"

"I have my hands full with one. You should keep her. You have a bond."

"I don't know. I need to consider Ben. He's allergic. The big question is, who dumped them there in the first place?"

Chelsea nods. "And what were they doing to them?"

"The vet wasn't sure. I hope he'll have some clues when the blood work comes back."

"I'm surprised Belinda wasn't cross-examining you about that this morning."

"Maybe the administration doesn't want anybody to know. I'm going to get my phone from my bag. I want to look some things up before the first patient arrives."

When I return, I find Chelsea and Harold whispering in a corner on the far side of the recovery room.

Chelsea spots me and busies herself counting covers in the blanket warmer.

"I heard you and Belinda chatting this morning." Harold taps his finger twice on his diamond-encrusted Rolex.

"I got caught in traffic."

"You live right next door. You can walk here in less than five minutes."

"I had to run an errand."

His brow pops. "At six o'clock in the morning?"

Did Chelsea tell him about the dogs? Do I walk away

like Ben said or stick up for myself? "There's a hurricane out there, Dr. Goss." I use his formal name to show him it's none of his business.

"Ariel, the weather people announce news about every little system as early as possible to keep their ratings up. Someone sneezes in Africa, and they make it into a huge storm bearing down on us so that softies like you stay tuned in to them twenty-four-seven."

He threw in sneezes. Has he seen Ben? I pull in a slow breath. "I'm not a sucker, Harold."

"You're after food and everything else you think you need while you're ragging on Ben to gas up his car and get cash. He's tired and irritable, and I have to deal with it in surgery."

Is he making this up? "Ben is very professional. He's not grumpy in surgery."

"How do you know? You're not there."

I unball my fists and force a smile. "I live with him. That's not his personality."

"Maybe you're starting to make him that way." Harold thumps his coffee cup on the counter, stomps into the OR.

"What an ass," I mumble. "I don't know how Ben puts up with him."

Chelsea doesn't answer. There's a funny look on her face.

"Are you all right? It looks like something's stuck in your throat."

She laughs. "Don't give me any Zantac, Bes. They've pulled it off the shelves."

I laugh, too. She's a whiz at comic relief. "Seriously, what's wrong? You don't usually have tête-à-têtes with Harold."

"I'm worried about my mother. I was asking him some questions." Chelsea fidgets with the hem of her scrub top.

"You remember she had to quit her job last year because of her cancer diagnosis? Now, she's getting short on money because she's not old enough to collect Social Security or get Medicare."

"I'm sorry to hear that. It's got to be tough for you. How is she doing physically?"

"Not bad. She's in remission. But we're both concerned about how she's going to pay her bills. Harold told me about a program that can help her get some money."

"Harold helping the nursing staff? That's unexpected."

Chelsea laughs. "Harold is nice to a lot of people. You and he butt heads too much to see the good in each other."

I want to believe her, but something's out of place.

Chapter 14

The urologist working in the OR today walks by, which tells me I have two minutes before his patient arrives. I dial Mom. "How are you doing this morning?"

"Your dad was tossing and turning during the night, so they gave him some Benadryl. He's moving slow."

"But my allergies have never been better," Dad jokes.

"Sounds like your head's still in the game."

"You should see what I look like before you say that." Dad's smile radiates through the phone.

It makes me smile. He's so brave. I can't stand that he's sick.

A stretcher clunks through the automatic doors of the operating room, prompting Chelsea and the other nurses to head my way.

"I have a patient coming, Mom. I'll stop by this afternoon." I click off as the patient rolls in front of me.

"Mr. Enns is a sixty-five-year-old who's had a prostatectomy under spinal. He's on Digoxin and Lasix," Dr. Johnson reports."

"Hi, Mr. Enns. I'm Ariel," I say after recording the first set of vital signs. "You'll be here with me in the recovery room until your spinal wears off and you can wiggle your toes."

"I'll try now. How are they doing?"

"No luck yet." I grin.

"I'm not fond of this area of the hospital." He scans the room as he yawns.

"The sedation doesn't seem to have worn off either. Why don't you take a nap? We can check again in an hour."

As we roll down the hall, Mr. Enns is chatty. "You should watch your back, pushing this stretcher by yourself."

"The orderly is busy. I don't want you to have to wait around." What I'm thinking is that, if I move fast, I can have a minute to clarify Sandra's theory. I roll Mr. Enns into a large private suite that faces the ocean.

"Thank you, that's very considerate of you." He scans the windows that show an undulating wall of gray. "Do they know anything more about the hurricane?"

I move his IV over. "Haven't had the news on today."

"Before I got here, it had strengthened to a category two, and it looks like it's heading our way. I'd like to get sprung in the morning. My son has arranged for a plane to fly us out tomorrow."

"Wish I could fly out of here."

"Maybe you can. I might need a nurse to help me over the weekend. I'll tell him to save room on the plane."

A ride on a private jet would be sweet. "That would be nice, but I'm on hurricane call. I need to stay right here in the hospital."

"I assume the hospital has generators to keep all those respirators in the neuro center running."

His comment catches me by surprise. "Do you know someone who's a patient there?"

"I heard Harold's spiel on how salamanders can regenerate their brain, heart, tails, and limbs. How the spinal cord is the master of that regeneration, so the same is possible in humans right here in Becham within a matter of months.

He's spouted about how he'll be able to save the lives of accident victims or people with cerebral hemorrhage."

I smile as I roll the stretcher up next to the bed. "Do you know anything about Harold's lab?"

"No. Nor do I care to."

So many questions. How do I word them without seeming rude? "He raised a lot of money at the opening of The Painted Muroid, but paying for the care of all those patients must be expensive, don't you think?"

"Don't trust Harold or his shady cronies. They said they created an Institutional Review Board in order to set up the unit. As far as I could find, it doesn't exist."

"How did you find out?"

"I did a lot of research when they asked me to be on the hospital board. I like the idea of participating in what goes on in my community."

My mind is stuck on *shady*. I jam my foot on the brake. "My boyfriend, Ben Guthrie, is the neurosurgeon Harold brought in because he's busy in his lab. I know Ben's not shady."

"If he's associated with Harold Goss, he will be soon. Harold will go to no end to save his wife."

That's more information than I can get looking up a regulatory panel.

I grab the sheet to heft Mr. Enns into his bed. "Ben does surgery on incoming patients."

"How do you think Harold gets his subjects?"

Subjects. That word again. "Ben's patients have all gotten better and gone home," I tell him while tucking in the draw sheet.

"Some healthcare system tried to buy out the hospital, and the board refused. Half the board quit. I swear some of the board members are being paid off."

I agree, but don't want to say it. "How do you know?"

"They asked me to be on the board. There's no way I want my name associated with that neuro unit. Either your boyfriend is naïve, or they've both got you buffaloed."

"That's a strong statement, Mr. Enns."

"Sometimes the truth hurts."

A woman with blonde highlights and a fancy, russet-colored suit hurries to his side. "Honey, you're back."

I have so many questions. Is there something personal that makes him critical of Harold? Is it the program in general?

Mr. Enns takes her hand, returns his attention to me. "You seem like a nice girl. Take care of yourself."

"Thank you. You, too."

I think about Ben as I head for the nurse's desk to give my report. His ethics are too strong for him to be corrupt, yet he sure does stick up for Harold.

Mr. Enns' story is outrageous. It's almost as bizarre as Sandra's theory stuff. Seems all the wackos have private rooms on this floor. Since she hasn't gone home, I'll pop in for a visit after I give my report on Mr. Enns. Maybe it will get me some points with Belinda.

"Ariel, what brings you here this fine morning?" Sandra's propped on her elbow, brushing her long, red hair with its natural highlights.

"I brought another patient to this floor. I thought I'd stop in and say hello. You look great."

"My doctor said I can go home today." She smiles, eyes twinkling.

I ease myself into a seat by her bed. "I was wondering about your theory. How would that apply to brain-dead patients in our neuro unit?"

As Sandra puts the head of her bed upright, a strong gust

of wind blasts a Japanese maple tree across the street, blowing red leaves everywhere. "Parse's theory is about becoming."

I don't know who Parse is, and I'm not going to ask.

"It would indicate that those people have had their transcendence messed with."

A handful of leaves get caught in a whirlwind, spiral up. "What do you mean?"

"They're bound to an earthy reality. They can't move on."

The mini-twister rises several stories off the ground and breaks up. A single leaf gets spit out the top and continues to rise.

"Like a twister?"

"No, more like a crossing."

"You're saying they're stuck?"

Sandra pulls back. "Why are you so intense about this?"

"It's new to me. I'm trying to understand."

She nods, takes a sip of water. "The principles of physics show our consciousness goes beyond our bodies, like heat waves."

I try to picture what she's saying.

"We can't see it, but animals are aware of the field."

I sit up. "Like dogs?"

Sandra nods. "That's why a dog will run to the window before her master's car turns down the street."

"My cat purrs before I touch him sometimes. I always thought he heard me coming."

"Animals are very adept. We don't know if they can see it or they sense it."

I recheck the window and the leaf is gone. "Sounds kind of like science fiction, completely way-out-there, like what Harold wants to do with his neuro unit."

Sandra grins. "Belinda told me you don't agree with his

principles. I've known her a long time. Management has changed her. She can be vengeful sometimes."

Where do I go with this? Is she fishing or being nice? "How so?"

"She's using you as an example for the other nurses, so they won't question the neuro unit or its practices."

"I never thought of that."

"Stay out of her sight. Switch workspaces in recovery with one of the other nurses at the far side of the room, and work in the pre-op area when you can."

She's trying to help. I lean closer.

"The hospital has the same view of its patients and medicine in general as Harold and Belinda. Getting yourself upset about it won't help you to find what you're looking for. Staying centered and in the moment will keep you open to opportunities."

"How so?"

"You'll be more aware of conditions that can be to your advantage if you don't get flustered by things going on around here."

"I appreciate your insight."

"I've heard you're an excellent nurse, Ariel. Stay true to yourself."

"I'm going to have to get back to the recovery room. Thanks for your advice." My mind churns. People stuck in their bodies, dogs in the dumpster, most everyone in the unit under the age of thirty. What next?

*

The recovery room is busy when I get back. Every nurse has a fresh post-op patient and two more are rolling through the door from the operating room.

I take a patient, get her settled and scurry to help with the others. It's lunchtime when we get the room to its normal flow.

"I'm going to the cafeteria to grab a salad," Chelsea says. "Do you want anything?"

"No thanks. I brought yogurt and an apple. I'm going to check on my dad and mom."

Chelsea gives me a wave, and I text Mom: *Have a lunch break. Coming to see you.*

We're not there. Your dad's in Xray and I'm getting him snacks at the grocery store.

I'll stop by at the end of the day. I answer. Pulling my lunch from the fridge, I wonder if security has had enough time to go through the tapes to see who emptied the dumpster. I don't want to be a pest, but the question is like a parasite eating away at me.

I tuck myself away where no one can hear my conversation and call security. "This is Ariel Savin. Did the night guard see who pitched the dogs into the dumpster?"

"The footage shows a Waste Manager truck emptying the dumpster at six-thirty. We called their office to find out why the pickup was so late. They said the driver had a personal issue early in the day and finished his route later than usual," a woman with a squeaky voice tells me.

"Is the driver's face visible on the tape?"

"They had a good answer for the question, miss. That doesn't seem necessary."

"Did anyone go back in the footage to find out who dumped dogs in there?"

She clears her throat. "No dogs can be found on the tape. It shows people tossing in bags of papers and a broken office chair."

"The dogs were on top of the pile. They must have been the last thing dumped in there."

"If there were any dogs, the guard would have called the police."

I jump to my feet and blare into the phone, "You think I'm lying?"

There's a long pause on the other end. "We can find no evidence of dogs on the security cameras."

This is so frustrating. I'm not getting anywhere with these people. "When did the chair go in?"

The woman starts drumming her fingers. "Tuesday. We had rain Wednesday. It obscured the camera."

"It wasn't raining when I pulled out the only living dog."

"The cameras show it was raining until before the dumpster was emptied. That's all I got. Come look for yourself if you want."

A sigh seeps out. "It won't make a difference if the tape only shows rain. Thank you for your time."

Somebody messed with that camera. Should I go back? I have no proof that there was anything but garbage in that dumpster. For all they know, I found the dog lying on the jogging path. Something around that dumpster will help me figure out where those dogs came from.

I grab my lunch and scarf down my food as I make my way to the back corner of the hospital, where the dumpster sits. I know I'll be able to find something in the daylight to show the dogs had been dumped in there.

My pulse picks up as I approach the dumpster. I snag the left lid and throw it open.

Nothing but bags of papers inside.

I grab the right lid and lift it high but find only a couple of empty water bottles. A handful of flies buzz past my head. "Damn flies."

Flinging the remnants of my lunch in, I slam the lid down and turn to the camera. I know someone will be watching the dumpster after my recent phone call. I want to shake my fist or throw a rock at them, but it won't do me any good.

As I stare, I notice something flapping on the side of the camera. Pulling my phone out, I zoom in and snap a photo of what looks like a piece of black tape. I smile and wave. At least I've got some sort of proof.

There's got to be something here to back me up.

Inching my way toward the jogging path, I search the entire area. At the edge of the parking lot, a wad of soggy papers lies in the weeds. Disappointed, I scoop them up because I've got nothing else.

*

Back in recovery, I head for the utility room and lay the wet paper down on the underside of an empty box, flattening it out the best I can so it will dry.

"What are you doing?" Chelsea looks over my shoulder.

"I found this paper near the dumpster." Pushing the pieces around, I line up the words to try and make sentences.

"What is *In sum*?"

"*In summary* might be part of a report."

"That looks like it says *cognitive values*." Chelsea points.

A rush of adrenaline hits me, and I scan faster. "This looks like *some of the subjects*, and here's *undetermined mental changes*." I search down the mushy page. "*Jake*. It says *Jake*. Is he involved in this stuff with Harold?"

"Hide it. Belinda's coming," Chelsea hisses.

I hunt for a cupboard with enough space for the box.

Belinda's voice is close. "The hurricane center announced the storm will be up to a Category Three by tomorrow."

"How far out is it now?" Chelsea stands in the doorway, arms and hands spread from her sides to cover for me.

Racing through two more cupboards, I find one and shove it in on top of a stack of ET tubes. "Done," I whisper and dart to the cupboard that holds our handbags.

Chelsea saunters out the doorway.

"Still two days, but it's gaining strength fast. I want everyone to be prepared to hunker down." Belinda snags the hurricane manual and heads back toward her office.

"Thanks, Chelsea. Who knows what she would've done if she'd seen me?"

"She would've ripped you a new one, that's for sure."

"I don't want anybody else to find that paper. I'm going to put it in my locker." As I fetch the box out of the cupboard, I notice half the E-T tubes I stocked yesterday are gone. "Chelsea, did you hear anything about the OR being busy last night?"

She gives me a funny look. "The opposite. Why?"

Do I tell her? Better to keep it to myself. She's questioning my ideas now, too. "Just curious." I tuck the upside-down cardboard box into my waist and hit the button for the automatic doors. Not wanting anyone to see, I dash through before it's opened all the way. The door smacks my arm, and I drop my bundle.

"What you got there?" Jake picks the box up off the floor.

"I, uh… dropped some papers in a sink. I'm trying to dry them out." I snag the bundle and keep walking, hoping he didn't have time to see anything.

"Ben told me about the dogs you found last night. What a horrible thing to do to those poor animals."

Heat prickles my face. I want to grill him, ask if he's in on it with the monster. Ben's advice to stay chill rings in my ear.

I slow my pace, breathe deeply. "Did he tell you how sweet the one I rescued is?"

"I think he's worried you want to keep her."

If he knows something about the dog from the lab, maybe I can trip him up. "Do you have any idea what her name is?"

Jake's brow creases. "How would I know that?"

"I figured you may have heard it."

His nose wrinkles. "Ben didn't tell me."

He is a good actor, but I can be, too. "I named her Grace since she's gentle in a terrible situation."

"That's nice." His eyes shift to the box again.

"I need to put this away and get back to recovery," I say and hurry into the locker room to stash my find.

A minute later, I roll a stool over by Chelsea and park myself to wait for the next patient. "I saw Jake in the hall. He was trying to see what was on the paper. And when I was putting it in my locker, I found the word *synapse*. This has something to do with the neuro unit," I whisper.

"You're presuming a lot, Ariel. There's no letterhead or reference to the neuro unit or to Jake.

"Come on, Chelsea. His name is right on it. Proof is right there on the paper."

"All you have is a bunch of words. They could be in any random order. It could be referring to Jake Farrow, the head of environmental services, for all you know."

"You're right," I sigh. This is so confusing. "I went through the security footage at lunch. The cameras only show a heavy rain yesterday afternoon."

"That stinks."

"In my gut, I feel that this is all connected somehow."

The lines on Chelsea's forehead deepen. "How?"

"The word *synapse* connects it to what Harold is trying

to achieve. Jake may not have anything to do with it, but he defends Harold and his plan all the time. What if Harold is experimenting on dogs at the lab?" I don't tell her Mr. Enns said Harold would stop at nothing to get Evie back.

My phone beeps in a text. *Dad has had an episode. He's okay. They're checking him out now.*

I hope he's all right, but that doesn't sound good. I go to ask her about it when my next patient arrives.

Chapter 15

I'm readying my patient for her room when the phone at the desk rings. Belinda answers and assures the person that it will be taken care of.

"Ariel, you forgot to take Mr. Enns' belongings when you transferred him to his room."

Great, one more thing she can pick on me for. "I'm heading up that way now. I'll take them with me."

"You've been rather scattered lately. A lot of things are going on around here. You need to focus."

You are part of the problem, I think, and smile as I load Mr. Enns's brown leather duffle into the bottom of my patient's gurney. I grab the foot of the stretcher and head out the door.

After getting my patient into his bed and finishing my report to his nurse, I shoot a text to Mom: *How's Dad doing?*

Doc just walked in.

Be with you soon. My shift is almost over.

When I look up, Jake is down the hall. Could he have something to do with those dogs? Should I confront him about the paper? There's not much to go on, and even though I'd promised Ben I'd avoid Harold, we hadn't said anything about Jake.

I slip the duffle into Mr. Enns' closet and catch up with Jake. "Hey there! You stop by to see Mr. Enns?"

"Yeah, nice guy." Jake leans against the rubber railing on the wall.

I smile. *Wouldn't you like to know all the dirt he told me?* "Mr. Enns was talking about Harold's progress. How's his research going?"

"He's been able to complete full synapse in his lab."

My stomach flips. Already? So many questions. "I'm sure Harold was happy about that. What was the change that made it work?"

Jake's shoulders come up, then drop like he doesn't care. "Some synthetic peptides he tried."

Were the peptides in the missing box? I would have thought Jake would be more excited, although it is more his personality to not really care what Harold does. "He's had success in test tubes?"

Jake checks a list of patients on the phone in his hand. "Yup. Now he's trying it out on lab rats and such."

Like dogs. I bite my tongue. "Wouldn't you have to work your way up in scale for something like that?"

Jake shrugs again. "I guess. Harold was so excited he was telling everybody in the neuro unit today. You should have seen him. It was like he over-caffeinated or something."

"He sure didn't look smiling and happy in the hall. Maybe because he saw me." I chuckle, trying to stay on the light side.

"Some other problem came up. He went from being ecstatic to depressed in about an hour. That's research, I guess. Two steps forward, one step back."

If I press him on his involvement in Harold's project, will I lose his friendship? After all we went through to help Ben almost ten years ago, Jake should know I'm persistent. I'll have to dance around it, though. "It seems strange that I found intubated dogs nearby. Does that have anything to do with Harold's newfound synapse?"

"He's doing trials on rats, Ariel."

"You said he's testing rats and such. I thought maybe *such* meant dogs."

"That's morbid. I wish you were on board with this. It offers a lot of potential for humanity. I know you don't like Harold, but don't start spreading rumors."

"I'm not. I'm asking you. You seem to know a lot about Harold's business."

Jake shakes his head. "Ariel, give me a break. I do my job. I don't follow the guy around after hours."

"Yet you champion his cause. Seems to me you're stuck to him all the time."

"That would be you. You dog it to the nth degree. I have a life outside the hospital, Ariel, even though I no longer see Ben outside of work since he shacked up with you."

"I'm sorry if you miss the after-hours camaraderie. Maybe you should get a dog."

"Like I have time for a dog."

"Dogs will love you forever. They're very loyal."

"Why are you so stuck on this dog thing?"

I'm not getting any more out of him. I smile wide and head for the stairs. "It's a pet peeve."

*

Pushing open the heavy fire door to the stairwell, I pick up, "Ariel! Ariel! Over here!" from down the hall.

Sandra is clinging to an IV pole and the railing for support.

Rushing to her, I slip my arm around her waist to hold her up. "Sandra, are you all right?"

"I was trying to walk a little more since I'm supposed to go home, but I ran out of juice."

"Let me help you back to your room." I think about Dad, glance at my watch.

Sandra leans heavily on my arm and puts her feet in motion. "Thank you so much, I underestimated how exhausting that would be."

"I know you're anxious to get well, Sandra, but you have to grant yourself time to heal." I guide her toward the foot of her bed. "Do you want to sit in the chair for a while, or would you rather go back to bed?"

"I need to lie down. You're angry with the guy you were talking to, aren't you?" Sandra asks as I lock in the safety rail.

"How could you tell from way down the hall?"

"I could see it in the sphere of anger surrounding you."

"I didn't think it was that obvious."

"I read people I pass in a hallway or in a park. It's amazing how much you can learn without talking to someone."

"Can you see dead people, too?"

Sandra bursts out laughing. "Oh, don't do that. It hurts to laugh."

"Sorry." I snatch a pillow from the chair. "Use this to brace your belly."

She places the pillow in front of her, wraps her arms around it. "I don't see dead people, although this would be a good place to practice."

Laughing out loud, I examine her eyes and wonder if she's messed up from the meds or if this is her. "Are you still getting shots for pain?"

"Very funny." She snorts. "They switched me to Tylenol this morning."

"That's best if you're going home," I say to fill in while I think about what she's telling me. "You told me you could *see* the anger. How do you do that?"

"You look for, or feel, waves coming off of someone."

I try and picture waves as I pull the covers up for her.

"Happy people have light-colored, rounded waves. Anger is darker, spikier, like how cartoonists draw people shouting."

The sharp lines of a stick figure meme come to mind. "Can you tell if people are healthy or sick?"

"Sometimes. Animals are better at it. They're using dogs to sniff out cancer." Sandra does air quotes around *sniff out*. "It's a combination of what they see, sense, and maybe a particular odor."

My mind goes to Grace. Were they testing her senses somehow? "I had a patient who arrested in ICU. After we resuscitated her and everyone was gone, she told me she was watching from the corner of the room. She described everyone who was present and what each of us did."

"There's a guy from Emory, Dr. Sabom. He lectures on out-of-body experiences. He did extensive research after a lot of his patients said the same."

"Does everybody who is unconscious have an out-of-body experience?"

"Some people have what's called Terminal Lucidity."

"What's that?"

"Their mental clarity increases before dying."

"Would the neuro patients have that?"

"They may, but I'll bet you they all have a sense of being trapped."

"Like a Keys' lobster right before they get clubbed?"

Sandra lets out a high-pitched hoot and grabs the pillow. "Don't make me laugh."

She may be laughing, but the thought of the neuro patients being trapped turns my stomach.

*

I hurry toward Dad's room after clocking out. X-ray doesn't sound good. Dad can't afford to break anything. A couple of nurses speed by me as I leave the stairwell. It must be busy.

I tug back the long, white curtain around the bed to see Dad propped on his side with a magazine and his favorite seltzer water. "You're looking pretty good."

"I've decided Becham is nicer than Miami, so I thought I'd stay," he says with a grin.

"He's got a fracture in his hip," Mom answers my blank look.

"It's not displaced, but I can't walk on it for six weeks." Dad sighs.

"You're lucky, Dad. That rarely happens." I give him a hug, turn to do the same with Mom.

Her face is taut, like things are spinning so fast in her head, it's stretching her skin.

I wrap my arms around her, whispering, "You okay?"

"I'm good," she whispers back, but her concern still shows.

"They tried to talk me into the stem cell thing. I told them it was a bad idea." Dad flips the page. "Maybe we can go on a cruise while we wait. I could check out all the locks in the Panama Canal from a balcony room with a lounger."

I laugh. "Do you think you can wait until the storm is over?"

"I don't know; that could add a little more excitement." He grins.

Mom takes Dad's hand. "The ortho doctor wants him to stay here on this floor."

"Didn't you say you were on hurricane call? Your mom got enough food for a party." Dad laughs.

"Get that party started. I'll be here." I laugh with him.

"My party animals," Mom deadpans.

Her words make me think of Grace. I wonder if I should tell them about her, then decide I shouldn't because they have enough to worry about. But I do need to check on her. "I have to run an errand."

Mom's eyebrows shoot up. "Now?"

Heat crawls to my cheeks. My mind toggles between Grace and my dad, guilt tugging at my heart. A picture of Grace's eyes, pitiful and longing, pops into my head. "I found a half-dead dog in a dumpster yesterday. She's at the vet. I need to check on her."

"You're going out in that weather to see a dog?" Mom sniffs.

"She was intubated and dumped with two other dogs that were dead. It's so sad."

Mom's brows knit. "What if she has some infectious disease?"

"The vet said she's weak, but otherwise, everything is okay."

"You know we love dogs, but wouldn't you rather stay with your dad for a while?"

"I'm fine," Dad says. "You gotta do what you gotta do."

The guilt returns. I know I should stay, but Grace is some part of the bizarre puzzle I have to put together. "Rain from the hurricane hasn't started yet. The roads should be workable. I'll peek in on her and be right back."

*

My hair slaps my face as I climb into the car. The wind has picked up. I wonder how far out Jacob is. I can't believe this hurricane has been named Jake. It's like our friendship which used to be a pleasant, gentle breeze and now is becoming more tumultuous.

The parking lot of the veterinary clinic is almost full. Claiming the last spot, I hurry inside to a waiting room packed with people and nervous-looking caged animals. I think of my conversation with Sandra, and a shudder runs through me.

"I'm here to see the dumpster dog," I tell the receptionist.

She removes a pair of bright pink reading glasses and looks up at me. "That was a brave thing you did. A lot of people would have looked the other way, not have the guts to climb in and save her. I'll buzz you in."

The door to the kennel chimes, and I scurry to open it before the door locks again. Bee-lining it past a row of four-by-four-foot cages, I search for Grace's kennel, spot her familiar paws. I kneel in front of her and stroke the paw that's close enough for me to reach. "How are you doing, girl?"

My dog opens her eyes. Her tail thumps on the ground.

"You must be the gal who found our trashy little friend."

"Haha, you're right." I scoot out of the way as the woman unlocks the cage door.

Grace's eyes never leave me.

"Is her blood work back?"

"She's a little anemic, and her liver enzymes are elevated. Her reflexes and affect are off, and we can't figure out why. She's super obedient, but her eyes are weird."

I sit down beside Grace and run my hand in long strokes along her back. "How long will she have to stay here?"

"Normally, we'd keep her a couple more days, but we're swamped because of the hurricane. I'll check."

She disappears before "I can't take her" comes out. Ben will have a fit if I walk into the apartment with the dog, but I can't leave her to be sent to one of those awful shelters with dogs whining and barking where she could get kennel cough and die.

"The vet said it's all right for the dog to go. He wants to see her back in a week."

I glance down the row of caged dogs. Some are bandaged and sleeping. The rest have sad eyes that beg to be helped. Not great, but better than a shelter. "My dad landed in the hospital, and I don't know if my partner is ready for a dog."

"You could foster her for a while. She's been so mistreated. She'll need a lot of love and attention."

"Could she stay in here another day or so?"

"We need this kennel, sorry. She's able to take in and put out food and water. She needs to regain her muscles. That may fix her reflexes, too."

What will Ben do if I bring her home, especially with hurricane call? I tell myself it's for a short time, and she'll be sleeping a lot. Our neighbor, Wendel, loves dogs. He'll check on her. "Well, Grace, seems you're coming with me."

"Feed her small amounts of canned dog food every two hours. She needs to get fattened up without causing stress to her digestive system. You can pick up supplies at the front desk."

"Can I put them in the car and come back for her?"

"That's a good idea. Carry her as much as possible and help her stand to relieve herself. She'll begin moving around on her own when she regains her strength. Call us if you have a problem."

As I take the dog food to the car, I spot a poster on the wall with all the dog breeds titled CANIS LUPUS FAMILIARIS. The whispers in the stairwell talked about working in the Canis Field. That means dogs. It had to be Harold.

Food in the trunk, I rattle out my presentation for Ben. "I couldn't leave her. You know we have a special bond. It's for a short time. She's been so neglected. She needs some love."

At the kennel, I drop to my knees and scoop my pup into my arms. "All right, girl, we're going for it."

Chapter 16

I tuck Grace into Victor's crate after feeding her. "This will have to do, my friend. You're small, and you can't stand yet. We can get you a proper one after the hurricane." My phone beeps with a text from Mom.

How far away are you?

I type back: *Be there in ten minutes. Is everything okay?*

Yes. Your dad is sleeping.

"I've got to see my dad, but I'll be back. Have a nap and get stronger." I give her a pat.

She tries to get up, but her legs won't work. She scratches at the door and whines.

"I can't stay, girl. I've got to see my dad."

Grace whimpers louder, clawing at the door like she's caged forever.

I sit down beside her, stroke her paw with the only finger I can fit through the holes. "It's all right, girl. I won't be gone long."

She cries, leans back, hits her rump on the crate, and howls.

"You can't do that here, Grace. I'll get kicked out of my apartment."

She claws and howls some more.

"I don't know how to help you, sweetheart." I squat beside her.

Victor pokes his nose around the corner but won't come into the kitchen.

"Don't let all that noise bother you, Victor." I fill his dish, put it down so he has to walk past the crate, adding an extra treat on top. "Come on, buddy."

The cat arches his back and gives Grace a dirty look.

"Yes, she's in your crate. You hate it anyway, and I know you're hungry." I scoop him up and bring him to his dish, positioning myself between the two of them. "She's in there, buddy. You're free to roam. Be happy."

Victor gives me his evil eye for a second, but his stomach takes over, so he launches into his food.

I sit down next to Grace, and she stops crying.

The cat eyes me again, head down, tail swishing. Grace lets out a boisterous bark, causing Victor to arch his back and hiss. Appearing to be curious about him, she tries to get onto her feet and falls. Victor is not sympathetic. He bats the crate with a guttural growl. Grace returns her own growl, starts to bark louder. Their fight continues with yaps and bats, howls and hisses that sound like screams. A neighbor thumps on the wall. I shoo Victor out of the kitchen and into the bedroom.

"Here's your dinner, buddy. You can use your box in the bathroom," I say as I close the bedroom door.

On my way back to the kitchen, I grab a washcloth. "Grace, you're going to have to hang in until I get back." I rub the dry washcloth over my arms and neck, toss it in with her, and place the towel over the top, hoping the scent and the closeness will help her feel safe.

She continues to whine.

"What else would calm you down? How about lavender?" I open the bottle of essential oil and place it next to the opening of the crate. As I pat her paw, her crying slows.

Within a couple of minutes, she lays her head down, goes to sleep.

Who knew? I tiptoe out the door.

*

The sun is unusually hot today. I feel like I'm being cooked in the car even with the AC vents aimed at my face. My phone beeps in my purse with texts several times while I'm driving to the hospital. Getting out of the car, I find it's Mom.

Something is going on with your dad. Where are you?

A minute later, she sent another one.

Ben is here. I thought you were on your way.

My stomach tightens. I break into a run, guilt eating at me for letting the dog take precedence over my dad.

I find my mother standing in the hall outside Dad's room. Strands of her hair are sticking out, and she's rocking sideways foot-to-foot.

"Did something happen in X-ray, Mom?"

"I went to get him some goodies while he was gone. He looked like he was getting sleepy when I brought the snacks in. I figured he was worn out. Now, they're doing all kinds of tests on him." The sideways rocking quickens.

I crack the door, poke my head in.

A tech is taking EEG leads off Dad's head while a nurse cleans up from having put in a urinary catheter. Ben and Dr. Mendez are looking at the EEG.

"It's Ariel. How's it going?"

Ben's look is grave. "He's not responding."

There's a thud in my gut. My legs are jerky and slow as I lunge to the bedside. "Dad!" I shake his shoulder.

No reply.

I grab my penlight to check his eyes.

His pupils are reacting, but they're sluggish.

"Dad!" I pinch his arm.

Nothing.

I search for Ben.

"He likes to be independent. Could he have fallen and bumped his head?" Ben asks Mom.

"Not while I was here." Mom is behind me like she's afraid to get close.

Dr. Mendez speaks up. "Stat blood work shows nothing unusual. Your dad had morphine for pain, but your mother said he had it for gallbladder surgery with no problem. The MRI machine is broken. EEG shows changes. I'm transferring him to ICU to be watched."

"ICU?" Mom's voice is a tiny squeak. "Which one?"

I tell myself not to react, to stay calm for her, as I grab her trembling hand and tug her to my side. "Not the one Harold runs," I say aloud to reassure her as much as myself.

The double doors to ICU bellow out our arrival. The monitor beeps are too loud, the sugary odor of IV hyperalimentation turns my stomach.

I don't want to look up and see all the people I know. It's too strange to be on the other side. I'm so dependent, so helpless. I can't go to the desk to look up results or do anything on my own.

"Room three, Ariel," the unit secretary calls.

The floor nurse, Ben, and I roll Dad into the room. I automatically start hooking him up to the heart monitor when a flurry of nurses arrives, giving me sympathetic looks.

With a glance of understanding, my old ICU buddy, Denise, places a warm hand on my arm. "It's all right, Ariel. We've got this."

My mouth opens to retort. Then it hits me—I can't do his nursing care here.

Taking Mom's hand, I ferry her into a corner while Denise and the floor nurse go to the desk for the report.

"I'll be at the desk for a minute." Ben strokes my arm in reassurance.

I nod, hand clutching Mom's, eyes glued to Dad.

"Sorry about your dad," one of my buddies says.

"Ditto," says another. "I've got to get back to my patient, though," she tells me with an awkward grin.

It's hard when another nurse's loved one comes in. Everyone knows the stakes are higher here. No one wants it to be their family. "Thanks. We'll catch up later." I offer an appreciative smile.

"Ariel, we need to find out what's causing this and how to fix it," Mom says like she's part of the staff.

"You're right. I've read all about ALS, and coma is not supposed to happen now."

She drops my hand. Her mouth is like a jellyfish in the surf as she tries to get words out. "He's in a coma?"

A lump forms in the back of my throat. I should have eased into it. "Well, we don't know for sure since this is new. It could be short-term from a reaction to the morphine." In the background, my brain argues that his breathing isn't shallow like an overdose, though.

"You have to get him out. He can't be in a coma now. He starts his treatment tomorrow." Mom looks desperate.

"We'll get him there. This is a little glitch. Ben and Dr. Mendez will get it fixed."

Mom steps to Dad's side, runs her fingers through his hair. "Yes. Ben."

I see movement from the corner of my eye. It's Ben. There's a flutter in my chest, hoping he's got new results. Maybe somehow, Dad can go back to his room.

"Mrs. Savin." Ben pauses a second, glances at me. "Mom."

A tiny thrill runs through me. He's never said that before.

He places his hand on her shoulder. "We're going to do

more blood work and get an MRI as soon as possible to see what the problem is."

"Dad, can you hear me?" I try again.

Ben slides his arm around me. "We'll get behind this soon. He'll be all right."

I clench my teeth. My jaw throbs as I hold back a sob. I know that morphine alone didn't do this.

Chapter 17

"It's been a horrible day, Grace. My dad was fine when I saw him. I go get you, and *boom*, he's in a coma." I pick her up and cradle her to me. "A *coma*, Grace. I had to get sedatives for my mom. She's at the hotel, sleeping."

I carry Grace downstairs, hold her up over a patch of grass as her legs bend and flop. "Dad's blood work is normal, his EEG's not. It's flattened for no particular reason. Does this have to do with Harold? Could it be in retaliation for the trouble I've created for him?"

Scooping up Grace, I bury my face in her fur and hold her close to my chest. "I believe it's all related to Harold. Am I losing my mind? You'd think people would realize whenever he shows up, something bad happens. Harold has crossed the line. This is my *dad*."

I stroke her soft fur over and over. "I hope Ben will warm up to you. I need you more than ever right now," I say as I lay her down in the crate. "There's so much happening at once. I feel like I'm going to explode."

"When Ben gets home, I'm going to invite him into the bedroom before I tell him you're here. You'll have to be quiet and stay in the kitchen."

The dog looks at me with her soft eyes.

"I wish I knew what the weird thing with your reflexes is and if it's going to get better."

Grace curls up, goes back to sleep.

I check the time. Eight-thirty. Mom will be out all night with the dose Ben wrote the script for. He should be home any minute.

I click on the weather channel, which tells me, "Hurricane Jacob's outer bands are expected to hit South Florida the day after tomorrow."

"More bad news." I click it off, pour two glasses of wine and turn on some soft music. I pitch my clothes into the laundry, hoping the memory of today's events go with them and slip into a silk robe.

"Hey there." Ben bursts through the door, tossing his keys onto the table. He eyes my glass. "I could use one of those."

"Right here." I hand him the wine.

Ben holds his glass up in a toast. "To my new raise."

I clink his glass. "You got a raise? I thought Harold was strapped for money."

"Simon pushed it through. Harold is doing so much research, I'm having to do more of the surgery and follow-up, they said I deserve it. Simon thinks driving a nice sports car will give people a good impression."

"You are definitely carrying the load for the surgical practice."

"After the storm, I'm going to look for a new car. How are you doing?" He tumbles onto the couch and brushes his lips across my cheek.

"I can't get over what's happened. It's too weird. Hear anything new?"

"No. We can call ICU later and check. For now, wine, and you will make my evening perfect." He shimmies closer.

Taking another sip of wine, I let it do its work, relaxing my tight muscles and easing my mind. "It's good to have you home." I lay my head on his shoulder.

Ben swallows a mouthful. He lets his head fall back on the sofa and seems to unwind a bit. Then he sneezes. “There must be remnants of that dog around here.”

I grab my wine, take a big gulp. Should I tell him about Grace? I want him to stay in the glow of his raise, and we need to talk about Dad. That’ll have to be later. I slip my hands under his shirt. “You’re worth every penny of that to Harold.”

Ben presses his chest toward me. “It’s so good to be able to come home to you.” He follows the curve of my breast with his eyes, and I fuse my mouth to his.

I run my fingers along his hot skin, kiss him deeper, tasting his steadfastness, absorbing his calm nature. Slipping his shirt over his head, I caress his defined pecs, running kisses along his neck.

Ben picks me up, carries me to our bed.

Releasing the drawstring of his scrubs, I take him in my hand.

His tongue traces its way around the curve of my shoulder, his breath hot. “What the hell?” Ben bolts upright in the bed. “What’s that dog doing here?”

A prayer for peace catches in my throat. “Grace! You’re standing!” I spring out of bed and kneel beside her. “I can’t believe it, Ben! She got up on her own and walked! This is incredible!” I wrap my arms around her quivering body. “Lay down, Grace.” I pat the carpet. “You’re still weak.”

She folds to the floor.

“*What* is she doing here?” He glares at me, eyes wide.

“They said her blood work was okay and that, even though she has a weird affect and slow reflexes, she’s going to be all right.”

“You bring her home in the middle of all that’s going on with your dad, knowing that I’m allergic to dogs, and you don’t even ask me?”

"They couldn't keep her at the vet because of the hurricane. They said she needs a lot of love, and we could foster her before we decide whether we should keep her."

"Yeah, what they meant is keep her until she seems like part of the family, and you can't give her up."

"I can't believe she's standing, Ben."

He sneezes, reaches for a tissue. "Ariel, we're at work all day and your dad is in ICU. How do you foster her from the hospital? And how do you know if there aren't other things wrong with her, like bladder control? I don't want a dog peeing all over." He sneezes again, blows his nose.

I sure messed up this intro. "The vet said if I put her in the crate, she won't pee. Wendel across the hall likes dogs. Maybe he'll take her."

Ben tugs on a pair of jeans and a T-shirt, walks into the living room. He blows his nose more. "It's bullshit you made the choice without me."

I grab my robe, cinch it tight. "I feel the same way about your support for Harold when he's torturing those poor people in the unit. He calls them *subjects*, for heaven's sake. He doesn't even think of them as people."

"Here we go again with the Harold conspiracy. You're like a dog with a bone." Ben takes a long pull on his wine. "You must be watching too many scary movies when I'm at work. You're starting to have delusions."

Heat floods my face. "How can you possibly believe he's innocent, knowing he's there every time something happens?"

"Ariel, you have no proof."

"Ben, a box went missing from the Fed-Ex truck. Harold's at the bedside when the guy codes, and he's with my dad before Dad goes into a coma. There's a pattern here."

"Harold is doing his job. Do you think managing that unit and kissing up to the hospital board is easy?"

I slam my hand on the dining table. "Putting my dad in a coma is over the top. What's he going to do next? Knock Dad off like he did Robert Young to fill the neuro unit?"

Victor bolts behind the couch.

"This apartment isn't big enough for a dog, a cat, and your attitude." Ben goes to the closet, starts shoving clothes into a duffle bag.

"Wait, what are you doing? What do you mean?"

"We have a difference of opinion on everything these days." He stuffs his dress suit, all his shoes, and his laptop into a suitcase, grabs his tennis racket, and he's out the door.

I run after him into the street, rain pelting my face. "Ben, stop!"

He hurls his bags into the trunk. "This dog and your accusations are over the top."

I put my arms around his waist and press my body against his, hoping the contact will jar him out of this. "Ben, you're tired. Have some dinner and sleep on it. You'll feel better in the morning."

He pulls away, my dry imprint visible on his rain-soaked clothes as he climbs into the car. "I've had enough. I'm out of here."

I shield my eyes from the driving rain so I can see him. "Ben, let's talk this out."

He puts the car in gear without looking up.

Where will he go? A hotel? A friend's?

My heart sinks as his car drives away, and my tears blend into the deluge.

Chapter 18

At six o'clock in the morning, the alarm goes off, reminding me I have to face the day even without sleep. I force myself into the shower. After gulping down a cup of coffee, I carry Grace outside, while texting Ben. *Are you okay?*

The only answer is a howl of the wind that plasters my hair across my face, making it hard to see. A palm frond crashes beside me. I jump.

Grace looks up with eyes that say, *It's nothing compared to what I've been through.*

Back inside, I re-check my phone. Nothing. What have I done? Will he ever come back? Will he talk to me if I see him at work?

I dial ICU. Dad's night nurse is new. I don't know her. "It's Ariel from recovery. You're taking care of my dad, Paul Savin. How's he doing?"

"There was no change in him, but we needed to make room for an incoming post-op trauma. The supervisor had me move him to the neuro unit."

My stomach lurches. "Is he intubated?"

"No, he's the same. They needed his room."

"You won't get the trauma patient until this afternoon. Somebody could get better and transfer out, or someone might die. This is ridiculous!"

"I don't know how it all works. I follow orders. Gotta go. My other patient is bleeding out." She hangs up.

I hit the hospital's main number. "I need to speak to the night supervisor." How can they do this? He shouldn't be in that hellhole. I need to get him out.

The phone clicks. I don't wait for hello. "This is Ariel Savin from PACU. You transferred my dad, Paul, to the neuro unit. Can we move him to step-down or CCU? He's not brain-dead. He doesn't belong there."

"I'm sorry, Ariel. I know he doesn't meet the criteria for the neuro unit, but that was the directive I was given from the top."

"Who was that?"

"The director of nursing said there was a meeting on it, and your dad had to move. It's busy here. I've got to go. Again, I'm sorry."

I feel like throwing up. Harold did this. He told the DON. I'll go there, talk to Janet Turner when she comes in.

I call Mom. "Hi. How'd you sleep?"

"I just woke up. I'm groggy from the pills Ben gave me. How's Dad?"

Ben. My heart sinks. I don't have time to think about that now. "No change. He's supposed to have more tests today, and they moved him."

"Back to his room?"

My throat goes dry. "No." I grip the phone harder. "They put him in the neuro unit." Silence on the other end. "You all right?"

"I thought you said he wasn't going there."

"He's not supposed to be in that unit. His mental function hasn't changed, and he doesn't meet the criteria. I'm going to check on him now. I'll talk to the director of nursing when she comes in."

"This doesn't sound good, Ariel."

I swallow, rack my brain for a good response. "It's only temporary, Mom, I'll get it worked out."

"I hope so. Your dad didn't even want to come here, and now this? I'm heading over there as soon I get dressed."

"I'll be at work by then. I'll stop by as often as possible." Clicking off, I wonder if I should have told her about Ben.

One thing at a time.

"Sorry to have to do this to you, Grace. Promise me you'll be especially good if Ben comes back." I tuck her inside the crate.

She seems content. Maybe she feels the heaviness in my heart.

I check for texts on my way to the car.

Nothing.

As I park at the hospital, I remind myself the ICU nurse said there was no change in Dad; they only needed the room. I take the stairs two at a time and bolt through the double doors to the neuro unit.

The sigh of a respirator hits me. I break into a run, search the board with bed assignments.

Room eleven, Savin.

Dad's room is stifling hot. There's no ventilator. *Thank you, God.*

I slip my hand in his. "Dad, can you hear me? It's me, Ariel." Lifting his lids, I check his pupils. The reaction is still slow, but they're equal. Good. I shake his arm. "Daddy, if you can hear me, squeeze my hand."

Nothing.

How do I get him out of here?

I go get the night nurse, the one with the blown-out shoe. She still looks tired, but there's something else in her eyes… a wariness. "What does his blood work show?"

"It's all normal. They even did a toxicology screen and found nothing. I know it stinks that he's here, but be grateful that he's breathing on his own."

You mean, be happy Harold didn't kill him? I take a deep breath. "Is he still going for an MRI?"

"Yes. And Jake has ordered more blood work."

"I'll have to thank him." I hear footsteps and look up to see Harold, brow furrowed.

"Good morning, Ariel. You're up early."

As the rage inside builds, I tell myself to be civil. "You know he doesn't belong here. This is outrageous!"

"I apologize for the inconvenience, but the administration decided with a hurricane coming, it's necessary to make room for acute care patients. He'll get more specialized care here than in a regular room."

I tell myself to walk away, bide my time, create a case, but the events of the past week keep tugging, gnawing, eroding at my composure. "My dad's ALS may be chronic, but his brain was fine. What did you do to him?"

Harold's fake grin turns into a scowl. "Those are strong words, Ariel. You wouldn't want that accusation to be circulated throughout the hospital because it *might* affect your job."

"That's absurd. Everybody knows what you are."

"And they love me for it."

"No, they don't. You've created all kinds of chaos around here."

Harold straightens his tie. "Gosh, there's so much turmoil I feel as if my sanity might slip." He leans in close and whispers, "But I'm going to make it look like it's yours, not mine." A smile creeps across his lips. "Better get along now before you get that fifth tardy on your record."

*

Chelsea gives me the once-over as I clock in. "I'm so sorry about your dad's fall."

"Thanks." I stash my handbag in the cupboard. I'm afraid to look at her in case I cry.

"Are you all right, Ariel? Your face is swollen."

"Allergies." I check my assignment for the day and remember Sandra's advice. "Would you mind changing slots with me today? I need to hide out in the back of the room."

"Sure, but I don't believe the allergy crap, fess up." Chelsea switches the numbers on the assignment board.

"Ben and I had a fight. He packed a bag and left. A few hours later, my dad was moved to the neuro unit."

Chelsea stops. "What?"

"Dad has a non-displaced fracture. He didn't hit his head. His brain stem is working. His blood work seems fine. Somehow, the administration decided they needed the space in ICU and transferred him."

"That's outrageous! Do you think Ben had anything to do with it?"

"Ben is not vindictive. It's all Harold, but Ben can't see it. He's caught up in building his reputation as a good surgeon. He's irritated by my thoughts about Harold and medicine in general. Bringing Grace home pushed him over the edge, I guess."

"Why don't you get rid of her? It's not worth ruining your relationship over," Chelsea clucks.

"I can't. The animal clinic is full, and she needs somewhere to go until the storm is over."

"They sucked you in. You're on call, Ariel. You could be here for days."

"I know. I'm screwed."

"Ben trudged through to the operating room a few minutes ago. He looked like crap. There's a trauma in OR six. Harold and Jake worked on the guy most of the night."

"How did Harold show up in the neuro unit when I was there?"

"He probably had Jake close the skin."

"Harold's timing was so perfect, it's eerie." *Unless Rebecca let him know I was there.* I make my way to the far corner of the room, where a respirator is already set up. "Let me take the trauma."

"That's a terrible idea. Did you get any sleep last night?"

Part of me wants to listen to her, but I need a diversion. "This will help keep me awake."

"Ariel, I don't think you should."

"I'll be fine." I check both of my oxygen flow meters, the respirator settings, the Ambu bag, and emergency drugs in my slot. "Over here!" I call to Dr. Johnson as the patient rolls into recovery with a throng of nurses—and Jake.

I wonder if they know about me and Ben already. I hope they do. I'm not up for any explanations.

"Carl Stanton had a boating accident on the Intracoastal. He hit the seawall when he was thrown from his boat, and he was run over by another boat. They left a piece of skull out to try to prevent herniation. His intracranial pressure is only up a bit with Pentothal, Versed, and fentanyl infusing. He has a fractured left femur, as well as left radius and ulna. Some nasty barnacle cuts are on his hands where he tried to climb the wall. We did a block for his arm and a spinal for the leg. He has no medical history, takes no medications."

Ten people surround the patient's bed. I can feel the eyes of each of them on me. I don't like how public my life is around here. "Was there ever a baseline mental status?" I ask as I hook up the patient.

"He wasn't conscious. His pupils are slow at three mils. I hope his brain isn't mush. He's supposed to be off-the-charts smart."

In an instant, all my senses are awake like something is going to happen.

The patient's body twitches. It starts to writhe.

"He's seizing."

"Eight milligrams of Keppra," Harold barks.

Where did he come from? Not the OR.

"I'll get it." Chelsea pulls the crash cart over, rips open the box, preps the syringe.

I push the Keppra and watch the patient's convulsions slow and stop. "His 02 sat is poor," I call out, hoping Carl will settle and they'll all leave.

"Increase him to sixty percent oxygen."

"Done." I blurt. "He's seizing again."

"Ten mg of Dilantin. We need a drip." Harold parks himself next to the patient.

"Got it." Chelsea runs to the medication room.

"PVCs are starting up," someone calls.

"A hundred milligrams of lidocaine!" Dr. Johnson hollers above the din.

I grab the lidocaine taped to the side of my supply cubby. Popping the lid off, I push it in.

He's in V-tach," Dr. Johnson calls. "One-fifty of amiodarone."

"I can't reach it. Somebody grab it for me." I eyeball the monitor.

"Here." Gloved hands pass me a syringe out of the box, all prepped.

"It's in," I say when I've pushed it through.

"We have a heart rhythm. Stop pumping," Dr. Johnson barks.

"He's seizing again," someone calls.

"Here's the drip." Chelsea returns with the Dilantin mixed into an IV bag.

"His intracranial pressure is through the roof," Jake growls. "Everyone be quiet. All the extra people need to get out of here."

A handful of OR staff slide their gloves off, tossing them into the trash next to me.

Harold paces by the foot of the bed. "This isn't going well. His heart rate is too fast."

The intracranial pressure graph flashes warnings as the spikes grow higher.

"Increase the drip. We need to keep that pressure down."

"It's already running at the maximum dose."

Pulling the penlight from my pocket, I check Carl's eyes. "His pupils are fixed and dilated."

Jake does a nipple twist on Carl. "Dammit," he spits when there's no reaction.

"Did you order atropine, Sam Johnson?" Harold demands.

Sam's face scrunches. "No."

"What's this empty syringe of atropine doing here?" Harold looks at me.

"I gave Keppra, lidocaine, and amiodarone," I follow his pointed finger.

"There's an empty syringe of atropine with the lidocaine and Keppra on the resuscitation cart. You do know atropine is contraindicated with brain trauma, don't you?"

"Of course." I snatch the empty syringes from the cart and examine them one by one. Could I have mixed up atropine with amiodarone? "Somebody handed me this syringe."

"Who?" Harold's voice booms.

I feel myself shrinking. "Someone with gloved hands."

"Everybody around this bedside is wearing gloves," Harold snaps.

I look around and find that he's right. "So were all the people from the OR," I murmur.

"This patient has herniated his brain stem," Harold glares.

Bile stings at the back of my throat. The boxes are different colors and easy to spot. The syringe I pushed was out of the box. Why didn't I check the label before I shoved it in? I can't believe this is happening.

"It was a bad head injury. He might have herniated anyway." Sam Johnson offers a shred of sympathy for me.

All I can do is stare at the patient. He's brain-dead, and I did it. I choke back the bile that returns to my throat.

Harold's lips flatten. "We're going to have to take this up with the director of nursing."

*

"Will you call the orderly?" Chelsea asks me when I return from transferring Carl. "This lady is ready to go."

"He's moving another patient. I'll go with you."

"What the heck happened, Ariel?" Chelsea asks as we wheel her patient away from the recovery room.

"I don't know. It's surreal." I follow her through the hall, one foot after another, trying to piece together snippets of the code. "The hand that passed me the atropine was much bigger than mine. It had to be a man."

"You don't make mistakes like that. Maybe you're distracted from everything else going on."

"Distracted is one thing. Oblivious is another. I am not oblivious."

"I wasn't in the room. I can't help you."

"The atropine is either boxed in a baggie at the head of the bed, or its box is in a drawer of the crash cart. Somebody opened it and handed it to me."

Chelsea rolls the patient into the service elevator. "There were so many people in the room; it's hard to know."

"Jake, Harold, and Sam Johnson were the only men in

the room. Harold was at the foot of the bed, Sam at my right elbow. Jake was on the left, the side the atropine came from."

Chelsea pushes the button, the doors close. "Could one of the OR nurses have thought it was lidocaine? They don't push IV drugs all the time like we do."

"The boxes are completely different colors. Did someone open them and have the syringes lying there, ready to go?" My stomach contracts just as the elevator dings its arrival at our floor. "I should have read the label."

"This kind of thing doesn't happen to a nurse twice in one week. Someone's out to get you, Ariel."

A shiver travels up my spine as we slide her patient into his bed. "I'm going to swing by Janet Turner's office for a minute. I'll meet you downstairs."

Hurrying down the hall, I text Mom. *How's Dad?*

No change.

I'm on my way to the director of nursing's office to see if I can get Dad a new room.

That would be good.

The secretary's hair is askew. She has a stack of folders in her hand, and her phone is ringing. She pauses with her palm on the receiver. "Ms. Turner is not in her office."

"Do you know when she'll be back?"

"Maybe in an hour."

"Lovely," I mumble, head back to recovery.

Belinda stands up from the desk on my arrival. "The pre-op area is all backed up and the surgeons in the OR are ranting that the patients aren't ready. Where did you take off to?"

"I went to help transfer a patient. There were no post-ops coming out. I thought there was plenty of time."

"Chelsea's been back for five minutes already. I need to have a word with you in my office."

I'm dreading the lecture I know I'm going to get as I

close the door to Belinda's office. I sit across from her desk in a worn khaki vinyl chair. Instead of going behind it, she parks herself on the edge, towering over me.

"The director of nursing and the head of human resources were here a few minutes ago. You've been placed on suspension until there's a formal review."

The breath gets sucked out of me as if she hip-checked me to the wall. "*What*?"

"You aren't allowed to come into work until further notice, and you have to leave the building immediately."

"Someone handed me the wrong drug."

"It doesn't matter. You are responsible for every drug you give to a patient. You've had fatal mistakes with two patients. Your frequent tardiness and your lack of respect for the hospital's neuro unit have all contributed. Security is here to walk you out." Belinda opens the door.

"You need to empty out your locker, miss," the security guard says.

My shaky legs don't want to hold me. I grab the railing meant for patients to steady myself. "I have to see my dad. He's a patient in the neuro unit."

"I can't let you do that. My job is to escort you from the hospital."

I open my mouth to protest but can't find words. I follow in stunned silence as he leads me through the main recovery room in a walk of shame. The staff line either side, pretending to be busy with patients or equipment. Why couldn't we have gone down the hall where all I might see are visitors that I don't know.

We arrive at the locker room, and he hands me a bag.

I want to put it over my head and tighten it up. How will I pay my rent, make my car payment? I have some money saved, but that won't last long. What if this prevents me from getting a job elsewhere?

Suddenly, I see Mom and Dad sitting us down at the kitchen table, telling us we need to move. *Dad's been trying, but jobs are hard to find. We're moving to a motel.*

I look at the bag in my hand. It's one that we put the patient's stuff in. It smells the same as the cheap vinyl furniture in a motel.

My hands tremble as I empty my career into a plastic sack like a homeless person. Extra scrubs, a sweater, a broken stethoscope… Things I've accumulated for years.

A picture forms of me as a child, packing my things in a pillowcase. A stuffed dog, my jump rope. The hollow feeling in the pit of my stomach.

How could this happen? A wave of nausea washes over me.

I stop, take a breath.

Harold set this up. He must have. I never thought he would stoop so low.

"I need to get my purse," I tell the guard. Shuffling into the pre-op area, I snatch my handbag from the cupboard.

"What are you doing?" Chelsea eyes the bulging sack that says *Belongings* under my arm.

"I've been suspended." I slide my ID badge through the computer to clock out.

Chelsea's face tightens. "Are you kidding?"

"You'll have to give me the badge and tell her later." The security guard extends one hand, hits the button on the wall with the other.

The automatic doors creek open with a noise that sounds like a jeer. The recovery room nurses stare.

Chapter 19

The security guard is kind enough to walk me down the back stairwell to an exit. He opens the heavy fire door and I run out into rain pouring down so hard the drops are bouncing three inches off the pavement.

This is my turf. I know so many people, all the ins and outs. Will I ever get reinstated? Water drips from my nose to my chest and trickles over what's left of my heart. Escorted from the building… How degrading.

The squall worsens, a wall of water blocking everything outside of the car, closing me in, same as when I was a kid. My ears start to ring. I tell myself it's from the rain. Lightheaded, I grab the steering wheel. I can't be homeless. I can't do that again.

Everything is caving in on me. I'm a bad nurse, a bad daughter, a bad girlfriend. Blinking back tears, I put the car in gear as the rain lessens.

As I dash to my apartment, the deluge batters me like punishment. How can I fix all these things I've screwed up? Where do I start?

Drying my phone off in the hall, I notice a message. I hadn't heard my phone ring. I hit voicemail.

"This is Samantha from the Florida Board of Nursing. Give us a call when you have a chance." She rattles off the number.

"Oh crap!" I hit the call-back button. Did I forget to renew my license? No, it's due in April. Shit. "This is Ariel Savin. Samantha contacted me."

"Hello, Ariel, thank you for calling back. How's your day going?"

"It's raining on my parade."

"These darn hurricanes are nasty, aren't they? Anyway, the reason I'm calling is that we're required to let you know a complaint of incompetence has been filed against you."

"What?" I grab the stair rail, steady myself. "Who did that?"

"We're not at liberty to say."

Whoever handed me the atropine. Sam Johnson wasn't close enough. I can't see Jake doing it or reporting me. The only one powerful enough to get it done that fast is Harold.

"The Board of Nursing needs to launch an investigation that will involve you as well as your employer."

Do I tell her that I'm not technically employed anymore? "Can I still work as a nurse in that time?"

"I'm afraid not. These accusations are quite harsh, so the Board of Nursing is required to suspend your license, even if it's on a temporary basis."

"How can you suspend my license with only an accusation?"

"I'm sorry, Ms. Savin. This is a courtesy call to let you know in case you apply for another job. The Board of Nursing will be sending you written documentation in the mail."

They know I'm out. That means someone at the hospital filed the complaint. I need to get my head together.

"Do you have any other questions?"

So many questions are spinning in my head that it's a giant jumble. "No" is the only response I get out.

"You should be receiving the packet in the mail in a few days."

What am I going to do?

*

I unlock the door to an apartment that's painfully vacant except for a skinny dog and a hairless cat. "Oh, Grace." I scoop her into my arms, hold her against the gaping hole in my chest. "Thank goodness I have you to come home to." I hold my head against hers. She licks the tears from my face as I tote her to a patch of grass.

Sheltering under the overhang, I dial Ben, hoping he'll change his mind about things if he knows what happened.

It goes to voicemail.

I'm not sure what to say. Is he not picking up on purpose, or is he in surgery? "I miss you, Ben. Please come home." Clicking off, I stare at the phone. I should let Mom know, but I can't. I tuck the phone into my pocket.

"Why do things never turn out the way they're planned?" I open a can of Doggie Digestives and sink to the floor as Grace scarfs the food down.

"I guess *you* could say that, too, huh?" I eyeball the incision on her belly. "What did they do to you? Will they do the same to the patients in the neuro unit? Are they trying to get my dad as a way of controlling me? I need to get him out of there, but how, Grace? I'm not free to roam around the hospital to get things done."

Grace licks my leg as if to heal my internal wound, then lays her head in my lap like she understands.

A knock at my door makes me jump. "Ben?" I scramble in the darkness to open it, only to find Chelsea's concerned face.

"You got caught in the rain, too? Bes, you've had a day." She envelops me in a hug, funneling compassion and sympathy through her rain-dotted scrubs.

I let her hold on, take some of the pain.

"I checked on your dad and spoke to your mom. She said don't worry about her. She wants you to take care of yourself."

"You told her about my job?"

"I said you'd had a bad day." Chelsea breaks away and fishes a bottle of La Crema chardonnay and two large bars of Ghirardelli from her bag. "What you need to do is to get drunk and eat a wad of chocolate."

She brought my favorites. A smile cracks my face. Chelsea's like the sun breaking through the gloom. "I'm lucky to have a friend like you."

"Come on, it's late. You need to get out of those soaking wet clothes." She grabs my arm and drags me toward the bedroom. "I should've brought red wine to warm you up. You've got to be cold after that drenching." She hurls my closet door open, rifles through my clothes. "Put on this pink cashmere sweater you love and those treasured beat-up jeans."

I follow her directions, happy not to have to think.

"You should see the commotion going on in the recovery room. All the nurses are pissed off. We started a petition, and we're going through the whole hospital to get every nurse to sign it."

"Don't bother. Harold will win. He always does. He won over Belinda and the administration. He's won over the families of all the patients in the neuro unit. He even won over Ben and got him away from me. I won't be able to beat Harold. I'm toast." My hands caress the velvety sweater sleeves, remembering all I've done with Ben while wearing it. My stomach knots.

"You're not going to be toast. You're going to get toasted."

"I can't. I need to check on my dad."

"I did that already. Come on." She nudges me with her elbow toward the kitchen. "I'm pouring you a large glass of wine, and you can introduce me to your new pup."

The thought of Grace jolts me into the present. "She was up by herself earlier. She must be sleeping." We enter the kitchen to find Grace cowering in a corner, eyes wide.

"I won't hurt you, puppy." Chelsea squats down and holds out her hand.

Grace pushes herself further into the crook by the fridge and starts to shake.

"It's okay, girl." I drop to my knees beside Grace, holding her close while I stroke her fur. "This is Chelsea. She's going to be my dog whisperer."

Chelsea lowers her hand and stretches it further toward my dog.

Grace's lip rises and a growl emits from deep in her throat.

Chelsea snatches her hand away. "Guess not."

"Grace!" I scold. "Sorry. She liked Ben. I thought there'd be no problem."

"Don't worry, Ariel. She's skittish after all she's been through. I don't blame her." Chelsea keeps her eye on Grace as she talks.

"Come on, girl, this is my bestie. You'll love her." I slide Grace beside me so she's a little closer to Chelsea.

Another growl emerges, and Grace scrambles back into the corner.

"This is weird." *Does she not trust Chelsea?*

"Don't strong-arm her, Ariel."

"All right. I'll leave her here in the kitchen. She'll come out when she's ready."

Chelsea snags a wine glass from the cupboard. She tosses a few ice cubes in the glass and fills it to the brim. "You need to get working on this wine."

"Whoa. I won't even be able to walk to the living room with that."

"Exactly." She grins, stuffing the bottle into my ice bucket and surrounding it with cubes.

Two gulps make the level safe to carry, and I maneuver my way to the sofa.

Chelsea settles into the green-and-white club chair and pops open a LaCroix.

"You want a glass?" I offer.

"Don't worry, I'm good. I love this stuff. Any old can will do." She takes a sip and smiles like it's the best champagne on the planet. "Have you thought about your next move?"

"Look for a new job, I guess."

"Plenty of hospitals in the area need nurses," Chelsea tells me with a reassuring look.

The heaviness in my chest returns. "Yeah."

"You'll work it out. At least you won't have to put up with Belinda or Harold or the conflict of you and Ben being in the same..."

My stomach wrenches. I reach for my wine.

Chelsea looks away. "Sorry," she whispers.

"It's okay. I do the same kind of thing all the time, wondering what he's doing or when he'll be home."

"It'll get better, Ariel. At least you get out of hurricane call." She laughs.

I eke out a laugh. "When this stupid storm is over, I'll figure it out." A picture of my dad scrolls through my head. I take another big gulp of wine.

Grace peeks out from the kitchen.

"Come on, girl," I call.

She doesn't move.

"What's your theory on the dogs?" Chelsea leans in as if my answer is important to her.

"Somehow, they're associated with the hospital and Harold. The vet tech said there's something wrong with Grace's affect. Maybe that's why she was acting weird around you."

"What do you mean, something wrong?"

"Sometimes, her reactions are slow, as if things aren't connecting."

"That's new." Chelsea looks like she's hanging on my every word.

"It's been that way all along. I must not have mentioned it to you."

Grace emerges from the kitchen with her eyes on Chelsea and starts to bark.

"Quiet, Grace, we have neighbors to think about."

Grace backs against the dining room wall and sits. Her barking stops.

Chelsea eases back against her chair, sips her drink. "Are you going to pursue your ideas about Harold?"

"I have to. Grace is all I've got left. I need to prove myself to Ben and Belinda and the people in security. If there *is* something wrong with her, other than being skinny and weak, I want to find out what it is and how it happened."

"You have a plan?" Chelsea angles an ear toward me, watches me closely.

Grace growls, moves over to the front door, never taking her sights off Chelsea.

"Right now, it's drink wine and don't lose it."

She chuckles. "Sounds like a good goal to me. Drink up." She raises her LaCroix in the air and I touch my glass to it.

The hollow sound it makes reverberates in my bones. Grace lets out another growl.

"*What* is up with you, doggie?"

Grace dips her head. Her lip goes down.

"You need a top-up there, Bes." Chelsea tugs the bottle from the ice bucket and fills my glass to the rim again.

"You do have a generous pour. Are you sure you don't want some of this?" I hold the glass steady while I sip out enough to feel comfortable putting it on the coffee table.

"No, I'm good, but like my mother says, 'Pack it to the rim, Jim. Those ice cubes need to swim.'"

I burst out laughing.

Grace shoots to my side, barking and baring her teeth at Chelsea.

Chelsea blanches, tucks her hands in close, shoves the chair back six inches.

"Grace, you need to chill out." I run my hand along her back, ease her into sitting. "How's your mom doing?" I ask when the dog calms.

"She's getting along." Chelsea drops her gaze to the floor. "How do you think the atropine appeared?" She takes a lengthy drink of her LaCroix.

A long sigh seeps out as the repercussions of the atropine debacle filter through my mind. I reach for the wine, take another gulp. "It was a big hand—a man's. Jake was standing on the side it came from, but it doesn't seem like Jake, though."

"I agree, not Jake's style." Shifting in her seat, Chelsea turns to face me. "Whatever happened with the guy you met at the restaurant opening? The one with hookers."

Grace's muscles tense, and I pat her faster, which seems to help.

"That's a big jump from atropine."

Chelsea spins the LaCroix can in her hand. "Yeah, it just popped into my head."

"The guy is sketchy. I looked him up. I think his investors were involved in a failed project to reprogram people's brains in Russia. They better not try anything on my dad." The thought of good times with Ben is like a kick in the gut. I take two more large gulps of wine.

"Doing better now?"

"If you mean getting a buzz, the answer is yes."

"Dessert time." Chelsea laughs and opens the chocolate

bar, breaking it into squares she arranges on the table in a smiley face.

Grace is on her feet again, barking and growling.

I scoop Grace up beside me. She squirms a bit and settles in with her stare locked on my friend. "Chelsea, you're too much." I laugh, taking a square from the edge of the smile.

Chelsea picks one of the 'eyes' up off the coffee table, takes a bite out of it. "I'd give some to you, Grace, but dogs aren't supposed to eat chocolate."

Grace's lip goes up, but she stays quiet.

"Do you think Ben knows about me being suspended?" I ask, letting the chocolate melt over my tongue.

"No doubt. He got called down to the ER when I was leaving. Sounds like he may be doing surgery this evening. That's probably why he hasn't called." She answers the question before I even ask.

Overwhelming fatigue invades my arms, my legs, my eyes. I slide my feet up beside me on the sofa as a yawn slips out. "What time is it?"

Chelsea checks her watch. "Twenty-to-eight. You look like you could use some sleep. I'm going to head out."

I squiggle down so my head is resting on the throw pillow.

Grace goes into a barking frenzy.

I wrap my arms around the dog, tug her in close until she quiets. "It's too early to sleep. We'll watch TV for a while."

Chelsea clicks on the TV. "Careful what you watch these days."

Careful comes out *carepul* and I smile. "You need to let go of your chronic worrying." My eyes drift shut, and I think she says, "You'd be surprised," but the wine has kicked in, and it doesn't register.

Chapter 20

A wet tongue on my hand wakes me. The room is dark, my head hurts. What does this dog want?

I roll over, bump the cat. Grace whines and I check the clock. Seven thirty. "I'm late for work!" Bolting out of bed, my head pounds harder. My mouth feels like I swallowed a dirty sock. "Don't pee in the house." I scoop the dog up, trudge to the living room, and spot the wine. It all comes flooding back.

Nausea sets in. No license, no job, no Ben, and my dad. "All I want to do is climb back in bed and sleep for a week," I tell the dog, ferrying her outside. It's not raining now, but I need to look at the forecast.

I climb into the shower, try to clear my head. Should I call the neuro unit, check on Dad? They probably won't tell me anything anyway and I can't get in until visiting hours. "This is awful, Grace," I say as I towel off.

Grabbing my phone, I text Mom. *You up?*

No answer. Is she mad I didn't go see them last night? My brain doesn't want to work. It bounces from Mom to Dad, to Ben, to my job. It's like I'm caught in a rope that's tangled so tight, I don't where to start.

Victor bolts under the bed as I plop down at my computer. Grace lies at my feet. "I'm not going on Instagram to see how wonderful everyone else's life is. There's nothing decent in my inbox. *Shit.* Shit everywhere. Harold is making my life shit," I tell the dog. "At least Simon is making his life shit, too." The thought brings a smile.

Grace thumps her tail.

"There's something about Simon. Yeah, he's the money man, but it feels like Simon thinks he owns Harold. Harold's got this God complex, and Simon's like the devil behind it. More shit! I need to find out more about Simon."

Grace's tail thumps faster.

"Right now, I need to clear my head. The gym will help. I'll meet Mom at the hospital when visiting hours start. You rest up while I'm gone." I settle Grace in the crate.

The gym is as empty as the apartment parking lot. It's kind of nice to have the place to myself. No waiting on machines, no sweaty backrests.

I plug in my earbuds and look for something on my playlist that will be a soft background. I start up John Mayer and step on the elliptical.

"Okay, Ariel, what have you got?" I ask out loud as I pump the pedals. "I'm a single unemployed nurse with a father who is comatose, a new dog, and a freaked-out cat."

Overwhelming sadness grips me, and the tears come. I glance around to see if anyone could be watching. No one is here thank goodness, because I can't stop them. They meld with my sweaty face and drip onto my chest, soaking my top, showing the world where the cavern in my heart is.

The machine slows. I can't stop, can't let the world see me like this. I crank up the tension on my legs, push the pedals, and grip the handles harder, grinding at them to drag myself out of this hole.

My legs turn so rubbery that I worry I'll fall. I stop and sit to catch my breath.

As I pant, Jake walks into the gym.

My stomach clenches. I don't want to talk to anyone looking like this, but if I bolt to the locker room, he'll see me.

I bend low and pull off my shoe, pretending there's something wrong with my sock, and hope he keeps his usual routine of going to the pool.

"Ariel?"

Busted. I shove my foot back into my runner and wipe the salt stinging my eyes as Jake saunters closer. His deodorant is sickening strong. My nausea returns.

He clears his throat. "What happened yesterday was bad. I keep running it through my head to try to figure out who might have handed you the atropine. You'd never make a mistake like that."

Jake is fiercely loyal, but I'm not certain his loyalty to his job hasn't become stronger than to his friends. I'm not sure what to say. "Well, it happened," I breathe.

"I can't believe they suspended you." His voice is strained like he's being sincere.

"You've got to help me, Jake. I'm so worried about my dad. What's going on with Harold's patients?"

"I'll keep an eye on your dad. The Weebly family announced they want to move their daughter out of the hospital. It put the other families on edge."

"Anything up with the patients?"

"Harold is moving forward with his plan since they've had a few triumphs in the lab."

"Where is the lab? I know you know."

Jake eases his duffle bag to the bench. "I had to sign when I was hired that I would keep the location to myself."

"That's creepy but not as bad as putting my dad in the unit. It's so vindictive."

"Maybe it's lucky there's a critical care bed for now. Simon wanted to bring in more patients, but the hospital refused because they didn't have the right paperwork."

I want to tell him being lucky they had a bed is a load of BS, but I decide to stay cool. "What does that guy do?" As I say it, a picture of Ben all dressed up at the restaurant opening appears in my head. A wave of sadness hits me.

"Nobody knows who Simon works for. Not Simon, not the guys he deals with. The big bosses somehow keep an invisible veil. I suspect they're foreign, but don't repeat that."

"How do you know?"

"Some of the biotech stuff that arrived was labeled in Polish or Ukrainian, one of those Slavic languages."

My guess is Russian. "What guys?"

"Employees, helpers, gofers. I've never met any of them."

"Simon has gofers," I mumble. Chelsea said cameras recorded a guy sideswiping Robert and another taking the box. "Is Simon around?"

"He's at the lab daily. Ever since the money started coming in, Simon took charge. He's in, checking on the progress of the patients, telling Harold what to do. Harold's been worrying about to filling up the unit ever since."

"Simon's flashiness is appalling. He must think he's some kind of big shot."

"Who always seems to have a new girl on his arm. Some guys have it made." Jake sighs.

I cough. "We have different definitions."

"A red Ferrari and a tall blonde with a charming accent will grab any guy's attention."

I fluff my towel and wipe my mouth to hide my disdain. "Does Simon direct your job now, too?"

"No. I still do all the things a PA in a hospital does. You may not like him, but Simon is a nice guy. He let me drive the Ferrari for an afternoon so I could do a few errands for him. Man, what a ride!"

I try for a genuine smile. "Sounds like you've got a new friend." I wonder if there's a new loyalty.

"Don't think so, but I'd do anything to take that Ferrari out again."

*

Climbing into the car, I fetch my phone from the center console. Nothing from Mom. Maybe she's still asleep, she *was* exhausted. I text her. *Can I meet you for breakfast?*

While waiting, I notice Chelsea called ten minutes ago.

"How are you doing this morning?" my bestie says when she picks up.

"I was a little foggy. I went to the gym and worked off that bottle of wine you forced me to drink last night."

Chelsea laughs. "You were doing a good job of slugging that wine down."

"You could've helped with some."

"I was on call. I switched my call time so I could get gas and some cash."

"I forgot to tell you last night, the Board of Nursing called. They're investigating a claim against me and have suspended my license."

"Bes, this is bad. What are you going to do?"

"I need to prove I didn't kill Carl and Robert."

"How do you do that? You need a lawyer."

"Maybe a lawyer would help. I wonder if any are open this close to the hurricane?"

"The truth will show up somehow. Get a good book and hunker down with Grace. With any luck, there's nothing contagious about her. You don't need some strange thing budding inside your dog."

"Such friendly support."

"Just kidding. I'm the one who'll be in jeopardy, camped out with a rabid Belinda, lathering at the mouth because we have one less nurse."

The visual makes me smile. "I don't know what I'm going to do about my dad. Harold would never let me or my mom stay there. She can stay with me, but I don't want Dad in that unit." My thoughts turn to Ben. I wonder if Chelsea saw him while on call. "Anything interesting happen in the OR last night?"

"It was quiet. The only thing that came in was a gallbladder."

"Is there news on Carl? Please tell me he's better and is being transferred to a normal room."

"I wish it were true, but you need to put this place out of your mind, Ariel."

"I can't. I need to get things straightened out, if only in my head. What have you heard?"

"Nothing."

"I know you, Chelsea. That means something's up."

"All right. There's a big to-do with the relatives of the patients in the unit. One of them called all the others when he smelled burnt flesh in the unit. They came in, demanding to see the patients three hours before the eleven o'clock visiting hours."

"Do you know what it's about?"

"No one would tell me anything. I went to check on your dad. He's unchanged."

"Thank goodness," I mumble.

"I saw Mrs. Young when I was leaving. She looked terrible."

"Did she say anything to you?"

"She was on her cell and said she was on her way to Publix."

"What time was that?" I start the car, head for Publix at the end of the plaza.

"About thirty minutes ago."

"Thanks for checking on Dad. I'll talk to you later." Jamming the car in park, I run for the entrance.

The grocery store is all but bare. The few people here are wandering with pained expressions as they decide whether to take something they don't want or go without. I need some more food if Mom and I are home. I want to find us a couple of good books in case the power is out. I hope they have some left.

I case the aisles in a grid, making sure I miss no one. Spotting Mrs. Young, I brace myself for the reaming out I might be inviting about the condition of her husband. Someone may have said Robert is in the neuro unit due to my carelessness, and now there's another patient going there because of me.

Snagging a box of crackers hidden behind a stack of ketchup, I steer my cart over to her. "Amanda, how are you?"

She stares at me through puffy lids, eyes searching for recognition.

"It's Ariel from the hospital."

A glint of pain shoots through her eyes. She turns her cart away. "I don't want to talk to anyone from the hospital."

She's several pounds thinner than when I'd first met her, with dark circles ringing her now dull blue eyes. Her blonde hair looks stringy and has lost its shine. I don't know what to say, but I can't give up.

I steer over to the next aisle, wait for her at the end. When I spot her, I inch forward. "You look tired." I offer a smile, ease my cart alongside hers.

She grunts. "I'm exhausted. I'm working, taking care of the kids, and trying to get to the hospital to see Robert.

There's nothing left in the effing store. I can't even feed my kids." Amanda turns her attention to a picked-over shelf of breakfast cereal.

Her cart has a jar of olives and two containers of apple juice. I look at the crackers in my hand, think of her kids. "Here, take these crackers."

"Keep them. You've got no food either." She marches away.

"My dad is the new patient in room twelve," I call behind her. "Please tell me what happened in the unit."

Amanda stops, eyes me up and down. "I didn't know that." She clears her throat. "One of the family members stayed in his son's room after visiting hours. He said the unit started to smell like burnt skin. He saw Rebecca doing tests on a patient with electrodes hooked up to a battery. The patient was contorting all over the place."

"On my dad?"

"It was the woman with no family in room two."

"Did the man call a nursing supervisor?"

"He contacted all of us. We met there at eight o'clock this morning and we called the supervisor. She called the risk manager. They examined all the patients. Only one burn was found. It was on the woman in room two. Rebecca told them the patient's temperature had dropped, and she put a blanket in the microwave to warm up. She said there was a glass plate from lunch in with the blanket that she didn't notice. When she put the blanket down, the plate burned the patient."

"That's a bald-faced lie. Blankets catch fire in the microwave."

"That's what we said, but the nursing supervisor stuck up for Rebecca. None of our family members had burns, so we're not sure if we can do anything else."

"That's disturbing." I don't think the supervisor is

aligned with Harold. She may not have much bedside experience and was sticking up for a staff nurse. "How is Robert?"

Amanda's eyes well up. "He's withering away."

"It can happen when people are confined to bed."

Wiping her tears, she straightens. "The weird thing is that, in the past couple of days, his brain seems more active. When I've gone in his room, it's like he's restless or agitated."

"That's different. What's he doing?"

"He has twitches around his mouth and eyes, which wasn't happening before."

"Have you asked the nurses what it's about?"

"They say he's the same, that the twitches can happen from electrolyte imbalances. It's weird, though, that the woman in the next room had the same twitches.

"You saw that?"

"I did. When I asked about it, the nurse was rude."

"Was it one of the regular nurses or someone who got sent there for the day?"

"It was Rebecca. She said they're specialized at what they do and if something had changed, she would know. When we protested, Rebecca told us we needed to trust the hospital's judgment." Amanda wipes her nose.

"The nurses used to be friendly and open. Now, they go around whispering and checking what we do while we're in the room." Her eyes well up again. "This has been terrible. It's like a bad dream that won't end."

"It's got to be hard for you." I grab onto her cart so I can guide it around the corner. "Did you talk to Dr. Goss?"

"I haven't seen him. The nurse said he's busy and unavailable." She searches an empty shelf for some granola bars. A tear runs down her face. "I don't know what to do."

I'm not sure if she means about Robert or the food

situation. "Take the crackers. There's some hard cheese on the next aisle. It'll last a while if the power goes out." I steer her cart alongside mine, and she follows.

"Here's the cheese." I put two bricks of cheddar in her cart. "All the chicken is gone. Will your kids eat pork chops?"

"Yes." She continues to follow as I navigate her cart. "I can't stand to see my husband like this. I'm sorry I agreed to ever let him in the neuro unit. At first, I wanted him to get better. That's what they sold me on. Now. I feel like I made a mistake. I don't want to go through life thinking that Robert hates me for keeping him alive like this."

I load the pork chops in and head for the produce department. "You can request he be removed from the program."

Tears spill from Amanda's eyes. "I thought I could, but that nurse, she said because we have no money, Robert became a ward of the hospital."

"Are you sure?"

"Rebecca said there's a clause in the papers we signed that said we agreed the hospital would take responsibility for Robert and the bills. Since they have assumed the obligation, they have the rights to his care."

"I didn't know that." I hold up a bag of apples and grab a bag of carrots across from them. She nods and I add them to her pile.

"I signed my husband's life away and now they're experimenting on him." Amanda wipes her face with her sleeve.

That better not happen to my dad.

"Thank you for your help," Amanda says as we near the cash register.

"Freeze the pork chops. The rest will last for a while without staying cold," I call as she walks away.

I need to help these people. No matter what it takes.

Chapter 21

"Hi, Mom. You all right? You didn't answer the texts."

"Sorry, I slept late. I'll be there when visiting hours start at eleven. How's your dad?"

Do I tell her about my job? "He's unchanged," I say, hoping Chelsea was right.

"Is he still in that horrible area where they whisper like a funeral home?"

"The unfortunate answer is yes."

"You've got to get him out, Ariel. Can Ben do anything?"

I swallow hard, try to keep my voice steady. "We have a lot to talk about, but I'm working on it, Mom. I'll meet you there at eleven." I click off and redial the hospital, punching in the extension for ICU and ask for the nurse manager. "Hi, it's Ariel. Did you happen to get any bed openings overnight?"

"We're so backed up, Ariel. The ER is holding patients for us. How's your dad?"

"He's the same. Hope it settles down for you. Let me know if a bed becomes available." I hang up, try CCU and the step-down unit without any luck. Pleading with the director of nursing isn't going to help. I need to figure out something else.

Walking into the front of the hospital with no ID feels so strange. They keep up appearances here with stylish chrome-and-white chairs and flowers left behind from when patients go home. At the desk, I give my name, say I'm visiting my dad. The gray-haired woman in a pink volunteer's tunic snaps a picture of me then plugs everything in to give me the printout.

Her face clouds. She looks from the computer to me and back to the computer. "Um, there's a notice here that you've been suspended and aren't allowed in the hospital."

The chatter in the line to check-in stops. My cheeks heat. "That's regarding my job. It doesn't have anything to do with my dad."

The woman angles her computer screen toward me. "This says we're not supposed to let you in."

"You have to. My dad has gone into a coma."

Someone in line gasps, and a buzz runs through the group.

"Sorry, miss, but I can't help you."

Mom appears from nowhere, waving papers in the air. "My husband is an ordained priest. He needs his family in his time of crisis." Mom shoves her face nose-to-nose with the woman. "Let her in, or I'm reporting you to the Catholic Church."

The woman pales, hits the button, and squirms as Mom breathes down on her. She hands the printed admittance to me.

"Thank you," Mom says while steering me to the elevator.

"No, this way." I nod as we speed-walk down the hall. We zip around the corner into the stairwell. "Wow, Mom, I didn't know you had it in you."

"I'm fed up with sickness and hospitals and doing what everyone says when all I want is for your dad to get better."

"Report her to the Catholic Church?"

Mom laughs. "I saw she had a cross pinned on her collar.

I figured it was worth a try. Do you want to tell me what's going on?"

As we slog up the concrete stairs, I tell her about Robert and Carl and the suspicious details.

"Oh, Ariel, I know you didn't do that."

"I need proof. I don't have any yet."

"What does Ben think?"

I want to spill everything about Ben leaving me, my fear of never finding another job, being homeless, my memory of being stuffed into the back seat with my sister while she and Dad slept sitting in the front of the old Ford when Dad lost his job. I want to confess that even though he has flaws, I'll never find a man that I admire as much as Ben. He dumped me because of my strange ideas and my stubbornness over a dog. But now isn't the time. Dad is the priority. Mom doesn't need anything else to worry about. I hit the button for the automatic doors as we arrive at the neuro unit. "We haven't had a chance to talk."

I check each patient's room we walk by. There's an odor of Lysol, and the rotting clay pot stench remains. I don't smell burnt flesh. I wonder if they're trying to cover it.

"Hi, Dad, it's Ariel and Mom." I rub his arm, kiss him on the cheek. "How are you doing today? I'm going to check everything out for you. The first thing is shining a light in your eyes." I lift his lids. "Your pupil reaction is good, Dad. I'm going to look at your skin." I halt. I've never seen his body naked. If I ask Mom to check him, she may not know a small change is untoward. I hope Dad's not aware enough to know what I'm doing. I steady myself, lift the covers, examine front and back.

No burns.

Mom pulls a chair next to the bed, takes his hand. "I found the mystery novel you were reading. It slid under the seat in the car. Your bookmark is still in it. I'll go from there."

She reads aloud while I take his vital signs and listen to his lungs with the stethoscope I brought in my purse.

"Dad," I say as Mom turns a page, "I want to see if we can get rid of this IV and feed your stomach. I'm going to talk to your nurse."

Mom nods, keeps reading.

It's Saturday, Rebecca's not here. I seek out the weekend nurse in charge. "Hi, I'm Ariel, Paul Savin's daughter."

She looks at me with suspicion. "He's the same."

"Do you have the results of his MRI?"

"He hasn't gone. The machine's been broken for a week. I doubt they'll fix it until after the hurricane."

What else can go wrong? "Can you ask Dr. Martinez to do a CT scan? And while you have him on the phone, see if he'll put Dad on tube feedings, please."

"Dr. Martinez signed off. Dr. Goss has taken over."

"That's ridiculous. My dad isn't one of your patients."

"I wish someone would tell Ariel the status of brain stem work is over her head." Harold appears, addressing the nurse as if I'm not there.

I hold my tongue. Why is he pulling this power play? The conversation with Jake about Harold needing bodies pops into my head. That's why Robert's truck was rolled. Harold needed a body to practice on aside from the box of protein. Dad is in this unit because Harold wants him for practice.

I stare into his eyes and say a quick prayer for his soul. "You'll never get away with this, Harold."

His eyes narrow as he smirks. "How quickly indiscretions are forgotten in the face of power and wealth."

My fists clench. I tell myself to play it down for Dad's sake and force my palms open. Turning away, I notice the heart is missing from the top of his pen where it sat on top of a caduceus. The same heart I'd found by the dumpster. "You lose something there, Harold?" I point.

He looks down. Red flags of color etch his cheeks. "It must have popped off when I was putting my coat on."

I want to throw in his face that I found the effing heart. That I know what he's doing and he's never going to get my dad.

Instead, I force a smile, try to sound genuine. "Your lab coat hides the indiscretion."

*

"You look like your head is about to explode," Mom says as I step back into Dad's room.

I close the sliding glass door. "Things aren't working in my favor at the moment." I take a seat on the far side of Dad to keep an eye on the unit.

"Can I do something to help?"

I shake my head. "I messed up. I never should have talked you into coming here. Dad should not be in this state. The MRI machine is broken, and his condition is not being investigated. I think he needs to get out of here for further evaluation. Emily, from nursing school, is at Delmar Hospital. If I can get a bed for him, is it okay with you that he goes?"

"I remember Emily. She's a sweet girl, but what about Miami?"

I think about Ben's friend. I don't know the guy. I can't call him up. "The weatherman said if the hurricane turns, it will head south toward Miami. I'm not comfortable with Dad being in this unit. We can get him moved by ambulance if we don't wait too long."

"I don't like the idea of going anywhere, but I agree that this is not the best situation for your father."

I punch in the number. “Hey, Em, it’s Ariel. Are you working today? I have a huge favor to ask.” I tell her everything about my dad, my patients, my job.

“That’s incredible. You can get a job here. Our recovery room would love to have you.”

“I need to clear up the suspension first.”

“Let me know when you do, Ariel. Regarding a bed, we have none right now.”

“I have to get Dad out of here before something worse happens.”

“We have patients scheduled to be discharged. I’ll put a note in the computer to save a bed. You’ll have to get a transfer order so I can confirm.”

“I will. Thanks, Emily. I can’t tell you how much I appreciate this.”

“Hey, you’d do it for me.”

I click off. “I’m texting Jake to ask for a transfer order. You remember him?”

“Of course I do.”

I read my text out loud. *Mom is in the neuro unit. She’d love to say hello to you. She didn’t get a chance the other day when I was reaming you out. Sorry about that. I was upset. I know it wasn’t you.*

Mom’s brow tightens. “Why don’t you ask Ben?”

My heart’s in my throat. How do I tell her what an idiot I’ve been? “Ben, uh… Ben and I had a fight. He left.”

Her eyes grow wide. “Oh my.”

“We’ve had some disagreements because I don’t trust Harold, and I’m not thrilled with medicine in some ways. Bringing the dog home put him over the edge, I guess.”

“Ariel, how could you? Ben’s the best thing that ever happened to you.”

The empty spot in my chest thuds. “I know. I messed up.

Now, he won't answer my calls." The phone pings, and my heart swells. Could it be him?

I'm right around the corner.

"It's Jake, he'll be here in a minute." I scan the unit. Harold has gone to his office and the nurses are in patient rooms.

The double doors swing open. Jake waves and heads our way.

Mom puts the book down, grips Dad's hand.

"Would you mind giving Jake a hug when he walks in to kind of warm things up? I kind of created a faux pas last time I saw him."

She glances at Dad, the door slides open, and Mom springs to her feet. "Hi, Jake. How are you?" She wraps her arms around him.

"Good, Mrs. Savin. You?" Jake backs away.

"Things have been better." She resumes her place at Dad's side.

Jake offers a smile. "I understand."

"Jake, I'm sorry."

He holds his palm up. "No need."

"We haven't been able to get an MRI since the machine is down. Do you remember Emily Brooks? She said Delmar could take him if we can get a transfer order. Will you help us so we can find out what's going on with Dad?"

"I'd like to help you, but Harold would have my head. He's all freaked out about the hurricane. He doesn't want anyone going anywhere."

"Please, Jake," I plead. "You know Dad doesn't belong here. What if Harold needs the bed for a real patient?" I don't dare say *subject* in front of Mom.

"Sorry, Ariel. I can't do it."

"Can you arrange for a cot so I can stay with Dad?"

"I'll have to ask Harold. That may work. Your dad's not one of the regulars."

I exhale, grab his arm. "Thanks, Jake."

Jake makes sure the door is closed tight, then focuses on Mom. "No one around here knows Mr. Savin coached me in Little League. Let's keep that to ourselves. I'll do what I can to help."

*

Resuming my place on the far side of my dad, I watch the unit through the glass slider. Jake's in Harold's office and the nurses are working in their patient rooms. I dial Dr. Martinez, leave a message and my number.

"Do you think they'll give you a cot?" Mom asks, picking up Dad's book.

"Chances are slim, but it's worth a try."

"I'm ready to try anything." Mom starts reading to Dad.

I check my texts, my voicemail, my email. Nothing from Ben. My mind wanders to our tradition of walks on the beach with a romantic dinner after all the tourists are gone. How could I have messed up so bad? It was stupid, selfish.

"That doctor hasn't called you back." Mom shatters my daydream. "The more I think about it, your dad would prefer to go to Miami instead of Delmar."

"The problem is I don't know anybody in Miami."

"Ben does."

My broken heart throbs in my chest. "I can't call him up and ask him to do that."

"He still cares about you and your father. He didn't ban you from his life forever."

"I don't feel right asking him. Besides, every time I've called or texted him in the last day and a half, he hasn't answered."

She puts the book down. "Can you try again? Blame me. It's your father we're talking about here."

"You're right. Maybe he'll do it for you. I wouldn't fault him for not wanting to do anything for me." I press the number. It goes to voicemail. "Hey, Ben, I'm sorry I've been such an ass about the dog and everything. I miss you. Mom says hi. She was wondering if we could transfer Dad to Miami. Can you help us?" I click off.

Mom smiles. "That's good, you reached out."

"I should have specified getting permission from Miami for Dad to go there. Ben won't write the transfer order for the same reasons as Jake."

Harold's door opens. Jake averts my gaze and walks out of the unit. Harold goes into Evie's room and draws the curtain.

I wonder what condition she's in. Has she had any changes, or is she still worse than the other patients here?

Dad's nurse scurries to the desk to answer a ringing phone. She nods several times, glances at me before hanging up and heading our way.

"That's not promising," Mom says.

The nurse scans Dad's monitor. She turns her focus to me. "Ms. Savin, you need to leave."

I jump to my feet and grip the bed rail. "This is my dad. You can't stop me from seeing him."

"You're flagged in the computer not to be allowed in."

Mom squares off with her. "That's insane! Patients and their families have rights."

The nurse lifts the tube emptying Dad's bladder, dumps urine into the bag. "I'm following orders from the administration, ma'am."

Mom's hands fly to her hips. "I want proof that this is legal."

"I didn't say that *you* have to go, only your daughter."

In the background, I see the Weebly family leaving. "It's okay, Mom. I have other things I need to do." I look at the nurse. "Can I have a minute alone with my parents?"

"Don't try to stretch it out," she tells me as she closes the door behind her.

I turn my back to the door and lower my voice. "I'm going to do some investigating and work on getting Dad out of here. Stay with him as much as you possibly can. We'll text."

Leaning over, I kiss Dad on the forehead. "Keep Mom company. I'll be back to get you both."

Mom wraps her arms around my shoulders. "You can do this, Ariel."

I saunter my way out of the unit, eyeballing every patient along the way. I wonder what Harold is doing in Evie's room. I look for his feet as I pass. The curtain flutters, and I see him cradling her head, his wife's hair streaming across the pillow as he runs a brush through it. It's sad she's in that condition.

At the door, I double my pace to catch the Weebly family in the hall. Mr. Weebly's hair rings his shining scalp in a one-inch band. He's clothed in shades of gray. His wife's skin is as creased as her black dress. Her eyes are weary. "Your daughter is in the neuro unit?"

"Yes," the man answers with a raspy voice.

I look up, note one of the hospital cameras, and hope no one is watching me. "Can I talk to you for a moment? We can sit in the lounge."

They nod, and we backtrack a few yards to the waiting room for the unit. It's empty except for some outdated magazines and the dregs of the morning's coffee. "My name is Ariel. My father is in the unit, too, but for a different reason. I heard that the families met this morning over concerns about goings-on in the unit."

"That's right. Our daughter and the others aren't being treated right, and they are agitated."

"I agree with you. I want you to know you have my full support." Down the hall, I spot a security guard.

His face looks angry, determined. I know he's after me.

I rip a corner off one of the magazines, scribble my phone number, press it into Mr. Weebly's palm. "I heard you want to remove your daughter from the program. Contact me if you need help."

The frame of the guard fills the doorway. "Ms. Savin, you were asked to leave. I'm going to escort you out. You may not return. I've been told you are a danger to the patients in this hospital."

Mrs. Weebly squeaks and covers her mouth with her hand. Mr. Weebly looks away.

I lock onto her eyes with a pleading look and follow the guard out.

Chapter 22

In the car, I think about Mrs. Weebly and her reaction. Will they think I'm a lunatic?

Across the parking lot, I spot the OR janitor, paper sack in hand, walking to the outdoor picnic tables. I relock the car to join him on a bench in the shade.

"How come I be the guy who knows everybody who done got fired around here?" He unwraps an egg salad sandwich.

"Haha. Lucky you. How are you doing?"

"Hopin' no one sees me talkin' to you."

"Do you think your buddy would like to talk to a fellow fire-ee?"

He laughs. "Bet he would. I don't know his number, but he lives on Pearl Way. Third house on the right, the gray-and-white one. You like eggs?" He takes a bite of his sandwich.

"They're okay. Not my favorite."

"Eggs are good for a lot of things." He waves his sandwich at me and nods in a strange way.

I smile, not knowing what he means, but anxious to talk to his friend who worked in the unit. "Hope you get to enjoy your lunch before it rains again." I scoot back to the car, plug *Pearl Way* into my GPS.

The house is right where my GPS said it would be. Its freshly mowed lawn and deep green landscape make it stand out on the street. The janitor from the neuro unit is on the side of his house, building makeshift hurricane shutters out of broken-down pallets. He eyes me when I park out front, puts down the shutter he's working on, but keeps the hammer. "I'm not looking to buy anything, lady."

"Wait, Bill. I want to talk, not sell."

He waves the hammer around. "You keep on driving."

"I'm Ariel, from the recovery room at the hospital. I sort of got fired, too. I thought we could compare notes."

There's a spark of recognition. Then, a bright smile lights his face. "Well, I'll be. Come on over here in the shade and tell me about it." He leads me to a pair of webbed lawn chairs under a tall pine.

I explain all the circumstances with my patients and my dad.

He clucks his tongue. "That Dr. Goss is under a spell. His ideas use ta be kinda crazy, but since that highfalutin guy came around, what they're doin' is downright evil."

My stomach tightens. "How did it change?"

"They started injectin' stuff in the patients at night when no one be around and torturin' them with what they called *stimulation techniques*. I never heard nobody yell, but I saw arms thrash and legs kick and smelled burnin' skin."

Amanda's story runs through my head. "Were they putting something in the IV or using a shot?"

"Shots, from what I saw. The patient heart monitors be going faster and the breathing machines beepin'."

"That's when those two nurses quit. Do you know where I can find them?"

He presses his lips together. "Nope."

"Did you see what was in the shots?"

He shakes his head. "They brought it from outside the hospital. It was in a big glass container, not them tiny jars with a rubber end you nurses use."

"How often did they do it?"

"Every night after the fancy guy showed up."

Dad didn't have any changes overnight. He can't be left alone. "Was the fancy guy there every night?"

"Only saw him one time." The man leans back in his chair, sizes me up. "You sure ask a lot of questions. I'm not gonna get in trouble for this, am I?"

"I want to help the patients in the neuro unit. Your information is very helpful to me. Did they say anything about what was in the solution they were injecting?"

"Unh, unh. Never."

"Do you know where they were getting the stuff?"

He snorts and crosses his arms.

"Please? I'm banned from the hospital. I have no other way to find out."

"It be from a lab for testing dogs."

I suck in a breath as I picture the dogs in the dumpster.

"You must like dogs. Not me, but I don't like to see nothin' treated bad."

"Are there any other details that caught your attention?"

There's a pause, a slow cluck of his tongue. "Dr. Goss say something about an extra fridge he keeps at home. Don't know if that's important, but it showed up in my brain." He looks to the darkening sky above. "I need to get my windows boarded up here."

"Of course, thanks for your time. I hope you find a new job soon."

"Got a real nice one lined up for soon as the storm's over." He grins.

"You're doing better than me." I wave, heading back to the car.

"Oh, Miss Ariel," he calls. "Be careful around those people."

*

Back in the car, I check my phone. Nothing from Ben or Dr. Martinez. I look back at the janitor. He said what's going on in the neuro unit is downright evil. I've got to find a way to stop it. I let that thought simmer while I head back home to grab a bite and let the dog out.

"You're walking a lot better today, Grace," I note as she pokes around the grass by the canal behind my apartment. I snap a photo of her happy face. "Don't go near that dam. The waterfall may sound nice, but it's dangerous when it rains a lot." I scoop her up, carry her back upstairs. "You have a rest while I give Victor some attention."

I plop down at my desk, sit the cat on my lap. "He said something about Harold's fridge," I tell Victor as I tickle the base of his tail. "Ben doesn't have a key, and I don't know Harold's housekeeper. How can I get in?"

Victor bats my phone across the desk with his paw. The motion reminds me of a sliding glass door.

"The house Harold lives in is on an amazing Intracoastal lot but it's old. He and Evie were about to tear it down and build a new one when her accident happened. I heard it's got sliding glass doors out to the water. Those can make a house vulnerable."

Victor starts to purr.

Plugging in a search, a video pops up on how to open a locked slider. "I can't believe I'm planning how to break into someone's house." Victor keeps on purring while I run through the video several times. "Turns out all I need is a screwdriver. I've got one of those in the trunk."

What if Harold has cameras and an alarm system? "I could dirty up the cameras like he did to you, Grace." The dog thumps her tail. "I'll have to figure that out when I get there."

I check Victor's water, tuck Grace back into the crate. "Okay, you two, wish me luck."

Harold's neighborhood has mansion after mansion, some Mediterranean, others contemporary, all with huge boats lining the Intracoastal Waterway. His, like most waterfront neighborhoods around here, are older and not gated. Doing a drive-by of his house, I note it's old and small compared to the rest. I guess that's why he'd planned to tear it down.

I find no car, no lights on inside, no activity in or around it. He told Ben he parks outside because the garage is full of junk. I look for a doorbell camera or security system and find none. There's a birdhouse that seems out of place in the garden. Its opening is pointed at the front door and nearby windows.

I think about my options while I circle back. If I park in the driveway, the neighbors will notice my car, but if I walk up and disappear around the back for half an hour, that seems pretty sketchy. I pull into the driveway but stop far enough back where I can get to the birdhouse undetected.

Opening the trunk, I wish I'd thought this through. I should have fished out what I needed before I got here.

With a quick glance around, I stash a screwdriver and latex gloves I keep in case I ever come across a bad car accident into my purse.

As I approach the back of the birdhouse, I notice the next-door neighbor's royal palm has shed a giant frond that's poking through the hedge. I tug at it and place the ten-inch-wide end that was attached to the palm on the birdhouse, so it covers the hole. Score!

Not finding any more outside cameras, I make my way to the front door and knock. My heart skips a beat. What if he answers? What's my excuse? I'll have to tell him I'm sorry about all the grief I've given him and beg to get my dad out. Can I do that with a straight face?

"Harold," I call and knock again so any nosy neighbors can tell I know him. Adjusting my bag on my shoulder, I head to the back.

The Intracoastal Waterway is busy with boats and jet skis zooming by. I can see why they would want to build a new house here. The setting is gorgeous, with tall coconut palms framing a sparkling water view. Thank goodness the hedges are old and tall, providing the perfect cover. I check the back of the house and slip onto the porch through an unlocked screen door.

Harold's sliding glass door is locked, and every window is latched down tight. I knock on the slider, encase my eyes with my hands to peer through the glass. The house looks messier than when I was here with Ben. I don't know what Ben would do if he saw me. I can't think of that now.

I scan for inside cameras or something like a hidden nanny cam and see none. The front door has an alarm keypad, but the green light is on like it's not armed. I spot a piece of computer paper with *Please clean out the cabinet under kitchen sink* written in large letters, with a check sitting beside it.

The housekeeper must be cleaning today. I need to hurry.

Dropping to my knees, I slip on my gloves and try to jam the screwdriver under the door. It doesn't go. With my other hand, I lift the door, shoving my thumb in a slot by the latch. The door is heavy. I can't budge it.

"Damn." I press my sweaty shoulder to the glass, pushing up with my weight and my fingers. The door raises, and I jam the screwdriver under.

I jimmy the door up and down while I tug on the handle. The latch clicks off, and the door moves. Wow, it worked.

The door stops. My eyes peer through the glass. He's put a stick in the track so the door won't open. "Shit!"

I lean on the door, stare at the track, and remember all the ways Harold has screwed me over. "I've got to get in this door."

If one latch opens, why not the other? I jump to my feet, throw all my weight at the other door. Sweat stings my eyes as I lift the opposing latch with all my might. The screwdriver slides under.

I crank with the screwdriver up and down. The latch won't trip. I crank again, up and down, up and down, getting nowhere. "Damn you." I kick the screwdriver. It jams in tighter. I hear a click, try the handle, and the door chugs open.

The faint smell of perfume greets me. It's familiar. I smell it whenever I walk past Evie's room in the unit. I shiver. Do I want to do this?

But then I think about my dad, who should not be in a coma in the neuro unit. I grab my screwdriver and step into Harold's living room.

It's large and formal. A blue oriental rug anchors a cream camelback sofa and a pair of toile-covered armchairs. What looks like original impressionist artworks adorn the walls. A bookshelf with expensive coffee table books and ornate ornaments flanks the wall beside me.

A gilded fish with one eyeball that protrudes more than the other is pointed at the front door. Must be a camera. Dropping behind the toile chair, I push it in front of the fish. A housekeeper could do that when cleaning.

I head for the fridge. It's empty except for a jug of half-and-half and condiments in the door. I check the freezer: Rocky Road ice cream. I pop the lid off. It is what it says. *Darn.* I've risked being caught breaking and entering for this?

There's got to be something else. He uses one of the bedrooms as an office. I'll look there. The office has a large maple desk with books and papers piled everywhere. A cold cup of coffee sits beside the computer.

One stack of papers is bills. The next is articles on the mechanics of automated physical therapy machines with pages of illustrations on how to work various muscle systems. Is he doing this off-site somewhere? There's got to be something here that will give me a clue about the lab.

Rifling through the desk drawers, all I find are stamps, a calculator, and a stapler. In a file below, I spot a tab with *Brittany Star* on it. I'd forgotten that Brittany had worked in the hospital lab, then got a job paying double to work in *Harold's* lab.

A door slams out front. I peek through the sheers and find a woman in the driveway tugging a vacuum cleaner from her trunk. The maid.

I drop the file into its slot. I'm about to bolt when I spot it, almost covered by full-length dresses in Evie's closet: a small fridge.

I stand up and see the maid fussing with something in her trunk. Do I have time? My brain screams *Get out! Get out!* But I want to check the fridge.

Keys jangle at the front door. My heart thumps against my chest. I yank open the fridge and spot vials of blood clustered in bins labeled *Stage one, two, and three*.

Snapping a picture, I dash for the sliding glass door. The latch on the front door wobbles. Sweat puddles around my gloved fingers as I chug the slider shut. The front door opens, and I race from the patio.

Did she see me? Even if she didn't, she saw my car. I strip off the gloves, burying them deep in my bag as I hurry to the front door and ring the bell. I can only hope that she thinks he moved the chair, and he thinks she did.

I wipe the sweat from my face and will my breath to slow. "Hi." I spread a giant smile across my cheeks. "Our church would love to have you come to services this Sunday."

"No, speak English." The door shuts.

A wave of relief runs through me. "Perfect."

It cracks open again. "You new doctor's wife?"

Oh, shit. How does she know?

"I see pictures from restaurant party." She grins. "I tell Dr. Goss you like his backyard."

I force the smile to remain as my mind flips through a string of responses. All I can come up with is, "Thank you."

*

I watch Harold's place in my rear-view mirror, half expecting the housekeeper to discover the open slider and come running after me. Did she notice how much I was sweating? Would she say that to Harold? I'm so focused on it that I almost run into a black truck parked on the side of the road that I hadn't noticed on my way in. Could that be the same black truck?

Calm down. Lots of people have trucks. Black is one of the more popular colors, and the maid only knows I was in the backyard. It'll be fine.

My mind goes to the refrigerator. Three stages. Are they of wakefulness or stages of synapse?

Brittany texted me about food for a party she'd had once. Let's see if she has the same number. I scroll through my contacts, hit Brittany Star.

"Hi, Brittany. This is Ariel Savin. How are you?"

"I'm nine hundred miles away from South Florida, so I'm doing great."

"Haha. That was smart."

"I moved to Nashville a couple of months ago. I love it."

"*That's* where you went. I heard you quit the lab. It's one of the reasons I called. Some changes have occurred in the neuro patients and Harold's been acting weird. Do you know what's going on with him and the lab?"

"What happens in the lab is supposed to be confidential."

"I heard that, but since you don't live here anymore, I thought you might help me out."

"To be truthful, I'm glad to leave it all behind."

"Did something happen?"

"There's a reason I quit and moved this far away, Ariel."

"Did it have to do with Harold?"

She doesn't answer.

"You're nine hundred miles away. You can tell me."

Her breathing quickens. "I found some paperwork by accident."

"What was it about?"

Brittany sighs. A rhythmic tic starts like a bump against a table.

"Can you tell me what the three different stages are that Harold would store blood for?"

"No," she states with a firm tone.

There's an awkward pause. The tic gets louder. My gut tells me to go for it. "I found three intubated dogs in the dumpster behind the hospital."

Brittany gulps. "They—" She stops.

I wait for a second, but she doesn't continue.

"One of them was still alive. I brought her home." I click on a close-up I took of Grace, text it to Brittany. "I should have Facetimed you. She's doing much better, but she's very thin. The vet said she'd been tortured."

I wait for a beat, but Brittany remains quiet. "Grace, that's what I call her, still has some delay in her reflexes. Do you know what it might be and what I can do about it?"

There's a sob on the other end. "I'm so sorry."

"Please help me, Brittany."

Another sob. She inhales deep. "Harold didn't want to

test on dogs. His grant ran out. Some guy from a biotech company came along and offered him money for the existing patients with bonuses for savant kids."

The breath sucks out of me. "He's selling the patients?"

"He was so desperate to get his wife back, he agreed."

My brain is numb. I tell myself to think. "There aren't any kids in the unit."

"He's trying to find some."

"When does he plan to do this?"

"They're going arrange a mass transfer to another facility as soon as they raise the level of consciousness."

It's already gone up. "Where are they getting supplies for the synapse development?"

"Don't know. A lot of things changed when the new money came along."

"You mean Simon?"

"You know about him? Simon plays like he's uninvolved. He's all about appearances and not getting his hands dirty. Harold's become his puppet and hates it. They hate each other, but they're like mutual parasites."

"Do you know what the long-term plan for the patients is when they get moved?"

"I've got to go. Stay away from them, Ariel."

"Tell me where the lab is."

She clicks off, and I'm left staring at my phone.

Chapter 23

I've got to find that lab.

At the red light, I search for spyware, find a shop in Fort Lauderdale, and speed onto I95 to get there before they close. I hit Mom's number. "Have you heard from Dr. Martinez or Ben?"

"Not yet."

"I checked with Emily again. She's got a bed saved for us, but we can't get Dad there without that transfer order."

Mom sneezes. "Sorry, this waiting area is musty. Once visiting hours ended, I stayed here in the waiting room all afternoon in case one of them walked by."

"I felt better when Jake said he'd keep an eye out, but I don't want to leave Dad alone, especially at night. I want to set up private-duty nurses to always be with him until we get him transferred. I'd be happy to pay for it."

"No, you're not. You don't have a job. This is a very good idea. I'll take care of it."

"Is it okay if I set it up? I'd like to know who will be with Dad."

"Please do. The four o'clock visiting hour starts in a couple of minutes. I'll go back in."

"Don't tell anyone we're getting a private-duty nurse. Better the nurse shows up unannounced. Stay with Dad as long as you can. The nurse will begin at seven and stay twelve hours."

"I'll do it," Mom says with determination.

"I will get Dad out. Right now, I need to run an errand. I'll touch base with you later." I click off, dial a nurse I know who started a company with home health and private-duty nurses. I explain the circumstances and tell her, "The neuro unit technically functions like a step-down unit since the patients are more chronic than acute. The hospital does allow a private-duty nurse in that type of setting. Does that work for you and your staff?"

"No problem. I've got a couple of people in mind already."

"Okay, but I don't want anyone to see me standing around outside the hospital. Can you have her meet me at my car? It's a white Camry. I'll be in the first row opposite the main entrance."

"I'm sorry to hear all that's happened to you and your dad, Ariel. You can have a job here any time. One of my nurses will meet you at six thirty before the shift begins."

"Perfect. I appreciate your help."

Back at the apartment, I wrap my arms around Grace. "I know who tortured you. I bought a car tracking set-up to catch him." I scoop food into her dish and Victor's.

As Grace eats, the idea that Harold could do the same to me wanders into my head. He does seem to want me silenced. I'd better check the car when I leave.

Victor pokes his head into the kitchen and stops.

"Come on, buddy. I know you're hungry."

He doesn't move.

I place his dish around the corner, next to him. "You win, but you're going to have to get used to her, Victor."

In the parking lot, I squat to check all the undersides of my car, under the hood, in the trunk, in the cab.

Nothing.

"Guess Harold's not as smart as I thought." I grin.

As I drive to the exit, I pass a black F150 pickup truck parked in a guest spot. It reminds me of the one I saw leaving Harold's. I watch for a second in my rear-view mirror. Ben would tell me to forget about it. There are hundreds of those trucks on the road. He's right. I need to let it go.

Parking near the main entrance, I look for the nurse. I'm five minutes late and don't see a woman in scrubs waiting to meet me. My chest tightens. Did I miss her?

I reach for my phone. A loud knock on the roof makes me jump.

The face of a burly man is at my window. I scream and lurch back in my seat.

"Ms. Savin?" He's wearing a navy scrub top with a top-of-the-line Lippincott stethoscope around his neck.

I power down the window. "You scared me. I figured you'd be out in front of the car."

"I'm Nate. My apartment is on the street behind. I walked over." The guy stands up.

His clean-cut, six-foot-plus frame carries two hundred and fifty pounds of muscle. He looks more like a bodyguard than a nurse. This is awesome. I can't contain my smile. "I'm glad you're here, Nate."

I give him the details about Dad, why Dad shouldn't be in the neuro unit, and his current state. "If anything changes with his status, please call me. My friends Chelsea, Jake, and Ben may swing by to see how things are going. Do not let Dr. Goss or the nurses be alone with my dad."

"I'll send you my number. Feel free to text me any time to check in."

"Thanks so much. I can't tell you how grateful I am that you're with Dad."

As he walks into the hospital, I text Mom: *The private*

duty nurse is on the way. You're going to be thrilled. Do you want to come to stay at my place instead of the hotel?

Appreciate your offer, but I like having my own bed and bath.

Do you want to come for dinner tonight?

Exhausted, going straight to bed.

I'll call you in the morning. Sleep well.

Glancing at the GPS bag in the seat beside me, I head out to the main street and into the doctor's parking lot in search of Harold's white Jaguar. His car is far from the building, but the security camera could still zoom in and see it.

I place my car down the row behind an oak that blocks the cameras. I twist my hair up under an old ball cap and tug on an oversized jacket. Hat tilted, stride long, gripping the device in my pocket, I near Harold's Jag. Peeking out from under the hat, I look for bodies.

All clear.

I duck down a few cars away, so the cars block the camera and waddle to his car. I slide my arm under the passenger door and the magnet grabs. "Yes!"

There's a soft thud. The tracker's on the pavement. Scrambling to my knees, I try again. The parts underneath are all rounded. The magnet needs a flat surface. I should have looked up where to put it on a Jag. I thought this would be easy.

The Jag rides low. Peering under the passenger side, I can't see much so I splay myself flat, shimmy under the car. My head needs to go sideways to fit, but I see a spot that would work. Grease smudges my face as I inch toward the flat area. I ready the hockey-puck tracker on my fingertips, stretch as far as I can and connect. "Yes!"

Sliding out, I hear two women talking. Shift change is over. It's usually half an hour. I thought there would be enough time from when Nate went in until others started coming out. I stay low and scramble to the front of the car.

The voices are closer. I hear footsteps, the jangle of keys. I hope it's not two doctors. My leg cramps from the squat I'm in. I dare not yell or stand up. I count to ten.

The footsteps and voices start to fade.

Inching up, I stretch my legs before I scurry back to my car.

Driving past the grocery store on my way home reminds me of what Amanda said about patients having muscle-twitching. Electrolyte balances can cause muscle twitching in patients, but the likelihood of it being in the exact same place in two patients is too high. Is there some sort of continuous muscle stimulation going on, or is the twitching residual? The only way I'm going to find out is to get into that neuro unit again.

Amanda mentioned there was someone who never had visitors. I think through all the patients in the unit and realize I know who it is: Mary Martel.

Giant globs of rain start to fall in a random pattern as I pull up at the apartment. I bolt up the stairs and look back as a wall of rain comes down the road. At least the black pickup truck across the street is gone.

Settling in after dinner, I search Mary Martel on my laptop and find a write-up about the accident a few months ago. Her only living relative is a sister who lives in Northern California. No wonder she doesn't visit.

Can I pose as her and pull it off? A few more keystrokes show Kelly Martel is about thirty pounds heavier than me, has darker hair, and works as a waitress.

If I'm not allowed to see Dad, at least I can get into the unit, maybe get into his chart, and check on the other patients and track down Dr. Martinez. It's good to have a plan.

How's Dad doing? I text the nurse as I get ready for bed.

No change. This place is definitely bizarre.

You can see why we need you with him.

They tried to tell me I couldn't be there. They even called the supervisor. Your mother was here and said if I didn't stay, then she would. Dr. Guthrie showed up and smoothed things over. Your mom was happy to see him, even though he wouldn't write a transfer order.

My heart flutters. Ben hasn't forgotten me. *Let me know if you need help or if anything changes.*

I climb into bed, hoping the little spark warming my chest is mutual.

*

A strange noise wakes me.

Grace growls low and purposeful in the darkness.

Muffled voices are coming from the living room.

The hair on my arms bristles. It sounds like two men. I don't understand what they're saying.

Pushing myself upright, my feet bump Grace.

She's standing with her ears pitched at the bedroom door.

Victor leaps from atop the desk to hide under the bed.

I grip the bedroom knob and depress the flimsy privacy button. Grabbing my tennis racquet, I flatten myself against the wall behind the door, Grace at my side.

Blinding light fills the bedroom. I duck, swing the tennis racquet, before I realize the light is coming from the parking lot.

There's a thud in my living room, heavy footsteps on the stairs. My heart slams against my chest.

"What the fuck?!" A voice echoes from the outside hallway.

"Shit!" A different voice coming from inside my living room.

Someone running.

I grip my racquet tighter.

"Ariel, you okay?" A gruff voice. Not Ben's.

Shuffling noise in the apartment.

"Ariel, are you there?"

It's Wendel, my neighbor.

The light blasting in the window goes out. I see movement in the parking lot and rush to get a look. A dark pickup truck pulls away. Am I being stalked?

"Ariel!" Wendel hollers, pounding on the bedroom door.

Grace starts to bark.

"I'm okay, Wendel." I breathe, opening the door. "I've never been so glad to see you."

"When'd you get a dog?" he slurs, holding onto the wall. His too-tight-over-the-belly Hawaiian shirt is sweaty and wrinkled, and his tawny Mohawk is askew. One of the shoelaces from his sneakers is ripped, with its mate trampled and dirty.

My hand reaches for Grace. "Did you see who it was?"

"Two low-lifes in black hoods."

The stench of alcohol is so bad I take a step back. "Did you see their faces?"

"I saw their asses. Running."

"Could you give a description to the police?"

He takes his hand off the wall and wobbles on his feet. "I ain't talkin' to police now. I got a DUI last year. Not sposta drive like this."

"Tell me what you saw."

"The door's open when I come up the stairs. I holler. They run before I get here. You okay?" Wendel swerves toward me. A sweeping arm gesture toward my door knocks him off balance. He grabs the wall.

"I'm okay, thank you. Come sit down. I'm calling the police."

"Not shickin' around for that." He lurches toward his place across the hall.

I halt at my doorway, scanning the hall and the stairs. There's no way I'm going out there. "The police care what you saw, not that you're drunk."

"Not drunk, jusht tired." Wendel closes one eye and slips his key into his lock.

"I'll make you coffee."

"Goin ta bed." He staggers inside.

I shut and bolt my door, then grab my phone.

"911 operator, can I help you?"

"Two men broke into my apartment."

"Are they gone? Are you all right?"

"Yes. A neighbor came home and scared them away."

"What's your name and address?"

"I'm Ariel Savin at eight hundred Oaks Road, unit twenty B."

"Will your door lock? Can you secure yourself inside?"

I peek outside and twist the knob. "The bolt holds."

"I've recorded the incident. Can an officer reach you at the number you called from?"

"Yes. It's my cell phone."

"I'll have an officer get in touch with you."

"Can they come now?"

"I'll let them know, but the city's hurricane protocol started at five a.m."

I check the time: Five-ten. Seriously? I want to blast her, but I'm scared they'll avoid me if I do. "Thank you," I mutter. As I click off, I race back to the window and stare into the darkness. No movement, no truck. Barely a car in the parking lot.

"What *was* that, Grace?" I sink to the floor, wrap my arms around her neck. "I don't care if it's five o'clock in the morning, I have to call Ben."

I hit Ben's number. The ringing seems to last forever. He's not going to pick up. Will he think this is a lame excuse to get him back? I hang up before it goes to voicemail.

The dog snuggles closer, licks my face like she knows.

"Oh, Grace." I bury my face in her fur, unable to hold back the tears.

*

My phone jingle goes off. I'm on it before the end of the first ring. I clear my throat, take in a deep breath. "Hello."

"This is Officer Kirk with the Becham Police Department. Are you all right?"

"Yes, sir." I wipe the tears from my face.

"You reported a break-in?"

"Yes, sir. It happened about twenty minutes ago."

"They're gone, everything is secure?"

"I think so."

"What happened?"

"Two men broke into my apartment. They got scared off by a neighbor. They were both wearing black hoodies. I didn't see their faces. They got into a dark-colored pick-up truck, but I couldn't see the license plate or the brand."

"Is anything missing?"

"I didn't notice anything, but I haven't looked closely." Pushing myself up off the floor, I scan the area. "My purse was on the dining table. It looks like it's been opened." I grab the wallet, rifle through it. "I had twenty-nine dollars in my wallet. It's all here. My ID and credit cards are here, too."

"Walk around the apartment. Check everything."

"It's a small apartment. The only place I haven't been is the kitchen." I flip the kitchen light on. "I had a small bin of canned dog food and some treats. It's been knocked off the top of the dog's crate, and the crate's been opened."

"Where's the dog?"

"She was with me in the bedroom."

"Anything else?"

"Let me check one more thing." I go back to the living room and open the bottom book in a stack of art books. The five one-hundred-dollar bills I got for the hurricane are still there. "The rest seems to be intact."

"Is there a chance you might have forgotten to lock your door? Opportunists tend to come out in times like these."

"My dog was wriggling in my arms. I remember bolting the door even before I put her down."

"Change your door locks today. The hardware stores are open until noon."

"Okay." Do I tell him about the black truck parked across from my apartment yesterday? I can't say I may have seen it after breaking into Harold's house. Better leave it alone.

"If you find something missing, let us know. This is recorded under case number BK-two eighty-three. We'll make sure patrols are stepped up in your neighborhood. It may not be until after the storm. Once the winds hit forty mph, we aren't allowed out on calls."

"Thank you." I click off and go back to the front door, maneuvering my eye around the peephole. This is way too creepy. I need to get pepper spray.

"I'll never get back to sleep now, Grace. May as well make some coffee." In the kitchen, I spot the dog stuff on the floor. What would they want in a kitchen? I check the cabinets and the fridge before picking up the scattered mess and placing the bin back on the crate.

Grace's tail thumps against me.

"I get it, you're hungry."

Fishing out the dog food, I catch my reflection in the oven door. "Looks like the grease on me from yesterday is gone. At least I don't have that to worry about," I tell her like she's Ben or Chelsea. "I'm losing it talking to a dog. It's time to get anchored back in the real world." I click on the TV.

The familiar local announcer is at his desk without a tie, like he's prepared for long days ahead. "Russian medical devices have been found in the US seeking to control human behavior. The full story at eleven o'clock tonight."

I wonder if those devices have something to do with Simon.

"Now, back to Hurricane Jacob," the announcer continues. "The eye of the storm is expected to come onshore tomorrow evening somewhere between Palm Beach and Miami. The National Hurricane Center is predicting it will strengthen to a category four as it crosses the Gulfstream waters after leaving the Bahamas. Mass devastation occurred overnight in Nassau, where the category three storm made landfall. Expect increasing wind gusts and squalls as the outer bands of the storm continue to hit South Florida today."

I click the TV off and eek open the sliding glass door to my balcony. The parking lot is wet from rain, and most of the cars are gone. I find no sign of the dark-colored truck. "Come on, Grace, there's enough light now. Let's get you outside before the next rain band starts."

I crack the door, check the hallway for anything unusual. The deadbolt works fine, not even a scratch. They must have been experts. A long shiver works its way through me. I gather up Grace, holding her close as I head downstairs.

Every shadow, every nook, spooks me. She's restless in my arms. I set her down in the grass, back against the wall, scanning… watching… hoping the only things I see are the familiar faces of my neighbors.

When Grace is done, we hurry upstairs. I slam the bolt shut and cuddle Grace close. Were they… after *her*?

My stomach knots. "This isn't good." I peek out the sliding glass door, re-check the parking lot.

"I'm going for a new lock right now. Home Depot will be open by the time I get there. You're coming with me, doggie."

In an hour, I'm back and done. Who would have thought an online video could make changing the lock so easy? I'll have to let Ben know and give him a key. I'd feel a lot safer if he was here, but I don't want to look pathetic, either.

"Perfect timing, Grace. It's time for shift change." I text the nurse: *How did everything go?*

It was an uneventful night.

The whole unit was quiet?

Very. The next nurse is arriving for the day shift. Should I give him your contact info?

Him. They sent another male nurse. Awesome. *Yes, please do and fill him in on the backstory as well. Thanks for being there.*

I catch myself pacing. I can't sit around. I need to talk to someone.

I punch Chelsea's number, force myself to slow my steps.

"Hey, Ariel, great call getting a bouncer to guard your dad overnight."

"Thanks. Dad's hanging in. Chelsea, two guys broke into my apartment this morning at five."

"What?"

"A couple hours ago, before it was light out."

"Are you all right? Did they take anything?"

"No. They were in my purse and knocked over Grace's bin of dog stuff. Wendel came home and scared them away."

"Did you call the police?"

"Yes. They said they'd have officers come by the complex during their patrols."

"I never thought something like that would happen." Chelsea's voice softens like her mind is far away.

"I'm still creeped out. I need to get out of here for a bit. Will you meet me at the beach? I could use some fresh air."

"Sure. The swells should be getting big by now. I wish we had a dog beach."

"Grace is sleeping. She's exhausted and isn't ready for walking in the sand yet. I checked the radar. It shows we have about half an hour until the next rain band. I'll meet you at the pavilion in ten minutes."

The parking lot is still. The complex is eerie with so many people out of town.

I do a lap around the car. Last night the truck parked behind it as if to block it in. Was that random or intentional? There doesn't seem to be any damage, no slashed tires or nails under them, and the doors are still locked. I click the fob, check the inside. It looks unchanged.

My breath stills as I push the start button, half expecting my car to explode. "This is ridiculous," I say to calm myself, yet I wonder—what's next?

Chapter 24

I pull up to a row of sea grapes perched on the dune. Their round leaves, masked in a layer of salt, shimmer and flap in the strong wind. I'm glad Chelsea is meeting me here. Her reaction was strange, though. Maybe she knows more of what's going on at the hospital.

Chelsea grabs me in a giant hug. "I'm glad you're okay. That must have been so scary."

"Terrifying. Wendel came home shit-faced and scared them off. I never thought I'd be grateful for his late-night drinking." A kitesurfer is picked up by a gust and flies for a hundred feet, landing his daredevil moves on the crest of a wave.

Chelsea laughs. "Wendel pulled it off? I like that guy."

"Yeah, but that guy likes living dangerously. I'm happy with a quieter life."

"It's not quiet now."

She makes me wonder if my life will ever be normal again. "When do you have to go back to work?"

Chelsea studies the kitesurfer. "I'm on call this evening. I'll bring everything with me and plan on staying there for a while."

"I always dreaded hurricane call, but after last night, the hospital would feel like a safe place to be. Well, except for the neuro unit." A gust of wind tosses sand, stinging my eyes. "I'm getting Dad out. I've got a bed arranged at Delmar."

Her brow tightens. "That would put Harold over the edge. He's already a nervous wreck that there'll be power outages and his patients won't do well."

"Dad's not on a respirator. Harold would have one less thing to worry about. Aside from his wife, he talks about the others like they're machines," I scoff.

"Don't say that. The situation Evie is in is heartbreaking." Chelsea's red windbreaker shrieks and flaps in the wind.

"What about all the other people in there?"

"Having their lives brought back will help them. The investors plan to move the people to rehab for mental restructuring to get them back to normal."

"Chelsea, that sounds like they're going to make the patients into robots or something."

"The patients would wither and die otherwise. At least, this way, they have a chance."

"When did you drink the Kool-Aid? You used to say those people were being tortured."

"The investors printed an article where people in other countries have had great success with this method. Relatives and employees can pick up copies in the waiting room or at the nurses' desk. Jake brought me one."

"Do you have a copy?"

"No, but you could look it up online. They have a website showing how their technology can help people with other neurological conditions and people with autism."

"You've all been buffaloed."

"Ariel, when you read the statistics, you can see how many people it will help."

"If they haven't done clinical trials, how can they have statistics?"

"Don't go poking around. I'm worried about you. You should go read a good book until the storm is over."

I need more. "The hospital has been my life these past few years. I feel so left out. You've got to keep me up on the news."

"In a couple of days, it'll all be over. You can get a new job, and I won't have to worry about you being in danger."

"What danger?"

A gust hits us, splattering sand across her legs, filling her shoes. "Yuck." She pulls the shoes off, flinging each foot as she dumps the sand. "The risk of not being able to pay your mortgage, your bills, that kind of thing." A bigger gust hits and Chelsea tilts.

Her answer doesn't fit. "You're losing your balance there, girlfriend." I steady her as she slips her shoes back on.

"Ariel, you're my Bes. I don't want bad things to happen to you. I'll talk to you in a week or so when things calm down. Stay home."

I breathe in fresh salt spray, hoping it will clear my mind. The kitesurfer sails through the air with another gust. He misses the crest he's aiming for and plows headlong into a wave, parachute collapsing beside him.

*

Climbing in the car, a streaming hurricane flag at the lifeguard stand catches my attention. It reminds me of Chelsea's jacket, big and red, flapping out a warning.

My mouth dries. Chelsea's mom is in a bad way, and Harold is helping her. Harold wants to know what I'm thinking. Could she be feeding him information? The thought slithers down, lands in my belly with a thud.

I stare at the huge surf as it crashes against the shore, dragging sand out to sea, eroding the beach with each wave. Chelsea would never betray me like that. She's too good of a friend. A gust of wind blasts over the Camry, covering the windshield with so much salt spray I can barely see.

Chelsea must be helping Harold, otherwise, why would she care if he went over the edge? She doesn't like what's happening in the neuro unit either. She's repeating what they've told her.

How long have they been playing me? My gut clenches like I've been sucker-punched. I open the door, vomit onto the street.

Chelsea was there when both of my patients arrested. She was getting drugs for me both times. Another tide spills from my stomach. How could she do this to me? I take a mouthful of cold coffee, rinse my mouth, spit in the street.

Rain begins to spatter my windshield. Big, sad drops smack against the glass, wash away salt in dollar-sized blotches. A sheet of rain barrels this way. I put my car in gear to head home, but the thoughts won't stop: Chelsea at tennis, nattering at me not to anger anyone. Chelsea in pre-op, going out of her way to make sure Harold's patients are ready on time. Why didn't I see it before?

I need to get Dad out of the unit today.

I hit the button for Mom and put a smile on my face to sound all right. "Hi, sleepy head."

She laughs. "It's only eight-thirty. I can't do all-nighters and recover like you."

My grin turns genuine. "I talked to the nurse. No change in Dad. They sent another male nurse for the day shift, which I hope is intimidating Harold."

"Dr. Goss came by to say hello last night. It was after the nurses called the supervisor and they all talked. He apologized for the misunderstanding about the private nurses. He was so nice, so concerned for the welfare of his wife and all the people there."

"Don't let his charisma fool you. The man is dangerous. I'm going to track down Dr. Martinez and see how we can get Dad out. Will you be around?"

"I'm heading to the waiting room as soon as I grab a bite to eat."

Should I tell her about the break-in? It would only upset her. More important to focus on Dad. "I won't be able to go in Dad's room, don't freak out if you see me in costume. I plan to impersonate a patient's relative. I'll let you know what I find out."

She giggles. "I can't wait to see what you come up with."

My phone rings before I even click off. Caller ID says DPR. It's a call from Tallahassee. Maybe they made a mistake. "Hello."

"This is the Florida Board of Nursing. We're wondering if you received a copy of the complaint filed against your license?"

This conversation doesn't have a good feel. "No…"

"It should arrive any day. We'd like to set a date for a review of the complaint."

I fish a pen and scratchpad from my glove box. "Do I need to have representation for this review?"

"It's a peer review, not one in a court of law. We'd like to set the date for May fifteenth."

"That's seven months away."

The woman on the phone clears her throat. "There's a backlog of reviews right now."

"You mean I can't work because of something I didn't do, that no one has proof of, with no way to defend myself until it comes up in seven months?"

"We know it's a frustrating process."

Effing Harold. I slam my fist on the steering wheel. "You don't get it. You have a job. You go to work every day, get a paycheck, and pay your rent."

"I don't make the rules, ma'am."

Shit, shit, shit. If I tell them my dad is mysteriously comatose and patients are being terrorized, it'll sound like I'm being vindictive. But how do I live with myself if I say nothing? "The patients they say I've killed or made brain-dead or whatever… They are being sent to a neurological unit where they're tortured and experimented on. The patients are being brought back to life, their memories wiped, and they're supposed to be sold. Soon."

"Are you all right, ma'am? It sounds like you're stressed."

"I'm fine. Please listen to me. We need to stop them."

"You'll have to wait until the review. I'm only the person who does the scheduling."

*

"SHIT." I whack the steering wheel. Seven months is ridiculous. Who would know about licensing? Not the director of nursing. She may have filed the complaint.

My thumb hits Contacts. "Hi, Sandra. Thought I'd call to see how you're doing."

"Ariel, it's so good to hear from you. My niece is here with me. I'm all set up with food, medication, and a generator."

"I'm sure it feels good to be home."

"I swear I'm healing faster already." She laughs. "How are things with you?"

There's a tug in my chest that makes me want to blurt out everything that's happened. To unload my problems and my worries so my head can think more clearly. I grip the steering wheel, shove the feeling back down. "The Board of Nursing called. A complaint's been filed against me. My license has been suspended until there's a review, which won't happen for seven months."

"Maybe it's a blessing. You were fed up with traditional medicine anyway."

"Nursing is how I pay my rent. I thought you might know how to proceed."

"You're young and smart. You can use those skills in other ways."

"Sandra, it's not my livelihood, it's my life. It's what I do. Where Ben and my friends are."

"If you lose your license, or your boyfriend for that matter, is your life going to end?"

"Sandra!"

"That might sound radical, but it can force you to think out of the box."

"I need stability right now."

"Why don't you come to the university and teach?"

"That's not me," I grunt.

"Oh, come on. You'd be perfect." Sandra chuckles.

I can imagine her green eyes twinkling. "Cut it out."

She laughs again. "I've heard rumors at the university of nefarious activity in Harold's lab."

I sit up, heart drumming in my chest. "Like brain-stem manipulation with AI implants?"

"At the university, we faculty have unwritten laws about the research of others."

"Is Harold on the faculty?"

Silence.

"Do you know someone at the university who could help me?"

No answer.

"Come on, Sandra."

"Let's say that I'm never far from the action."

"*You're* not involved, are you?"

She laughs. "Definitely not."

"You know more. Where's the lab?"

She sighs, "Remember, everything is symbolic. In the down-and-dirty world, the calmest person in the room wins."

"What do you mean?"

"It's time for me to show my niece how to do this dressing change. There's due process for everything. Good to hear from you."

"You've got to give me more, Sandra."

"Stay safe."

Chapter 25

My new door lock works great when I slide the key in. Cool air spills out into the October heat as Grace shoves her head through the doorway, happy as can be. She's got a line of scratches the length of her snout and the cat's asleep on the sofa, a circle of fur stuck to the pine-colored velvet around him. "Well, Victor, it looks like you two have figured it out."

He rolls over, and Grace thumps her tail against my leg.

"Come on, doggie, let me take a look at that." Holding her muzzle, I wipe the scratches with peroxide on a cotton ball.

She flinches but stays still.

"You're a good girl." I toss her a treat, head to my computer.

"I need to figure out what Sandra was talking about. *Due process.* Lawyers use due process in a filing. Did she mean I should get a lawyer?"

The dog's ears perk.

"What if I filed an ethics complaint against Harold?"

The dog barks.

"You're right. He's too powerful. I won't get anywhere with that. What about the ASPCA? You and the vet are proof there's a problem."

Grace's tail goes non-stop while I fill out an online form on the ASPCA's website. A confirmation email pops up when I finish. "That's one little deterrent, but I have to stop Harold and Simon. I need to find the lab and a timeline. Harold's office is the only place I can think of to look. It's Sunday, the least likely day for him to be in the hospital. I'm going in to find it."

Pulling out my phone, I text Mom. *How is Dad?*

Visiting hours just started. The nurse says he's the same.

I've discovered Harold has nasty plans for the patients. If I tell you how to get to the doctors' door, can you let me in?

You shouldn't be sneaking in here. Things are stable now. Don't rock the boat.

I don't want to worry her, but we—Dad—could be running out of time. *Dad may be included in Harold's plan. I haven't been able to get in touch with Dr. Martinez.*

What's Harold's plan?

I can tell you at the doctors' door. If you go down the main elevators and, instead of turning left, go right and through a door. Keep going down that hall. There's a self-locking door at the end. Ten minutes? I can almost hear her sigh.

I don't like this, but, okay, ten minutes.

I pull out a container of spray tan I tried, but didn't like to give my face, neck, and hands a new shade. Donning jeans, a long-sleeved shirt, an old lab coat of Ben's from med school, one of his fishing caps, and some old sunglasses, I head out.

Cruising by the doctors' door, I don't see Mom. I check my watch, notice I'm a few minutes early. I saunter to the side with no camera and wait.

At the far end of the doctors' parking lot, I spot Harold. It looks like he's talking to Simon. At least, I *think* it's Simon. I've only met him once. I'd love to hear *that* conversation, but Harold would recognize me for sure.

There's a scraping sound and a thud on the sidewalk. A

kid on a skateboard has jumped the curb and is cruising toward me. "Hey, buddy, stop." I hold my palm out.

The kid eyes me and slows.

I slide a twenty from my pocket. "Find out what those two guys are talking about. Do your thing. Don't let them know you're listening."

The kid gives his skateboard a push, snatches the money on his way by without saying a word. It makes me wonder if he'll take off.

The flies find me. I swat them while the kid weaves his way through the cars, heading straight for Harold and Simon. He does little circles in front of them, jumps on and off the board.

Harold does a backhand through the air and points like he's shooing the kid away. Or was it a fly?

The kid ignores him and does a couple more circles.

Simon throws his hands in the air, gets in a black Mercedes.

Harold climbs in his white Jag next to it, and they leave.

When the kid pops the board into his hand beside me, Harold and Simon are out of sight. "What did they say?"

"They were arguing about an old man. The one in the lab coat said he was too old for an accurate result. The one in the suit said to do it anyway because they need the trial no matter what the result."

My stomach catches. They're talking about my dad.

"Lab Coat said kids that are savants would be the best, and he stared at me. What's a savant?"

"A savant is someone who is over-the-top smart."

The kid continues, "Suit Guy told Lab Coat he's more trouble than he's worth, and that he was out of options. Then Suit Guy got in the Mercedes."

"Thanks for helping me out. I appreciate it."

The kid holds out his hand.

"You think I'm made of money?"

"You're the one wearing the lab coat, not me."

I groan, fish out another twenty for him, and he rides away.

*

What does Simon want to do to my dad? Make him brain-dead? I've got to get Dad out of there.

I head back to the doctor's door, pull out my phone. *Mom, are you close?*

There's a click, and the door swings open. I dash around the corner and up the stairs.

"Oh my gosh, you look ridiculous," she says. "Go home and wash that stuff off."

"Do you have a better idea?"

"Yeah, go home," Mom spouts.

"I need to find Dr. Martinez."

Mom sighs. "What's the big secret?"

I don't want to tell her what the kid said. I steer her away from the door and down the empty hallway. "Harold is going to sell the patients. I know we have a private nurse, but Harold has so much power in the hospital."

"Say no more. I'll sleep in the waiting room to monitor things if I need to."

"I'm still trying to track down Dr. Martinez for a transfer. I'm confident we can make that happen, but there's something else. I found out that Harold wants to start experimenting on savant children and others." My flesh crawls, wondering what's worse, children or my own dad.

"That's disgusting, I agree, but you are my child. I don't want anything happening to you."

"I'll be fine. This place is as familiar as our backyard

was, Mom. Once I know we can get Dad out of here, I want to find out where the lab is and Harold's timeline. Will you distract Rebecca if I come into the unit for a few minutes?"

"No. I don't want you to get in any more trouble."

"I've tried everything else. I've pleaded with Ben and Jake. I've talked to old employees. This is my last hope."

"Just focus on getting your dad out of here."

"I will, but you don't want the fate of innocent patients and children on your conscience, do you?"

Her head tilts, and she looks at the ceiling. "My gosh, you're relentless. Fine, I'll try."

"Thank you. If you see me in the unit, ignore me."

"Got it."

"I'm going to duck in the doctors' lounge to see if Dr. Martinez is in the house."

"Get us out of here soon. Please." She heads back to the unit.

As I slip into the doctors' lounge, I smell stale coffee permeating a rack of lab coats. I slip off Ben's and place it on a hanger. A list of checked-in physicians on a light board makes me smile. "Dr. Martinez, so glad you're in the hospital." I grab the in-house phone and dial the operator.

While I wait, I hear a click. The bathroom door screeches on a set of rusty hinges. I hang up the phone, heart in my throat.

"This room is for the doctors, ma'am."

Relief floods through me. "Hi, George. It's me, Ariel."

His eyes squint while he cranes his neck. "You sure get around," says the operating room janitor.

I let out a laugh. "I talked to your buddy. He was very helpful."

"He told me you done stopped by." George cranes his neck at me. "I didn't think you was this crazy."

"I'll do whatever it takes to get my dad out of here."

"Seem so."

"I'm calling Dr. Martinez to get a transfer order."

"I don't want to know." He plunges his mop into the bucket, rolls his rig to the exit door.

"Promise you won't tell anyone?"

"Not unless they ask. I ain't losin' my job over this."

"Fair enough."

He continues on his way, and I redial the phone.

"Operator."

"Will you page Dr. Martinez to extension 1024, please? His cell phone doesn't seem to be responding."

"Certainly."

The page zings through an overhead speaker, and the phone rings.

"Hi, It's Ariel Savin. I'm uncomfortable with Dad being under Dr. Goss's supervision."

"I'm sorry I couldn't do anything about it."

"I have a supervisor friend who is getting a bed for Dad at Delmar Hospital where he can ride out the storm. The staff in the neuro unit said you're off the service, and they won't transfer him."

There's a pause and a sound like an unshaven beard scratching against the phone. "I'm still your father's primary physician. I was overridden because of beds for the hurricane. Dr. Goss said he would cover for me because I had a personal issue that came up yesterday."

"You have admitting privileges at Delmar, don't you?"

"I do, but I'd prefer he stay here."

"Dad shouldn't be in neuro unit. He's not one of their subjects."

Dr. Martinez is quiet for a second. "I hate that term. I'll write the order. You know he'll have to go in an ACLS ambulance."

"No problem. I'll set it up. My mother is with Dad now. You can confirm with her."

"I'm almost finished my rounds. I'll be there shortly."

"Thanks."

I hang up and text Mom. *Dr. Martinez is on the way. He said he'll write the transfer. I'll set up the transportation.*

I text Emily next. *Martinez is writing the transfer. Is the bed available? I'll call an ACLS transport company.*

Emily replies. *Ready for you any time. Will notify admitting and ER.*

I give her a thumbs-up, arrange the ambulance. Spotting a puffy black jacket someone must have forgotten last winter, I slip it on. It's huge but hides my shape.

The only way to the neuro unit from here is past the recovery room. I pull the cap down over my eyes as I approach.

A heavy steel door at the end of the hall opens. I turn my face as if I'm studying the framed print on the wall. A nurse I know passes me without a glitch. All is good.

Rounding the corner, my stomach clenches. Ben is talking to an equipment rep outside the recovery room. My heart thuds against the jacket that's not mine. I want to talk to him so badly, but I don't know what he'll think of me sneaking around the hospital.

My sunglasses slide from the sweat on my nose. As I try to adjust them, there's a rattling noise, and before I can react, I trip on the leg of a walker.

The elderly woman attached to it groans. I reach to steady her, knocking my cap sideways. My hair tumbles out.

She wobbles and goes down on one knee.

"Oh my gosh, I'm so sorry. Are you all right?"

"Don't you look where you're going?" she growls.

"Let me help you." I lock my arm under hers and try to lift her upright.

It doesn't work.

"I gotcha, honey." Ben arrives on the other side. He slips his arm around her, and together, we lift her to her feet.

"Do you need to sit down? There's a chair in the visitor's lounge," I blubber as I straighten the cap on my head.

"You've done enough. I don't have time to sit." She shoves her walker forward, disappears around the corner.

Ben grabs my arm and marches me away from the recovery room. "What the hell are you doing?"

Do I tell him I think Dad is in danger, that patients are being scorched and might be sold? I don't want him any angrier with me than he is already. "I want to check on Dad. They won't let me in."

"So, you put on a hat and sunglasses? You need to get out of here before anybody else sees you." Ben's phone beeps with a text.

"I have a commitment," I blurt. It sounds so lame that he's going to hate me even more.

"You can get arrested for trespassing. Do you think your dad wants that?"

I want to talk with him, work this mess out. I grab his arm. "Ben, I—."

He cuts me off. "They're ready for me in surgery. Hurry up and leave the hospital before someone sees you in that get-up." He rushes to the OR.

I readjust the cap and find myself breathing in the scent of him. A wave of sorrow courses through me. How do I ever get him back?

I lean heavily on the wall as his advice rings in my ears. He's right, and so is Mom. I should leave. I'm in enough trouble already.

Down the hall, from the direction of the neuro unit, an argument starts. I strain to hear what it's about, but the voices are muffled. I can't tell what they're saying. I watch Ben as the OR doors thud shut. The arguing resumes. With one more glance toward the OR, I re-tuck my hair and head to the neuro unit.

*

No one is in the hall or the waiting room outside the unit by the time I get there. The eleven o'clock visiting hour is well underway and everyone has gone in. I take a deep breath and hit the button to open the automatic doors. I'm lousy at disguises. Ben knew it was me. I can't make that mistake again. I text Mom. *I'm thirty seconds away.*

The rotting pot smell greets me when I enter the unit. The curtain is pushed back in my dad's room where I spot my mom and Rebecca. Rebecca's back is to me. Mom gives me a nod.

Room eight is empty. That was Zora.

A lump forms in my throat. Where is she?

As I hustle toward Harold's closed door, the knob turns. He's in there. I do an about-face and make my way further into the unit.

What to do?

I zip past Evie's drawn curtain. Room two is empty, cleaned out. That was Lydia from Jackson. Shit.

I don't dare check to see where Harold is. I duck into room six as the glass door to Dad's room slides open.

From behind me, a familiar voice calls, "Do you have a minute, Rebecca?"

It's Amanda bringing Rebecca into Robert's room. Perfect.

Tina is in this room. The screen from her chart hasn't faded away yet. I spot an *M* on the page where there was a *P*. Does that mean move? I blink, and the screen is gone.

Tina starts coughing and bucking the respirator like she can breathe on her own. That's new.

Footsteps nearby. I can't be found here. I need a story. Mary Martel's family has never been to visit. Flipping up the collar of the coat to hide my cheek, I step from the room almost bumping into Rebecca. "This isn't Mary," I bark, facing toward the patient and away from Rebecca. I turn toward the nurse's station like I'm looking for the boss.

Rebecca backs up. "We haven't met. I'm Rebecca, the charge nurse."

I clear my throat to make sure my voice sounds deep and avoid eye contact. "Kelly Martel."

"Mary is in room seven." Rebecca ushers me in. "You heard the circumstances of her being here with us in the unit?"

I nod, grasping the hand of my apparent sibling, letting my shoulders sag and my head droop. The room has a strong scent of peppermint oil like the OR staff use on their masks when a surgeon opens a gangrenous bowel. "She's so skinny," I murmur, trying to sound gravelly.

"Our patients often look different because they lose muscle mass. We have a new routine to prevent that using muscle stimulation."

So that's how they're explaining away the burnt flesh. "Hmph," I grunt, not wanting to speak.

"You live on the other side of the country, don't you?"

I nod and keep my head down.

"You've traveled a long way. Here's a seat so you can rest." Rebecca pulls a chair behind me. "Can I get you some water or something?"

I shake my head and sit, reaching for a tissue to dab my eyes.

"There's something familiar about you. You haven't been here before, right?"

I shake my head, hoping she's worried that the other families called me.

"I'll be close by if you have any questions."

"Thanks," I sniff and wipe my nose.

When Rebecca leaves, I start rubbing the arm of the patient. Rebecca will be watching so I won't be able to check Mary's legs. She doesn't have any twitching. I wonder if that makes her more advanced than the others, or less.

Caressing her arm, I inch the covers over and find no blisters or burns on this arm. Her skin is warm like she has a low-grade fever.

"Rebecca." Harold's voice is clear. He must be close by. "One of the hospital's main generators quit during testing. They've set this wing up on a reserve generator, one of the old ones."

"Dr. Goss, if it fails, we're sunk. I don't have enough staff to bag all these people by hand."

"They said they tested the generator, and it works fine."

"Are you ready to take bed six off?" Rebecca whispers.

I glance at Tina's room. She has an *M*. Are they taking them off the respirator and transferring?

"The research isn't far enough along yet. I haven't got the report from the lab. I don't care if there's a hurricane out there."

What report does he need that's so important?

Head down, I squint through the glasses, but I can't see Harold.

Rebecca parks herself at the nurse's station, watching me as she pretends to be charting on a computer.

Should I leave while I'm ahead, so I don't make things worse for Dad? He's got the private nurses taking care of him. He should be okay. Someone must help the rest of these people.

I'll need some sort of diversion. A stack of plastic measuring containers is piled on the end of the desk. I dig around in my purse for something to toss at them, and while doing so, smack my elbow on the bed railing.

Pain shoots through my funny bone. I rub it hard, thinking Rebecca is probably laughing, and notice that the railing is loose.

Positioning myself so Rebecca can't see my hands, I spin off the loose bolt.

Amanda Young asks a question, and Rebecca's focus changes.

I toss the bolt.

The stack of containers tumbles to the floor with a crash.

Rebecca jumps. "Geez! What was that?"

Another nurse calls, "Sorry! I meant to put those away."

"I'll get it." Rebecca reaches for a trash bag.

"Rebecca, what happened?" Harold's voice.

I hurry with my penlight to assess the patient. Her pupils are fully reactive. Her eyes follow like she knows what's going on, then she blinks. *Holy shit!* She's not supposed to be able to blink.

"Harold, we have a problem," Rebecca blurts.

I look up to see her staring in my direction. My heart pounds. I shove the penlight into my pocket and grab my bag. Tucking my head low, I hurry from the room.

"We have an intruder." Rebecca points. "And I know who it is."

"Call security!" Harold barks, rushing at me.

I see my mother watching from Dad's doorway as I break into a sprint and bolt out of the emergency exit, setting off the alarm. I race to my car and out of the parking lot.

Chapter 26

I park the car in my spot at the apartment. Thank goodness Mom is with Dad. Guess I'll never get my job back now. I wonder if she wants to disown me. I shoot her a text. *An ambulance is required to transport Dad. It's set up.*

Dr. Martinez was here while Dr. Goss and Rebecca went looking for you. He said your dad is stable enough to move and wrote the order. The private nurse informed the nursing supervisor. Dr. Goss is furious.

A picture of Harold fuming pops into my head and I can't help but smile. *The ambulance people want to do this before the storm gets bad. They should arrive within the hour.*

Morning visit time will be over by then.

Go buy lunch for the private duty nurse and have him use the bathroom while you stay with Dad. After that, hang out in the waiting room. I'll meet you by the ambulance when you come down with Dad.

As long as you wash that horrible spray tan off before anyone at the new hospital meets you.

I laugh out loud. *Deal.*

My phone buzzes with a different noise. The GPS. Harold is on the move. I need to find out where his lab is. Watching his direction, I see he'll have to pass by my complex to reach Dell Road. I keep my car hidden near the entrance.

When he drives by, I let a couple of cars pass, then I follow.

Harold turns east. He lives that way. Is he going home?

At Southern Highway, he spins into a Mobil gas station. I pull over at the office building next to it and park my car around back.

The wind has picked up, and it's hard to walk. Lucky for me, the storm is between rain bands. I duck behind a cocoplum hedge as Simon arrives at the station. I see them talking as they fill their cars, but all I can hear is the howl of the wind.

Two guys emerge from the convenience store and stand under the overhang. A skinny one in jeans with worn knees and a gray shirt with STOLI VODKA on it has long, unkempt hair. The other one has more meat on him. He's in a dirty, red T-shirt with a raised middle finger on the front and black shorts that have a hard time staying up. The skinny one lights a cigarette and leans against the side of a freezer with ICE on its front. They both stare at Harold, talking with their heads down like they're discussing how to steal his Jag.

Harold replaces the pump nozzle, walks to the store. He looks nervous as he stops to talk to the guys.

Simon finishes gassing up and joins the group. He sticks out his hand to shake Skinny's and palms him something.

What the heck?

I strain to hear their conversation above the wind. It's impossible.

Crawling along the hedge toward the back of the building out of their sightline, I zip across to the gas station, creep beside the giant ice chest.

"You want 'em today?" a deep voice asks with a puff of smoke. I assume it's Skinny.

"Is that a problem?" Simon hisses.

"Only that a hurricane's supposta hit us in a couple hours," a raspy voice whines.

I know that voice. It's not from the stairwell. It's the voice from inside my apartment. These are the guys who broke into my place. Simon sent them. Goosebumps cover my arms and legs. I'm being hunted.

"All the chaos should make it easier. You can dump them in front of the ER in the pouring rain, and no one will see you," Harold says.

I peek through the crack behind the ice machine. Red T-shirt Guy is leaving. Why?

"You want a man and a woman. What'd you call 'em?" the deep voice questions. More cigarette smoke wafts by.

"Savants. That doesn't matter for today. Right now, we need two bodies over the age of eighteen. We can work on the children next month," Simon tells the guy.

Harold glances around, spots the camera, positions his back to it. "They need to show up alive, with enough damage to their skull to go brain-dead."

My stomach churns. They're going to kill people for the neuro program. I *knew* those deaths were no accident. Thank goodness Dad is leaving.

"When do we get the rest of the payment?"

"When do you think?" Simon growls.

"Arrogant asshole," Skinny mumbles into the crack behind the ice machine. Smoke billows my way.

I hope he didn't see me.

"Done!" Red T-shirt Guy hollers over the wind.

Three doors slam. I peek from my hiding spot to see Harold driving away and the two guys getting into a black pickup truck. I knew it was them. I grab my phone, snap a picture of the truck. It's too far away to read the plate on the back, but maybe it'll help ID them.

Simon's car is still here. He must be inside. Maybe I can chat him up and find out where the lab is. Smoothing my hair, I breathe deep and step into the convenience store.

The store smells like stale beer and Slim Jim sticks. It's big enough for five rows of snacks and essentials that have been picked over, except for the more expensive items.

Simon is a couple of rows over, looking at white wines in the refrigerator section. I saunter toward him, pull open a fridge door, and stick my head in, hoping my spray tan hasn't melted from the heat.

Grabbing a container of orange juice, I head for the cashier. "Do you have any half-and-half in the back?"

"What you see is all we got," says a man with big bags under his eyes and grayish skin.

"You look just as good in jeans as you do in taffeta," Simon says from behind.

Heat rises in my face. I wasn't expecting that. I spin around. "Simon? What are you doing here?" I feign. "They don't have champagne and caviar, do they?"

"The champagne is cheap but good enough to go with orange juice." He nods to the jug in my hand.

I laugh, glad he lightened it up. It makes things easier for me. I notice the chocolate and wine in his hands. "Are you having a hurricane party with one of your friends?"

"They went back to Russia. Their visas ran out."

"Zalj." I pronounce the word for "what a pity" in Russian, remembering to shorten my vowel.

"You know Russian?"

"From my grandmother."

"You're becoming more interesting all the time."

He's such a womanizer. "Was that Harold I saw pulling out? Is he riding out the hurricane at the lab?"

"He's going to be at the hospital. Keeping an eye on his patients."

"And you?"

"I'm spending it with two lovely ladies."

"I should have known."

"You ought to get going before the rain starts and ruins your hair. Here, take my half-and-half. You might be needing the caffeine."

I wonder what that means.

Simon throws down a fifty. "This should cover the young lady's bill also. Keep the change," he tells the cashier as he opens the door for me.

"That wasn't necessary but thank you."

"You stay safe. There's a lot of nastiness coming." He climbs into the Mercedes.

"Not just weather," I mutter as he drives off.

Raindrops splatter on the pavement, chasing me as I run for my car. That got me nowhere. I still need to find the lab.

Checking the GPS tracker to see how far Harold got, it shows him turning west on Design Street. Do I follow or go catch up with Mom and Dad? I check the time, ten minutes before I need to meet the ambulance in ER. The sky opens and my wipers beat double-time as I gun it after Harold.

At Couple Avenue, the light changes. I hit the brakes. My foot sinks to the floor.

I pump on the brake pedal, push down with all my might. The car's not slowing. Cranking the wheel, I swerve around a car in front of me that stopped for the light.

A car throttles in from the side. I lean on the horn and swerve into oncoming traffic. An SUV on the other side jams on the brakes. Horns blast from every angle.

My car flies over a two-by-four in the road, slamming down on the other side. Pumping, pumping. Nothing. The road curves, and my car shoves me against the door. I hang on to the steering wheel with all my might. How to stop this car?

Grabbing the shifter, I push it into low gear. The car jolts and starts to slow. I guide the car to the side of the road and downshift one more time. Making a big round turn into the parking lot of an apartment building, I tug on the emergency brake and slump across the steering wheel.

*

"Ben, can you help me?" I holler into his voicemail over rain pounding on the roof. "My brakes went out on the car. I'm parked at an apartment building west of Design Street and Couple Avenue. Is there any way you can pick me up?"

I click off and my whole body starts to shake. That was the scariest thing that's happened in my entire life. It must be ninety degrees in the car, but I can't stop shivering. What happened? It wasn't wet brakes or a simple hydroplane across a puddle. My brakes failed. Why? I had them changed a few months ago.

The call doesn't come. I check the time and think about Mom waiting for me with Dad.

Why didn't I fill out that AAA application a month ago? I can't call Chelsea, and Ben's not answering. I have to figure something out. I call the dealership, hoping someone answers.

"Hello. Hello? Sounds like the rain is ready to come through your roof."

"I'm sitting in my car. The brakes went out. I was wondering if I can get a loaner?"

"Don't have any right now."

"Can the dealership tow my car in for repair? I'm near Design Street and Couple Avenue."

"I don't know. We're supposed to be outta here by one o'clock."

"Please, I can't leave my car. They'll impound it."

The guy grunts. "Screen shows me there's a tow truck five minutes away. He should be able to get here before we close."

"Thank you so much." I tuck my hands under my legs to stop the shaking. Rain nails the roof so hard it almost hurts my ears. It's like I'm in a paint can in one of those shakers at the paint store, bouncing, beating, stripping every one of my nerves.

I dial Mom.

"Where are you? The ambulance is ready to go. I've been stalling them."

"I'm so sorry. The brakes went out on my car."

"Oh my. Are you all right?"

"Definitely a little shaken. I called a tow truck. Go ahead with Dad. Emily will meet you there. I'll catch up."

The driver stops beside me, powers down his window. "Leave the key inside and get in the truck. I'm going to park it in front of you!" he yells.

I nod and gather up my bag, dash twelve feet from my vehicle to his. Wiping the rain from my face, I push my hair back as puddles form around my feet on the black plastic mat of the tow truck.

He climbs into the truck, tosses back the hood from his heavy-duty yellow raincoat. His hair is much thinner than his frame and is plastered against his face even with the raingear. "Damn, that's nasty," he grins. "Hey, you're shaking. Here, I have a towel." He hands me an orange beach towel with a big rip that smells like old socks.

I tell myself to suck it up and wrap the towel around me. It feels good, like the warm blankets at my job. I miss my job, and Ben, and Chelsea, and warm blankets.

"Are you okay?"

I force my brain back. "The brakes going kind of freaked me out. I was afraid I wouldn't be able to get the car stopped."

"Heavy rain can be a problem unless you had your brakes done yesterday. Sometimes, air in the line can do that."

"The brakes felt absent rather than sluggish. I had the pads done a few months ago."

"The car is getting older, maybe a line came loose, or it was cut. Have any enemies?" He laughs.

My throat dries up. Red T-shirt Guy had disappeared. "The car is old," is all I muster.

He starts the truck, checks his mirrors. "What are you doing out in this weather?"

I hear the question, but my mind is doing re-runs of Red T-shirt Guy leaving the conversation early. If Simon wanted my brakes cut, I must be on to something.

"You sure you're okay?"

I can't tell him I was tracking a well-known brain surgeon. "I was on my way to the hospital."

"You a nurse?"

"Yes. Is there any way you could drop me off at the hospital?" He's driving slow, heavy-duty wipers shoving rain off the windshield like buckets. I'm not going to make it on time. "On second thought, that's not along your route. My apartment is closer. If you would let me out near there, I can get some dry clothes."

"Sure." He brakes, peering through the rain. "My sister was diagnosed with multiple sclerosis last year. They put her on a ton of drugs that gave her headaches and nausea all the time, so she went off them. What's your opinion on that?"

"Sorry to hear about your sister." I shift to get a read on his face. "How's she doing now?"

"Amazing. I was terrified and tried to talk her out of going off the drugs, but she wouldn't listen. She started eating different, doing exercises and stuff."

"I used to think that everything we did was helpful to

patients. A lot of it is, but I'm glad that people are looking at alternatives, too."

"I can't believe the difference in her. Those drugs were so expensive, even when she got them at a discount. Why don't they tell people these things?"

Through the rain, I see a black truck pulling out of my apartment complex. I get a bad feeling in my stomach. "Thanks for the ride." I leap out and sprint to my place.

Chapter 27

Flying up the stairs to the apartment, I notice the door is crooked like it's not shut right. An alarm rings in my head. I back away, go to bang on Wendel's door and find that it's open. "Wendel, are you home?" The deluge of rain drowns out my voice. "Wendel!" I yell into his apartment through the space in the door. I get no answer.

My dog isn't barking. She would know my voice. "Grace, GRACE!" I scream and rip my apartment door open.

Everything looks all right but feels so wrong. I stay in the doorway and call, "Grace!" She doesn't come. What if someone is still here?

I glance back at Wendel's door. Did they break in there, too?

Leaving the front door wide, I dash to the kitchen.

The crate is closed. I left her out with the crate open in case she felt more secure there.

"GRACE!"

I run from room to room to check the closets, the bath.

She's not here. SHE'S NOT HERE.

*

"911 emergency. What's the problem?"

"They stole my dog!"

"Miss Savin at eight hundred Oaks Road, unit twenty B?"

"Yes," I sob. "I changed the locks. They came back. They stole my dog."

Wendel appears at my door. He's fish-belly white. "I couldn't stop them."

The breath sucks out of me. My knees buckle, and I hear a scream. I know it's me, but it's like I'm far away.

"Are you all right, ma'am? Are you hurt?"

I can't get my tongue working.

"Are you injured? Do you need an ambulance?"

"Not hurt," I chug out.

Wendel grabs the phone. "I saw them. They took the dog. I followed when I heard the noise. They threw Grace in the back seat and drove off in a black pickup truck."

"I'm sending the crime unit for prints," I hear the dispatcher say." Do you want me to stay on the phone 'til they get there?"

"No!" I wail.

"I'm her neighbor across the hall. I'll stay with her." Wendel clicks off, hands me the phone.

A fresh wave of tears comes like a tsunami. "My dog! My poor, tortured Grace!" I sob, puddling on the floor.

Wendel crumples beside me. "How could anyone be so awful?"

"She was only here for days, and already she's like family." My breath catches in my throat. *Victor.* I scramble to my knees, look under the couch, the chair. "Victor, are you here?" I check behind the TV console.

Nothing.

"Victor." I run to the bedroom, flip up the bed skirt.

Victor is crouched wide-eyed, back to the wall, ready to spring.

"It's all right, kitty, Momma's home," I murmur to soothe him. "I found him, Wendel. He's terrified. He'll never come out. Will you help me lift the bed?"

"No problem." His heavy-footed steps slog my way.

"Take the side near the foot. I'll lift near the head so I can reach him. Ready?"

Wendel groans as we lift. "I didn't think this would be so heavy."

I peek at Victor. "I'd hoped he'd run out, but he scooted to the far corner. Can you hold it by yourself while I get him?"

Wendel sidesteps toward the middle of the bed with another groan. "I got it. Go ahead."

I climb under the bed, hoping Wendel doesn't have a major league hangover and drops it on my head. "Come on, Victor. It's okay, baby." I manage to get both hands around my cat. "Gotcha." I tug him in close, crawl back out.

"They wrecked your artwork." Wendel pants as he lowers the bed. "I should have stopped them."

An ache fills my chest. Half a dozen of my drawings have been splayed wide with a knife.

Gritting my teeth, I keep walking. "They're dangerous. You did the right thing, Wendel." I drop onto the sofa with Victor clutched to my chest.

My gaze falls on the coffee table. Something's not right. "The books. They're in the wrong order. The one with the money was in the middle."

"What money?"

"Five hundred dollars for the hurricane. Flip open that top book."

"There's nothing here." Wendel lifts the book, fans through the pages.

Rage flashes through me. "Damn you, Harold."

Wendel squints at me, his forehead wrinkling. "How do you know it was him?"

The phone jangles in my hand. "Hang on, Wendel. It's Becham police. Hello."

"Miss Savin, this is Officer Kirk. You called about another break-in?"

Another. My mind goes back to being in the apartment with them, hearing their voices, locking myself in the bedroom with Grace, hoping she wouldn't make a sound. The hair on my arms stands. I can't make any words come.

"Is this Ariel Savin?"

I tell myself not to cry. "Yes, sir." I swallow hard and try to be calm. "My apartment was broken into again. They stole my dog and five hundred dollars cash I had to ride out the hurricane." A sob sneaks out. I breathe fast to make the ones building behind it go away.

"Are you all right?"

"Yes. I changed the locks." A second sob escapes. "I got home and… and she's gone."

"Is there anything else disturbed or missing?"

"The crate, it's closed. I left it open, and they took a knife to my artwork."

"Could you have left a window open? Maybe the dog ran off."

"My neighbor saw them take the dog and throw her into a black pickup truck."

"I'm sorry, miss. We get lots of calls near hurricanes because bad guys know people keep cash on hand. Is there a possibility someone saw you at an ATM and followed you home?"

"No. I'm very watchful." Do I tell him what's going on with Harold and Simon and the patients? Will he think I'm crazy? "The truck has been hanging around even before I got the money. They wanted the dog. I found her abandoned in a dumpster after they left her for dead. She was part of a lab experiment that's now being done on humans. I could really use your help to stop them."

"Whoa, there's a lot to unpack in that statement, miss. Our priority now is to get people evacuated from the island because the bridges across the Intracoastal are being closed. I'll try to get to you right after. Don't touch anything."

My mind goes to Grace. Why would they take her but not kill her or let her run away? They must want her for some reason. Would Harold want to study Grace because she survived when the other dogs died? I bet they took her to the lab. Before they do anything to her, I need to find them.

*

I've barely hung up, and my phone rings again. The cop must have forgotten to tell me something.

"Hi, Bes, it's Chelsea."

Does she seriously think I want to talk to her? I should make a bunch of background noise and hang up. "You're calling to tell me something?"

"Yeah, you got a minute?"

Wendel pushes himself off the couch. "I'm going to put some dry clothes on. You should, too, before that cop gets here. I'll be back in a few."

I nod and wrangle the door on its hinges to get it to close. "Is it going to take more than a minute for you to tell me you're helping Harold? You're feeding info to the guy who has ruined my career, put me out of a job, broken into my apartment, and stole my dog."

"What?"

"That's right. The police are on their way over to investigate."

"I'm sorry, but you're wrong about how all this happened."

"Of course, you'd say that. You're going to defend him no matter what."

"Ariel, I can explain."

"Go ahead. Enlighten me on how my neighbor saw the same thugs in the same black truck running away from my apartment with my dog."

Chelsea gasps. "They took her?"

"They wanted the dog, but they stole my hurricane money to make the police think it was a robbery. After Harold orchestrated all that, how can you think I'll listen to your excuses?"

"I haven't been honest about some things lately. I admit that. You know I'd never do anything to hurt you. The people you're up against are dangerous."

"Tell me something I don't know. Prove to me whose side you're on."

"Harold's desperate. He told me Simon's only a broker, a middleman. His buyers have threatened Harold and Evie. They want more patients, Ariel, smart, young subjects. They plan to use the neurotransmitters to program people's brains like robots."

"Why didn't you tell me at the beach?"

"I didn't know then. That's why I'm calling. I had to call Harold about my mother. He's super-stressed and blurted it out. These goons have no problem rubbing out other people. Do you think they'd be worried about murdering you?"

Gooseflesh covers my arms. Would they kill me? I've been so busy trying to figure things out I didn't think about it. How can I have confidence in what she's telling me? I want to believe in the old Chelsea, but everything is such a mixed-up mess, I don't know. "That sounds kind of far-fetched."

"So does keeping brain-dead loved ones alive in hopes of bringing them back. You need to come and stay at my place. I have to go to work, but my next-door neighbor has a key."

How can I trust her if she's aligned with Harold? This could be a setup. "I appreciate you thinking about me."

"I'll see you when the storm is over. Be careful." Chelsea hangs up.

I dial Mom. "How are things going?"

"Pretty good so far. Emily met us in the ER. The nurses are getting your dad settled. When will you be here?"

I look at my soaking wet clothes, my messed-up door. "Someone broke into the apartment and stole the cash I got to ride out the hurricane." I don't dare tell her the rest.

"Ariel, this isn't looking good. First, your car, now, a break-in. You need to come to stay here with us."

"Because of Emily, they're letting you stay. Both of us would be too much. Chelsea offered me her place."

"That's good. Keep me up to date. Something else, when we were leaving, Harold was telling Rebecca they needed to get the woman in bed six and the girl in bed seven ready to move to phase B and have surgery."

"Tina and Mary were in those rooms. They were responding to Harold's treatments also. What kind of surgery?"

"I don't know. Rebecca said she couldn't get the transport people. Their transfer would have to wait until after the storm."

"Did you hear where they're sending them?"

"No, but Harold was really angry."

"Thanks, Mom. I'll keep in touch, although I'm not sure how good cell service will be in a hurricane."

"I'm worried about you, Ariel."

"I'll be fine. You and Dad are safe. That's all that matters." As I hang up the phone, the image of George waving his egg salad sandwich at me reappears. "Eggs! Harold wants oocytes. He's going to carve the eggs out of those women."

Chapter 28

I'm halfway dressed when the tracking system beeps. "Shit! I don't have a car." I pull some shorts on, grab a rain poncho. Putting Victor in his crate, I snag a big container of his food and pound on Wendel's door. "It's me, Ariel."

I can hear the Weather Channel on inside: "A very strong band will be hitting Palm Beach County in the next forty-five minutes, increasing the wind strength to ninety miles an hour and dropping three to four inches of rain in a short time. You must shelter in place."

Enough time for me to find the lab before this gets bad.

Wendel cracks his door for a peek, opens it wide.

"Can I borrow your car? Mine is shot, and I'm desperate."

"I'd give it to you, but it's on fumes. I meant to get some gas last night but got, uh, a little carried away."

The light of the GPS map is shining through my bag. "I need a car."

"I have a bad habit of waiting until the car says it's empty. After that, I go twenty more miles. It's already past twenty."

"Geez, Wendel. Can you watch Victor? The cops may not show up until after the storm." I tug the key off my ring, give it to him with the cat. "Take them inside and tell them what happened if they arrive."

"Where are you going?"

"To stop Harold."

I go to hit speed dial for Ben, but I see that he called. I didn't hear a ring.

Bolting down the stairs, I play it back.

"Are you all right? I'm on my way to get you."

The sound of his voice melts my heart. He called me. Cradling the phone to my ear, I redial his number.

The call goes straight to voicemail and cuts off before I can leave a message. His call was half an hour ago, the complex where I was stranded is ten minutes away. Did he change his mind?

How do I even begin to tell him everything that's happened? My thumbs fly across the screen with a text. *I'm okay. I miss you. Can I borrow your car? I think the brakes were cut on mine. I can meet you at the hospital. I had to change the apartment door lock. Wendel has a key.*

I remind myself that even though Ben offered to help in an emergency, the offer doesn't mean that he's moving back in.

Taking a deep breath, I check the GPS. Harold has left the hospital parking lot and is on a side street.

Tucking my phone under the poncho, I lean into the wind and head out in the rain. Thankfully, the hospital is only a five-minute walk.

The parking lot is almost empty. I spot Ben's Civic and go to the lee side of the wind to check my phone. Nothing from Ben. Harold is on the university grounds across Dell Road, only six minutes away. Sandra wouldn't talk about what she'd heard, but I bet his lab is there.

I fish my key ring from my bag and watch Ben's fob swing in the wind. Do I call him again?

"Don't hate me for this." I hit the button and climb into his warm dry car. Mounting my phone on the dash, I peel after

Harold. He's in the research section when the tracking blip disappears. I hope all this water didn't short it out or knock it off.

I peer through the rain. The light is red at Dell Road. The research section is two minutes away. If he's not parked, he could be all the way to I-95 by then. I grip the steering wheel harder, lay on the horn, and blast through.

Sandra said that she's never far from the action and that she can't talk about the research of others. What she meant is that Harold's lab is here at the university in the research section. That makes so much sense. Why didn't I think of it sooner?

I pause by a sign showing the main buildings in research. Harold wants to make patients into robots. Dodging a giant puddle, I head for the robotics lab. As the rain lessens to a mundane drizzle, I circle the building. No cars, no lights on.

I park, press my face to the hurricane glass. Inside is a wide-open area with sections of metal parts. This lab is mechanical, not biological.

I walk to another building that's smaller and more discreet. The windows are covered with sliding metal shutters. A sign at the door reads MECHANICAL ENGINEERING DEPARTMENT with a list of who is in each office.

Clomping back to the car, I drive around each building. The place is battened down, abandoned. I was wrong. I messed up. He's gone.

I hold back the emotions fighting to get out, fetch a napkin from the glove box, and wipe my nose. "Damn it, Harold, where are you?" Driving in a grid pattern, looking for the Jag or any type of clue, I hit a puddle. It's deeper than it looks. The car slows like a splashdown.

"DON'T STALL!"

A trickle of water seeps through the door, and the engine dies. "I cannot believe this is happening."

The puddle will get worse and fill the car. I need to get it out of here.

Scanning the puddle, I notice that it's shallower to the rear. "Sure hope this road doesn't have a big slant." I press the brake, click the gear in neutral, take my foot off the brake with care. There's no movement. "You've got to stay put, car," I say. Climbing to the back seat, I cross my fingers and open the door.

No water comes in. The puddle is mid-calf as I slog to the front.

Shoulder to grill, I push.

Nothing happens.

I wrap my hands around the bumper, try to rock the car and build momentum. The car jiggles but won't start to roll. Panting, I straighten, stretch my muscles, try again.

The car rocks an inch but rolls back.

"No, you don't! I. Am. Not. Going. To. Ruin. Ben's. Ride!"

I grit my teeth and shove with all I've got.

A gust smacks me in the back. The cold wind feels good.

The gust strengthens.

The car starts to move as I push.

I roll it twenty feet up and out of the puddle before the wind fades.

Looking to the heavens, I pat the hood. "Thank you."

I put it in PARK and turn the key. The engine doesn't turn over. It doesn't click like a dead battery. It can take a day inside a garage for an engine to dry out. I'll have to leave Ben's car out here in the open, where it can get flooded or hit with debris. "Shit." I bang the steering wheel. "Harold, you win again."

*

With phone and wallet tucked under the poncho, I trudge toward home. The rain is still light, the wind a constant. I lean into it as I head south. I think about calling Mom, but my phone is running low.

Passing some buildings with tractors and mowers, I notice one with a light on next to the canal that's overgrown with Florida holly and trees.

The wind slows for a moment, and I hear a faint buzzing sound. It's familiar somehow, but I can't place it.

A few paces later, it hits me: *Flies*. It's flies, like at the hospital. Harold's Jag is nowhere in sight. I wonder if I'm wasting my time.

The building is concrete block, with no stucco and a rusted tin roof. Iron bars cover two small windows. A couple of flies are under the overhang near a peeling red steel door, but the sound is coming from the rear of the building, near the canal.

A whiff of feces swipes my nostrils as I round the corner. There, I discover a giant mound of dog doo. The stench turns my stomach. A horde of flies hovers over it with a tenacity that's amazing in this weather. "This is the place."

Scanning for cameras, I find one in the eaves, pointed at the door. If I knock the camera lens so that it's pointing at the wall with the next big gust, they'll think a branch fell on it.

I grab a branch blown from a dead tree, line up, and swing with the wind. The camera moves a couple of inches, not far enough. I poke it the rest of the way, hoping they think it's another branch.

The old door has a new deadbolt attached to an electronic key system. I think about combo options. Harold likes simplicity. I hit 1234. It doesn't work. I try his house number, then the address of the hospital—7095. No luck.

It's got to be something important to Harold, something easy for him or staff to remember.

My mind goes to their wedding anniversary. I punch in 0725.

The bolt hums out of the way.

"Yes!"

This *must* be Harold's lab, or that number wouldn't have worked. Should I call the police?

A huge gust shoves me into the wall. "That was nasty."

I straighten out my crumpled poncho. The wind speed has got to be over forty. The police won't come. If I let Ben know I'm here, I'll have to explain the car, plus he wouldn't want me here anyway. I take a deep breath. "Here goes."

The old, round, aluminum doorknob is locked. Looking around for a stick to pry it open with, I spot the pickup truck. I root around underneath until I find its spare tire and the tire iron. "Score."

As I head for the door, another huge gust hits. I throw my weight into it, flinging out my arms for balance. The wind rips the cheap plastic poncho. I struggle to keep it on. "Man, that's vicious."

The old doorknob lets go on my second try.

My heart slams against my chest. What if there are people in here? No one would stay in a dump like this during a hurricane. Just in case, I tuck the tire iron in my belt and slip into the building.

As my eyes adjust to the darkness, a dog whines. Could it be Grace?

Trying to ignore the pounding of my heart, I tiptoe toward the sound.

A door hinge creaks. The light flicks on.

I gasp.

Zora and Lydia are naked on the edge of a bed, arms and

legs hooked up to some type of physical therapy machine that's shocking their muscles to react. Their eyes are open with blank stares. There's a makeshift OR enclosed in plastic beside them, and they both have new gauze dressings over their ovaries. I'm too late.

"Looking for this?" I whip around to see Harold with the GPS tracker in his hand. He deadbolts the door. "Seems it fell off my car when I hit a pothole here in the yard."

Sweat trickles down my back. Behind the women, there is a row of steel tables, a dog attached to a ventilator on each. Then I spot her, Grace, in a cage with a muzzle on, tail thumping as she whines.

"No, just looking for my dog. I'll get her out of your way and be gone." I slap on an innocent smile.

Another creak with a scraping noise. My heart races faster. Simon appears in the doorway. "I don't think so," he says.

Shit. Two of them. I finger the tire iron.

"You believe you're so stealthy. You broke into my house and didn't think I'd find out?" Harold laughs.

A chill grips me. He knows. What's he going to do to me?

Harold nods to the women. "Our two advanced subjects, the ones with the *P* you read about in the charts, have graduated. What do you think of their lucidity? Amazing, isn't it?"

He doesn't care about his house. Don't react. Stay on the offense. I fake a cough to buy time to think. "Where's your car, Harold? You didn't walk here in a hurricane, did you?"

"It's holed up safely in the building next door."

They don't know that Ben's car isn't working, but now I know where to look for one. I put my hands on my hips. "You mean to tell me you're so desperate you don't even have staff for these poor girls?"

Simon leans against the wall. "We have very competent staff who we sent home to be with their families. Our main guy went to get his things so he can stay for a couple of days."

"How thoughtful of you."

"I knew you were on your way." Harold puts the GPS down, walks my way. "Two can play the tracking game."

I square my shoulders. "Your program has been reported to the state. You and Simon will be shut down in no time."

Harold keeps coming. "They won't shut me down. Everybody knows this technology will save millions of people."

I back away from the machines that are pumping the limbs of the two women.

"Besides, you won't be around to tell them anything."

I back toward the dogs, trying to feel my way around the equipment.

Harold lunges just as my feet hit something. He shoves me over it, and I land on my back, my tire iron skittering away.

"Did you think you could outsmart me? Like in the stairwell on the day of Robert's accident? I figured you overheard my conversation with Simon. I feigned leaving the hospital and have watched you since." He steps on my throat, kicks the tire iron under a cabinet.

I cough, unable to catch a breath.

He wrenches my phone from my pocket, grabs my index finger.

I dig my nails into his flesh, clawing for air.

He leans harder on my neck.

Stabbing pain shoots through it.

He holds the phone in front of my face to unlock it. "I know how to handle your meager boyfriend."

I hit him behind the knee, which bends his leg so I can roll away, coughing.

He seems enthralled with my phone. "Such a lovely home screen, you and Ben." His smile is pure evil.

"It's me you're pissed off at. Leave him out of this."

Harold steps away, keeping his eyes on me. "The city calls the low-head dam structure in the canal by your apartment a drowning machine." He grins and starts to thumb my phone screen. "I'm texting Ben that you went to look for your dog by the dam."

I scramble to my feet. "Ben is on to you. He called me this afternoon and said he was coming to get me. He knows how to locate my phone."

"I heard his message when we were in the locker room. Before Ben left the hospital, a portable X-ray machine got out of control, crushing him against the wall and breaking his shoulder socket. They're prepping him for surgery now."

Rage burns through me. Planting my feet wide, I search for something to swing at him. "You didn't have to hurt Ben to be successful."

Simon rips the phone from Harold's hand. "Quit the BS and get to the hospital. My investors want living proof to present at their annual meeting."

Harold snorts, turns to hide the snarl on his lips then opens a cupboard, gathering sterile containers and putting them in a plastic bin. "A wise friend once told me that, before hiring anyone, you should find their weakness and make sure you can live with it. Jake's is his naïveté. Chelsea's is her love for her mother. With Ben, his only flaw, besides you, is that he carries the malignant hyperthermia gene."

Having general anesthesia with MH triggers the person to cook himself. *He's going to kill Ben.* The room spins. I brace myself against a table.

"That was the main reason I went to medical records when you saw me there. After you left, I circled back and expunged the report from Ben's medical record." His laugh is dry, purposeful.

The calmest person in the room wins. Sandra said that. I steel my nerves. "Ben is your partner, an asset. You can be successful and still maintain the integrity of your team."

Harold adds a few more containers to the bin. "I don't want to do this, but I'm up against a wall."

"Because the latest prospect was moved to another hospital." Simon glares at me. "Harold, cut the BS and wrap this up for my investors."

Harold shoots him a look. "I need ten more collections of oocytes. That is if your guys bring in more subjects."

Was this two? Would Tina and Mary make it four? No more young women are in the unit. Where are the rest coming from? "You're getting carried away, Harold. The state is going to investigate you. They'll find out you killed Ben."

Simon crosses his arms over his chest. "No, they won't. They didn't figure out the FedEx driver's accident was because we needed the peptides on his truck. A lot of influential people like this research. They want the mind-reprogramming to continue en masse."

Harold puts the lid on the bin with a loud *pop*. "Ariel, you can see how far we've come. Evelyn will be back home with me, and Simon and I will be famous."

"She'll never be what she was before. Your Evie is not coming back." I regret the words as they leave my mouth.

Harold's face turns crimson. "Neither are you."

Simon steps in front of him. "Get out of here and get on with it. I don't care if you kill everyone in the hospital. If you don't pull this off for my people, I'll crush you and your helpless little wife."

Harold's jaw sets. He dons a heavy-duty raincoat and looks back. "You're the guy who doesn't like his hands dirty. You better get it done."

"No problem," Simon retorts, bolts the door as Harold leaves.

I glance at Grace. It's thirty feet from the kennel to the door. I'll have less than ten seconds to get her and get out.

Simon tucks the end of his tie between the buttons of his shirt. "I shouldn't be doing this kind of manual labor." He pushes a lever on each therapy machine. "Wind down, ladies."

Simon loosens the straps on Zora. "It's a shame these women didn't take care of themselves. Appearances are important in this world. You take care of yourself. I admire that."

I consider trying to sweet-talk him but decide it won't do any good now. He does seem to have a low tolerance for problems. Maybe I can distract him by helping with the patients.

I step closer to the women so they can see me better. "Zora, it's Ariel. I was your nurse."

"She won't listen to you. Her memories have been wiped clean. She only does what she's programmed to do. These young subjects work the best. Their muscles recover much more quickly. Watch." He looks at Zora. "Subject one-o-one, bed."

Zora pivots, places her bottom on the bed, scoots herself back with her arms. She then flops onto her side, pulling her legs up into the bed.

I'm amazed at the obedience. She's like a well-trained dog.

Simon loosens the straps on Lydia as rain pelts the windows. "My Russian investors are happy with how this girl turned out."

Harold said an hour. Simon's car wasn't outside. It must be in the landscape building. I need to get his keys.

"Subject one-o-two, bed."

As Lydia starts, I race past him, fling open Grace's cage. "Heel!" I holler and sprint for the door.

"STOP!" Simon lunges after me.

As I fumble with the deadbolt, Simon jerks me from the doorway.

I land a stomp on his foot.

He lessens his grip, giving me the chance to flip the bolt.

Kicking the door open, I shove Grace out.

Simon yanks me back by the hair.

"Let go!" I yell. Swinging hard, I punch his stomach.

He folds, releasing my hair.

I shove my hand into his pocket, grab his keys, race out the door.

I look for Grace but can't see her through the rain. "Grace, come! Grace!" I'm almost to the landscape building when I spot her by the canal, snorting and clawing at the muzzle like she sucked in water. She won't survive out here.

I check over my shoulder and don't see Simon. "Come on, girl!" I call through the rain. "I'll get it off for you."

Grace doesn't come. She's choking on the water.

I look for Simon again.

All clear.

I run to her, get the clip undone when a whack on the head knocks me off balance. My arms flail for stability on the edge of a giant culvert gushing into the canal.

"Too bad you're a sucker for dogs." Simon palms the tire iron, rips his keys from my hand then shoves me in.

Chapter 29

Can't breathe. Water.

Coughing. Water.

Air. Need air.

I claw through the water, pushing and shoving me out of control.

Something hits my arm. I get my fingers on it.

A branch. I grab hold with both hands and pull.

My face breaks the surface. A fresh breath.

The branch snaps. I'm being hurled down a canal by the water.

I hit another branch, grab it, catch a breath.

The branch breaks.

Wild water. Butt down, feet forward.

I claw my head to the surface and see the dam.

It's a waterfall now. The other side is bad. *Don't go over.*

Spotting a branch hanging from shore, I know it's my last chance before the wall. I stick my arms out. Twigs scrape my flesh. The branch hits my arm, and I latch on with both hands, pulling my head from the torrent.

A loud *crack.*

The branch comes with me.

I push my legs downstream. My knees hit the wall. Fighting to keep my head up, I shove the branch down in front of me.

It catches something.

Water gushes, debris, and twigs sting my face. I get another breath and spot a ladder of cemented rungs.

If I let go of the branch, I may not make it to the ladder and get pushed over the edge, where I'll drown from suck-back. If I stay, the water will rise until I'll drown.

The current sucks me down. *I can't let go of the branch!*

I kick my legs, dog-paddle with my free hand, and break the surface. Coughing and sputtering, I catch my breath. I only have one chance.

I grab the top of the branch, bend it away from the ladder as a spring.

My hand finds the metal handle on the side of the structure. I lock the other hand on and try to pull my legs in. There's another handle above it. I grab the rung. Fragments of metal dig into my hand.

The rung breaks.

I'm dangling one-handed. I don't have the strength to hold on for long.

Pulling with all my might, I get my arm around the third rung. I fight to get my knees on the first and keep my head above water.

A knee hits, and I get some leverage.

Both knees on.

I get a big breath, let my fingers loosen, wrench myself higher.

The rusted metal cuts into my leg.

I push with my knees, claw my fingers up the concrete.

They connect.

I heave myself up higher and get my feet on.

Two more rungs, and I'm out.

Blood runs off my hand, disappears in the rushing water. It's raining full force, making it hard for me to see anything.

I push with my feet and get a hand on the next rung. With the water at my waist, I feel more in control.

I drag myself from the rushing water and collapse.

*

I lie, panting on the bank, water crashing over the dam below. My head hurts. I finger a sticky gash by my temple, wincing. Forehead on arm, I keep my face out of the water draining past me and try to clear my head. The wind bends a Florida holly. I grab the limb for fear the rushing rainwater might wash me back into the canal.

Ben. Harold is trying to kill Ben. A wave of nausea hits me, lurching my stomach contents out into the river-like current flowing beside me.

Get to the hospital. Get Ben.

I roll onto my hands and knees.

The ground tilts.

Shutting my eyes, I drop to my elbows, tightening my grip on the holly. My head throbs, my hand throbs.

Signs of a head injury are nausea and confusion. Fear grips my arms, my legs, making them want to wobble to the ground, but I need to stay out of the dirty water with this open head wound. I should rest for a minute.

A picture of Ben on a stretcher rolling into the OR flashes through my mind. My eyes fly open. I reach higher on the branch. *Get to Ben.*

Hand over hand, I drag myself up the canal bank.

The wind is fierce at the top. I steady myself against it as sideways rain pummels me. I want to curl up and hide somewhere, anywhere it won't sting my skin.

Get to Ben.

Crawling further from the bank, the silhouette of a

building appears through the murkiness. It's my apartment building. Relief rushes through me. I know where I am, only five hundred yards from the hospital. If I can find the jogging path, it will lead me right there.

Weeds scratch my face as I tuck low to keep the rain from hitting the gash in my head.

Something moves beside me.

My insides jump, and I scramble away.

It's a duck hunkered down under a log. I wonder if it will survive. If *I'll* survive.

I think of Grace out in this weather, and my stomach knots again. *Don't vomit. It increases intracranial pressure*. I need to breathe fast, make it go away.

A dog has instincts, like the duck. She'll be okay.

Where am I? Focus. Don't let confusion rule.

I'm in dirt, not weeds. *Dirt.* That means the path. I found it. *Thank you, God. Please help me make it to shelter.*

I'll have to get up and walk to the parking lot. Balance is an issue with a head injury. I wonder if I *can* stand. *I can do it. I* have *to do it.*

Pushing one leg back as a brace, I start to raise myself up, but my balance is poor. The rain slams like rubber bullets against my skin. A fresh gust blows me sideways into the weeds.

I should keep my hand off the ground to prevent infection. How am I going to do this?

Gathering my legs underneath me, I throw my arms out for stability. The wind is so vicious I'm at a forty-five-degree angle against it.

Attempting a step, I get knocked down by the wind.

I'm behind a big piece of coral. It's protecting me from the wind. I curl in a ball. I could stay here.

Get to Ben. All I need to do is follow the path fifty yards to the parking lot.

I push myself to my elbows and knees and make my way through the tunnel of weeds. A picture of Ben and me on the beach, laughing, teasing, splashing, falling onto the soft sand in each other's arms.

A fresh gust blasts me.

I hug the ground like the duck.

There's a loud smash, and red shards of roof tile dig at my skin like shrapnel.

Please don't let me die out here.

My elbows are raw, my knees scream with pain.

I wonder if I'll make it in time if I'll ever see Ben alive again. I press on as rocks and twigs tear into my skin.

My hand throbs worse than my head, now begging me to stop. I wonder if the path will ever end. Will I run out of steam, and they'll find me floating, face-down, in the canal?

Suddenly, the path forks. I'm at the parking lot. A rush of hope energizes me. My eyes well up. I know I can make it from here.

A plastic lawn chair spirals toward me with a huge blast of wind. I crouch, but it knocks me to my side in the mud. Will the jolt make my head worse? I'm so close. I can't let that happen again.

The wind is so relentless that I don't know if I'll be able to stand.

Tucking my arms in, I roll a dozen feet to the first car. Using the bumper, I tug myself upright. I keep low to the wind and wait for a break in the squall, stagger past four cars. Behind a minivan, I stop to rest and survey my hands.

One is bright red, with nicks and scratches that the rain has washed clean. The other has deep gouges that are still bleeding. My pants have ripped through both knees, which are scraped and bleeding.

A shadow appears in a hospital window. Waving like a madman, I scream, "Help! I need help!"

The wind sucks it away, along with the small hope that the person in the warmth of the building would come out in a hurricane to save me.

Get to Ben.

Taking a couple steps backward in the lee of the van, I bend down, fight against the wind from one car to the next, making my way to the nearest hospital door.

A white SUV is the last vehicle. I pause behind it to wait for the end of the gust. Gathering my strength, I stagger to the kitchen door.

It's locked.

I kick it and scream for help as I grip the handle, so I don't blow away.

No one hears me.

A tree goes down, hitting a stack of wooden pallets. The rope securing them snaps. Loose pallets come flying.

I turn my face to the wall as one of them smashes next to me.

Burning pain sears through my leg. A four-inch stake is sticking out of my calf. The muscle spasms, and my leg starts to shake. Blood saturates my sweats. I need to get it out.

Maintaining my grip on the door, I slide my other hand down. It's the one with the deep gouge. I hope I have the strength to pull out the spike.

Doing a little test, I find the spike won't come out easily. My palm sends shooting pain through my fingers as I strengthen my grip. I grit my teeth and yank with all my might.

Blood gushes. *Uh-oh!* Should I have left it in?

Chapter 30

I bang the door, pleading, while airborne pallets mutilate cars in the parking lot. Glass breaks, car alarms blast.

The steel door cracks open.

"Help me."

An arm reaches out and hauls me inside. "You're hurt." A man with round cheeks, a white apron, and a hair cover guides me to a seat at a desk surrounded by boxes of canned food. "I'll call the ER." He reaches for a phone on the desk.

"Don't," I snap. "I'm a nurse from the recovery room. I need to get up there."

"What are you doing out in a hurricane?" The guy steps back.

"My um… car stalled in a puddle on my way in for hurricane call. This door was the closest one to my apartment."

He tilts his head. "Really? That don't sound right." He hands me a stack of towels.

Would he know I'm suspended? Gossip travels fast around this place. A clock on the wall says it's four o'clock. An hour since I was in Harold's lab. If Harold is in the hospital, he can't know I'm here.

He squints and leans closer. "Your hair looks different, but I remember you."

"Good memory." I smile. I hope he doesn't call security. I whisk a kitchen towel over my soggy body.

The guy is staring at me. "You can't go to work. You got a big gash on your head, and your leg's bleeding all over the floor. I'm calling the ER."

"It looks like more than it is from the rainwater." I drop the towel over the blood pooling next to me. Looking down at it makes me dizzy. Is that because of the head injury? *Don't think about it.*

"I need to use this phone," I say while punching in the operating room extension. "It's Ariel," I tell Sheila when she answers. "Ben's got malignant hyperthermia. Don't let him go to surgery."

"Is this a prank? It doesn't sound like Ariel."

"I found out Ben's got the gene for MH. He can't have a general."

"He's already in there."

"Tell anesthesia!" I drop the phone and run toward the hospital's central stairs.

*

"Stop Ben's surgery!" I holler as I run through recovery toward the operating room.

Belinda gapes at me from behind the desk. "Ariel, you're not supposed to be here. Why are you a bloody mess?"

The OR doors blast open. I see Ben on a stretcher, with Dr. Johnson bagging at his head.

Panic slides down my throat. My feet stop. I'm too late.

"Bes, what happened?" Chelsea spots Ben and sprints past me to an open slot. "Put him here!" she yells.

I grab the MH cart and drag it over. Cranking open the oxygen, I realize that I don't work here.

As the OR team approaches, the portable heart monitor beeps fast, showing the strain on Ben's system. His color is ashen. Guilt floods my brain, and I blink back tears.

"He'll be okay." Chelsea's words are surer than her tone.

"I'll get the ice," someone calls from behind me.

Sam Johnson's mouth is tight. "I asked all the questions about previous anesthesia and family history." His voice is an apology.

"I did, too, when I put in his IV," Chelsea murmurs.

I know I should reassure them. All I can do is stare.

Nurses rush over.

I stay by Ben, stand my ground. No one asks how I got here or dares to make me move.

Somebody slips a blood pressure cuff on. "His muscles are rigid. His skin's on fire."

"Give him Dantrium 10." Dr. Johnson bags one hundred percent oxygen into Ben's lungs.

"BP is 204 over 165. Heart rate 152. Temp 106."

Chelsea pushes in the Dantrium.

"Here's the iced saline." Someone hands it to Chelsea.

As she changes out the IV, the monitor screams. Ben's heart is in an irregular saw-toothed pattern.

"Lidocaine 100!" Dr. Johnson barks.

"The IV's kinked." I tug at the tubing.

The monitor screeches.

"It's caught under the monitor." I go to lift it when pain shoots through my head.

"I got it." A hand lifts it away.

Chelsea pushes in the lidocaine, opens the iced saline wide.

Ben's fingers twitch. The twitch spreads to his arms, his legs, until his whole body is convulsing in a grand-mal seizure.

The monitor screams.

"Valium 10! Get some Dilantin running!" Dr. Johnson hollers as he tries to hold the ET tube and bag stable while Ben's head bangs against the stretcher.

Chelsea pushes in the Valium.

I hold my breath, eyes glued to the monitor.

The static dissipates, and I see a beat. Then, a few more.

"Sinus rhythm with a few PVCs." Ben's limbs cease their clonic contractions.

"Start a lidocaine drip." Dr. Johnson pushes in a lungful of air.

Chelsea inserts another IV into Ben's arm.

"BP's 185 over 140."

I spot Belinda at the foot of the bed as I put two ice-filled gloves on the back of Ben's neck and two in his armpits. It's not medication, and it's not a procedure. Let her try and stop me.

"You're not supposed to be here, Ariel," Belinda says.

I ignore her.

"Temperature's still 106," Chelsea calls.

"Don't die, Ben. Don't die."

"Ten more of Dantrium," Dr. Johnson responds.

Chelsea pushes it in. "Come on, Ben. Break this."

She still cares. A flicker of trust in her rekindles inside me.

I can't stand here. I must do something.

I fetch more ice-filled gloves. "You're going to hate me for this, Ben." I stack the ice along his sides and on his groin.

Dr. Johnson stops squeezing the bag and lets it rest in his palm. "He's breathing on his own."

"Probably so he can yell at me for the ice bags." A chuckle runs through the crowd, and the tension in my shoulders ebbs.

"Oxygen saturation is 95 percent. Temp's down to 104 and his heart rate's down to 92."

Dr. Johnson looks up from his patient for the first time and sees me. "You look like hell."

"I had to break my way in here."

There's a murmur through the staff around the bed.

"You need to get that head wound checked."

"After he's settled." I nod to Ben. "Did they even do the surgery?"

"They were closing skin when the call came. I shut everything down right away, but it wasn't soon enough. I'm so sorry."

"You didn't know." I slide my hand into Ben's.

"Let's pull this tube, see how he does." Dr. Johnson, tears the tape off, removes the ET tube from Ben's lungs.

He monitors Ben as Chelsea slips an oxygen mask on. "Ben needs to spend the night in ICU. I think he'll be fine."

Tears of relief flood my vision. One splashes onto Ben.

He opens his eyes. "Ariel?" He squeezes my hand. "I'm so cold."

"That's a good thing." I return the squeeze as Ben falls back to sleep.

*

"Ariel, what happened to you?" Chelsea asks as she scurries around the stretcher, tending to Ben while he has nodded off to sleep.

Belinda inches closer to adjust Ben's blood pressure cuff.

I think about her alliance with Harold… her collusion with the hospital administration… the fact that she suspended me. Chelsea betrayed me. Yes, it was to help her mother, but it makes me hold back the truth. "I had to abandon the car and get here on foot."

Belinda straightens an IV tubing. "You're bleeding. You need to go to the ER."

I can't even allow the thought of leaving Ben alone to

enter my head. "Harold tried to kill Ben. I'm not leaving him."

Chelsea's eyes grow wide.

"Oh, come on," Belinda groans.

My jaw tightens. I can't hold back. "Don't you dare launch another speech about how wonderful Harold is. I went to the lab to find Harold. He told me he needed another patient to meet his quota." The two of them stiffen when they realize I've been there.

Chelsea stops retaping the IV she had put in. "He tried to take out Ben?"

"My dad was transferred, so he went after Ben. Harold plowed into Ben with an X-ray machine so he would need surgery. Ben had a basil cell biopsy a couple of weeks ago. Harold must have had the tissue sample tested, so he knew about the MH."

"Strike me dead," Chelsea gasps.

"That's horrible." Belinda glances at a scar on Ben's ear where the biopsy was done. She disappears.

The thought of him dying chases all the way up my spine. I grip his hand tighter.

"Your leg is bleeding pretty bad." Chelsea hands me a wad of gauze and a roll of Coban. She peers over my shoulder while I clean, steri-strip and bandage it. "That looks like it needs stitches."

"It'll be fine."

"You've been through a lot, Ariel." Belinda wraps a warm blanket around my shoulders.

I can't remember the last time she did something kind.

Waiting for a verbal blow, I tug the ends over my chest. The heat radiating through my wet clothes feels so good. "Thank you."

"Let me see that sliced-up hand." She grabs a spray can of antiseptic.

I keep my hand under the blanket. "You've caused me enough pain."

"You're right. I'm sorry." Belinda sighs. "Your dad being sent to the neuro unit didn't make sense to me. I started to ask questions. Harold was not polite with his answers."

"He's like a God to you."

"I was enamored with his dedication to his wife and to the hospital. I figured you were being rebellious because of your relationship with Ben."

I tighten my lips so I don't blurt a retort on her assumption.

"I understand how you might be angry, but you can't bandage your hand while your other one is rightly occupied."

She means that I'm holding Ben's.

My cut-up hand starts to throb. A drop of blood slides off it and splatters on the floor in the shape of a heart with battered edges.

I need to forgive and move on.

Tucking my thumb out of the way, I grit my teeth as she sprays.

Belinda starts wrapping my hand in gauze. "One of the OR nurses said Harold bribed her to go back into the OR. He stepped in her place between the crash cart and you right before the atropine was given to his patient who coded. The administration is investigating."

I hold back my anger. None of that matters now that Ben is okay. "Harold has a deadline to wake more patients up by next week. He's partnering with a group of investors who have Russian biotech guys creating implants to reprogram the patients' brains. The most responsive ones are being transferred to an offsite lab. He needs a constant supply of fresh meat, like Ben." I caress Ben's face, run my fingers down his arm.

Belinda's gaze goes to Ben. "This is outrageous. Harold needs to be stopped. I'm calling security." She hurries off.

Chelsea's eyes well up, and her gaze drops to the floor.

Something's up, but I can't tell what. I slip my hand back into Ben's to check his temp. "What is it you're not telling me, Chelsea?"

She clears her throat.

I brace myself.

"Harold gave me money for my mom. I told him about you trying to get to his lab. I didn't think he would ever do something like this to you."

The room swirls, I hold tight to Ben's hand. "*You* told Harold? I realize your mom needed money, but…"

"It was bad. I'm a terrible person. I don't know if you can ever porgive me."

I gape at my friend, my tennis partner with the funny little *p*. She's betrayed me and put Ben in danger, yet she's kind and fun and, until now, loyal. I want to hate her, but I can't. It's Chelsea.

"Dr. Goss to the emergency room immediately. Dr. Goss to the emergency room immediately." The voice booms through overhead speakers.

The announcement hits me like a shot of adrenaline. *Simon's thugs have dropped off a new victim.* "Watch Ben for me. Don't let him be anywhere alone."

Chapter 31

Racing down the stairs, I remember Harold at the lab when I was by the dog cages. He'd been gathering equipment and talking about getting cells like it was from the hospital, not the lab.

What's he up to? Whatever it is, he needs to be stopped before anyone else gets hurt.

There's a cluster of staff around a room in the ER. I make my way there.

"Someone dumped this woman at the front door and drove away," a nurse reports.

And I know who it was.

Jake is examining the patient's head. "She's got a huge gash with skull fragments in her hair. Her pupils are fixed and dilated."

"Tube's in." José, the ER doc, listens to the patient's lungs as he squeezes the Ambu bag.

"I've got a line." A nurse tapes down the IV she put in.

"Jake, where is Harold?" I demand.

People gasp and stare at me.

"Ariel!" Jake stammers. "Are you all right?"

"Harold did this to me, and he tried to kill Ben."

Jake's face goes bird-splat-white. "Not Ben." He pushes his way to the foot of the bed. "I was so worried about you."

I examine Jake's face. "Really?"

"I went to the lab. Harold hasn't wanted me there for the past month. I found the door combo changed and your wallet lying in a puddle. I knew something was wrong." Jake's voice is shaky.

"Why should I believe you?"

"I thought you blamed me for your fallout with Ben. When Ben got hurt and couldn't reach you, he asked me to find you."

Jake looks crushed, his eyes pleading. I remember the fierce loyalty he had toward Ben in college. It's time to bring him into the fold. I could use some help. "Harold's deadline for his contract is up. Simon hired thugs to do that to your patient because Harold needs more bodies to experiment on." I project it loud enough so everyone can hear.

Jake grips the patient railing. "That can't be."

"In the lab, he said he needed more cells to complete his last step. He must be in the hospital because I heard him paged."

"He's here. He called me to answer the page for him." Jake's gaze sinks to the patient. There's a look of terror on his face.

"Excuse me." The voice comes from the hallway. It's George, the janitor from the OR. "She my cousin." He nods to the woman on the stretcher. "I got a text to come check on her."

"I'm sorry. She's not in good shape," Jake admits.

"I know 'cause I been standin' out here a few minutes. There's somethin' I need to tell you. I saw Dr. Goss switch the oxygen on the patient in the recovery room. He knowed I saw him, and he said he get me fired. I need this job bad, so I didn't say anything."

My eyes flick to Jake. "It wasn't you with the oxygen."

Jake nods. "Thank you, George. We'll make sure you don't get fired."

The doors to the ambulance entrance fly open. "We've got a baby coming right now!" someone shouts.

A woman in labor groans with pain.

A baby wails.

A *baby*. There's a flutter in my belly. "George, your egg salad. Harold is stealing eggs?"

George nods.

"I've got to go."

"Jake, we need your help here," a voice says from down the hall.

Jake grabs my arm. "Get your head wound cleaned up. I'll go with you."

As soon as he leaves, I run for the cryo center.

*

Emerging from the stairwell, I see the lights overhead flicker then go out. A red exit sign glows over the stairs. The lights blink again, come on at half-power. The generators must have kicked in.

I spot a shadow down the long hall. I'm too far away to tell if it's Harold. I pick up my pace.

The profile is close to Harold's. He looks up as he badges in access to Cryogenics. It's him.

"Stop right there!" I shout.

Harold ducks inside, and the door locks.

I have no ID card to use. I can hear him chatting up some nurse inside. "Open this door!" I shout, pounding on it.

Nothing happens.

I grab the hall phone and call security, hoping they'll send someone if they find out it's me.

"This is Ariel Savin. I'm a nurse from recovery. There's a problem in the cryogenics center."

The door clicks.

A kick to my thigh wound knocks me off my feet. Pain sears through my leg, and fresh blood appears.

Harold cuts the phone off, then replaces the receiver. "You're pissing me off."

I roll to my hands and knees.

He kicks me in the stomach.

I gasp for breath as I fumble to reach the handrail and pull myself upright.

"You called about a problem?" a security guard shouts from the stairs.

"Did you see what happened?" I pant. "He knocked me to the ground."

Harold throws his shoulders back, straightens his lab coat. "Thank you for coming, officer. This nurse was suspended from her job in the recovery room last week. She's got mental problems. She even snuck into the hospital in the middle of this hurricane to stalk me."

The guard squints at me. Recognition crosses his face. "What are you doing here?"

I need to convince him that Harold is lying and I'm not. "My boyfriend had emergency surgery because Dr. Goss tried to kill him."

The guard gawks at Harold.

Harold leans on the wall with an air of nonchalance. "If I killed my business partner, I'd have twice as much work to do."

He's such a liar. "You don't care. You'd get a new partner, anyone who'd go along with the neuro unit puppets you're selling."

"That's obscene. I'm helping my wife."

The guard faces me. "Why aren't you with your boyfriend if he had surgery?"

"I need to stop this man from doing more harm."

"Alone? Shouldn't the police be doing that?"

"See?" Harold sneers. "She's not making sense. She needs mental help. I'm not wasting my time with this. I need to see a patient." Harold slides his card and disappears into cryo.

"He's not a reproductive endocrinologist. He doesn't belong in there," I blurt.

"Attention all security officers," comes through the guy's radio. "Becham police would like to question Dr. Goss. Keep an eye out for him and report back."

The guard's face drains. He pushes the button on his radio. "Dr. Goss went into cryo through the east door. I'm following him now." He slides his card to open the door.

I need to convince the guard I can help. "I'll check the rooms on the right. You take the left."

He hesitates.

My heart skips a beat. "It'll go twice as fast."

"You come back out here where I can see you after every room!" he shouts.

After the third room, I spot the tail of Harold's lab coat as he rushes out the opposite exit with a container under his arm.

"He's got to be heading for the neuro unit," I tell the security guard. We dash back the way we came. "We can cut through the OR and take him by surprise."

"That's a restricted area. I could get fired." The guard pauses by an adjoining hallway.

I sprint past him through the OR and toward the neuro unit.

Opening a janitor's closet in the hall, I feel my way along until I find a mop. Screwing the handle off, I wait with the door cracked. My heart hammers in my chest. Footsteps are coming closer. The light is poor. I strain to see through the crack. I'm coiled to spring as Harold's form appears.

I heave the door open and swing, smacking him in the chest.

He drops the container. It smashes on the floor.

"My oocytes!" His nostrils flare. "You've ruined the chance of recovery for so many people. You're going to pay for this."

Harold grabs my stick and swings at me.

The room tilts as I duck. I reach for the wall and spot a fire extinguisher.

Shoving my elbow through the glass, I pull the pin and aim for his face.

He screams and lunges, body-slamming me against the wall. "You killed them!" He gets hold of my jacket, spins me into a chokehold.

I try for a breath. It won't come. My head pulsates with pain. *Think.*

Shoving my hip sideways, I get a foot in front of him and thrust my elbow into his stomach.

Harold doubles over but doesn't let go. He spins me closer, clamping down on my head.

Searing pain shoots through the open gash. He's got me in a headlock. I back up, trying to wiggle out of it, but nothing works.

I spot an exit door. If I shove him out into the storm, will I be able to get the door closed?

Harold wrenches my neck toward him, and my nose smashes into his hip. I see stars. "Those cells were lifesavers! You destroyed them!" He jerks a tie from his pocket and uses it to cinch my neck in one swift move.

I get two fingers under the tie and kick the back of his knee. It buckles, making him stagger toward the exit door. Sandra said, "Flip a bad situation on its ear." So here goes.

I kick the door open. We're sucked outside.

The rain's so intense that it's hard to see. The wind drags us, and I struggle to keep my two-finger grip.

Harold grabs a tree limb, holding us back from the wind. I yank on the tie, finally able to catch a breath.

He lifts me up higher, attaches the tie to the tree limb. I writhe and twist but can't break the headlock.

A huge gust of wind hits, knocking him over. As he falls, he kicks out my feet.

Can't breathe. Can't breathe.

Throwing my arm over the limb, I'm able to catch a short breath. I spot a piece of broken glass below me. The wind bows the limb. I try to reach the glass but miss.

The limb bends again. It tightens the tie around my neck. I won't be able to last long. Slamming my shoe onto the shard of glass, I peel it out of the rubber sole and slice at the tie with the raw edge.

Slashing away one-handed is taking forever. I'm not getting enough air. I'm going to pass out.

Ben comes to mind. We're floating side by side.

I'm losing strength. One more slice. The tie breaks and I land in a puddle, wheezing, coughing, breathing wonderful air.

There's a crash, and huge hunks of metal spiral past. Harold grips a piece that looks like a spear, tucks it under his arm, then crawls toward me.

Rolling to my hands and knees, I scramble to get away.

He grips my leg and flips me on my back.

I search the ground for something to grab. Harold's eyes are wild as he raises the spear, his jaw set.

I need something heavy. My fingers graze a roof tile. A new gust hits. I swing with the wind.

The tile connects. Harold falls, screaming over the wind. The spear has pierced his eye and is sticking out the back of his neck.

Chapter 32

Several days later, every part of me still hurts. It feels like my body was thrown into one of those rock tumblers I had as a kid. I gaze out our apartment window at the aftermath of Hurricane Jake.

"You're looking good this morning." Ben walks into the kitchen, wraps an arm around me.

I breathe in the scent of bay rum on his skin and feel his heart beating against mine.

Stepping back, he inspects the ten stitches on my shaved temple. "That's doing well, considering."

"Becham Police called a few minutes ago to let me know that Simon was killed in a plane crash on the way to Grand Cayman yesterday. I bet his cohorts had something to do with it. How's your shoulder feeling?" I check the dressing on the left side of his torso.

Ben adjusts his sling. "Pretty good. I still can't believe what you went through. You were right about Harold all along when I let his reputation blindside me. I'm going to have to do the chores around here for a long time to make it up to you."

I laugh as I slide my new phone into my pocket. "Chelsea told me the neuro unit is not being shut down to satisfy community outcry."

"It's a short-term fix," Ben says. "I heard the hospital is

going to be sold to a larger hospital group. That'll get rid of the board members and clean up the hospital's reputation."

"A lot of controversy is happening about how the patients will be cared for and whether or not to take out the neurotransmitters. Since the patients are no longer brain-dead, they can't be removed from the respirator and allowed to expire. The governor has stepped in to help the families by keeping the unit open with new staff while everyone figures out what to do."

"Evie didn't respond to any of Harold's cellular treatments and was twenty years older than the rest. She never got an AI implant like the others. Her sister had Evie removed from the ventilator and cremated the same day."

Ben shakes his head. "Your dad had another decade on top of that."

"Harold put my dad there out of spite. He had some kind of plan to kill his brain. I'm glad Dad got out."

"Jake did some snooping in the unit after you told him what was going on. He notified the police when he discovered the nurses were hand-injecting barbiturates in your dad's IV bags and not labeling the bags."

"And switching blood vials so toxicology wouldn't catch it. Rebecca and her cronies will never get their licenses back, and they'll be in jail a long time." *So well deserved.* "When Dad was transferred, he started waking up because his IV bags weren't being tampered with."

"He's made a remarkable recovery."

"Dad's especially happy they made room for him in Miami."

"The whole medical community knows about this. Miami called me after they heard what happened to him to say he could go there for treatment whenever he's ready."

I reach for Ben's hand, grateful that we made it through

this ordeal. "I haven't been outside for days. How about a walk?"

Ben laughs. "Since both of our cars are in the shop?"

"I'm sorry."

"Hey, I'm amazed you got it up and out of the water. The fluids need to be changed, but the mechanic said it would be fine. Besides, the car was better off at the university. All the cars at the hospital were ruined by loose pallets and roof tiles flying off people's houses."

Piles of landscape rubble line the courtyard alongside torn-off tree limbs and bushes without leaves. Other piles have broken chairs stacked next to green garbage bags stuffed with plastic bottles, children's toys, patio accessories. Anything that could blow away did. Our world was stripped like Mother Nature thought we needed cleansing.

I think about taking Grace here as she healed, how she was so happy to put her paws in the grass. My eye goes to the apartment on the far side of the courtyard. "I'm happy Wendel offered to keep Grace after she showed up at his door during the storm. It's a great arrangement. I can see her, take her for walks, even dog sit when he's gone, and you don't have to be sneezing all the time."

Ben laughs and gives my hand a squeeze. "Thanks for being understanding about the dog." He lets out a sigh. "Simon's dudes will rot in jail for a long time."

"Yes, they will. Between Wendel, people at the hospital and me there are lots of witnesses. I wrote down every detail yesterday, so I don't miss a thing when I'm deposed." The canal is still swollen, and I can hear water running over the weir. "Let's go over by the dam."

Ben tightens his grip. "Are you sure?"

I'm *not* sure; in fact, I'm terrified. I think about Harold behind the hospital, and how I ever had the strength to overcome him. *Don't dwell on it*, I tell myself. But my mind keeps going over the moment when the wind was right, and the tile just heavy enough to save me.

I inhale the morning air, carrying a touch of crispness, a promise that the hot, humid days of summer have come to an end. "It's time to move on with life, and this is a good start."

The wildflowers I like to paint are flattened from their two-foot height to about four inches. Debris litters the entire area. I make my way toward the canal, holding tight to Ben's hand.

He hesitates. "What are you looking for?"

"A duck. It was hunkered down near here. I want to see if it's all right."

I take a few more steps, the duck squawks and takes off in flight.

I burst out laughing. "You made it, buddy."

Downed trees and bushes have jammed up against the dam. Water spills over the upstream banks, fighting its way past them, over and around the dam in a vicious flood.

Ben pulls me close. "I don't know how you survived."

A stillness descends, a state of awe that I've been given a gift. "I've been thinking… I may not go back to the hospital."

Ben's brows shoot up. "They'll miss you". He stares at the windblown wildflowers. "You could sell your artwork. Everyone raves about it."

"Who makes a living in art?" I laugh. "My license is going to be reinstated. A friend of Sandra's offered me a job at New Health and Healing Hospital in Fort Lauderdale. They have acupuncture and massage, as well as biofeedback and yoga, for emotional help with stress. Blood work includes checking for trace minerals, along with a standard complete count and electrolytes."

"That's different."

"I'm excited because I feel like traditional medicine is… *severe* in some ways?"

Ben coughs.

"Okay, that best describes Harold. Traditional medicine has its place, like when your appendix ruptures or someone crushes your shoulder." I run my fingers along the edge of his sling. "This new hospital has alternative treatments alongside traditional ones, and it's only half an hour away."

Ben gapes at the rushing water and his gaze drifts toward the path I'd crawled. "Getting out of this hospital might be good for you."

I chuckle. "You wouldn't have to worry about me getting into trouble with the administration."

Ben gives my hand a squeeze. "I'm here for you no matter what you decide."

"People thought I was crazy. They believed what Harold was doing wouldn't happen here."

The water rushes by, fighting for its equilibrium. I fought for mine and found my truth.

The End

I hope you enjoyed TERMINAL LUCIDITY. Find deleted excerpts from the book at www.JoLoveday.com. Please write a brief review wherever you bought this book.

Acknowledgments

I am so grateful to those who have supported me through the many stages of my writing journey.

To my critique group, THE TUESDAYS, who gave advice that initiated change week after week. My writing process made leaps and bounds during our time together.

Melody Maysonet
Cathy Castelli
Faran Fagan
Stacie Ramie
Jonathan Rosen
Joyce Sweeney (our writing coach)

I am forever thankful for the people who offered to read my entire story and offer feedback. Your knowledge and input helped me immensely.

Dr. Deborah Shlian
Dr. Victor Aquista
Karen E. Osborne
Robert Young RN
Sherry Bates RN
Cathy Castelli

Thank you to you, dear reader, for supporting me on my journey. I could not do this without you. Yes, you!

About the Author

Jo Loveday is the author behind those thrillers that keep you up way past your bedtime, with just enough romance to make things interesting. She loves diving into concealed secrets with themes of integrity, morality, and the mysterious stuff that goes on in our heads. With a background as a registered nurse, Jo brings a whole lot of compassion and medical know-how to her writing, giving you an authentic peek into the human condition.

When Jo picks up her pen, she takes you on a wild ride through suspense and intrigue, with moral dilemmas and hidden truths lurking around every corner. She strives for captivating storytelling that will open your heart and mind for a long time after you've turned the last page.

Born in the frosty tundra of Winnipeg, Canada, Jo decided she'd had enough of freezing her tail off. Landing a nursing job in Florida, she made a beeline for balmy weather. Now she's spinning spellbinding novels, penning heartfelt poetry, and occasionally creating some hilariously bad artwork lakeside with an undocumented number of alligators. You can find her multi-genre work at JoLoveday.com.

Follow Jo Online

Website – https://www.JoLoveday.com
Facebook – https://facebook.com/JoLovedayAuthor
Instagram – https://www.instagram.com/jolovedayb/
X – https://x.com/JoLoveday
LinkedIn – https://www.linkedin.com/in/joloveday/
Pinterest - https://www.pinterest.com/JoLovedayBooks2Art/

Questions for Discussion

1. Is it right to keep people alive on respirators for research purposes?
2. Is it possible that someone medically deemed brain dead could still have a state of conscious awareness?
3. What moral questions would you ask if you were a member of the hospital board?
4. If your family member had an accident and became brain-dead, would you donate their organs or sustain your loved one with the hope of a cure?
5. Would you recommend using donated stem cells to help a loved one?
6. Would you trust the administration is doing the right thing, not being a whistleblower, so you keep your job?
7. Would you pull strings to get a loved one medical care even if it meant someone else, ahead on the list, got bumped?
8. Did you find yourself criticizing Ariel, empathizing with her, or both?
9. Do you think Rebecca knew Harold's plan all along or took the job out of pity for the patients?
10. How do you feel Harold handled his guilt?
11. What did the kite surfer crashing into a wave at the beach act as a metaphor for?
12. Do you think Harold sought out Simon and company, or were Simon's investors looking for a situation like Harold's?

COMING SOON

CAMPUS OF SHADOWS:
A Psychological Thriller On The Seduction Of College Life.

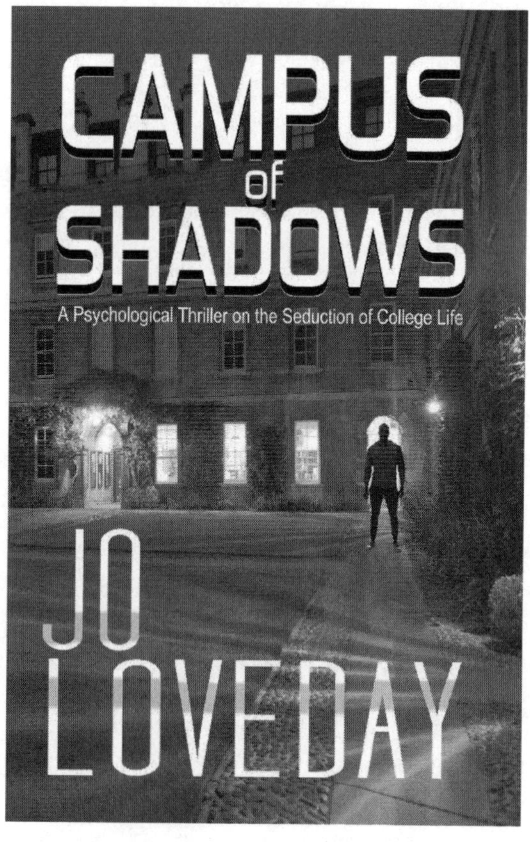

Order from your favorite bookseller or at
www.JoLoveday.com/books

Made in the USA
Middletown, DE
04 September 2024